The children cried out for a mother. He wanted a wife...

The more Kelsey tried to shake the idea of asking Meg to marry him, to come and make harmony of his chaotic days, to share with him the raising of his children, the more the idea grew.

Meg. Pretty and sweet tempered in a way that was seldom seen in this day and age. Yet a nineties woman for all that, smartly intelligent, efficient and seemingly tireless.

RUTH SCOFIELD

became serious about writing after she'd raised her children. Until then she'd concentrated her life on being a June Cleaver-type wife and mother, spent years as a Bible student and teacher for teens and young adults, and led a weekly women's prayer group. When she'd made a final wedding dress and her last child had left the nest, she declared to one and all that it was her turn to activate a dream. Thankfully, her husband applauded her decision.

Ruth began school in an old-fashioned rural two-room schoolhouse and grew up in the days before television, giving substance to her notion that she still has one foot in the last century. However, active involvement with six rambunctious grandchildren has her eagerly looking forward to the next millennium. After living on the East Coast for years, Ruth and her husband now live in Missouri.

In God's Own Time
Ruth Scofield

♥ *Love Inspired*™

Published by Steeple Hill Books™

STEEPLE HILL BOOKS

Steeple
Hill™

ISBN 0-373-87029-9

IN GOD'S OWN TIME

Delight yourselves in the Lord and He will give you
the desires of your heart.

—Psalms 37:4

God is our refuge and strength, an ever-present help
in time of trouble.

—Psalms 46:1

I can do everything through Him who gives
me strength.

—Philippians 4:13

For my daughter Karen,
who gives all of her heart wherever it is needed—
especially to children.

Chapter One

Meg Lawrence almost tripped down the step when she glanced up and saw Kelsey Jamison pull his nine-year-old road-dirt blue car into the far side of the church parking lot. He shut off the motor and remained where he was, eyes to the front, obviously waiting for his children to emerge from the crowded church.

She stood for an instant, letting people stream around her, and ordered her heart to right itself. His profile showed her a familiar straight nose, both sunburned and tanned, and the edge of his mouth—a mouth she most often remembered in laughter—before he dipped his head and his straw cowboy hat hid her view.

Did his green eyes still dance with teasing humor when he told a funny story? Did he, she wondered, still have the knack of turning around an innocent comment someone offered to suit himself, and then laugh gently as if they shared an inside joke?

Those mossy colored eyes had made her feel those moments were ones of personal sharing when she was young; memories she'd held close.

Kelsey hadn't seen her, and Meg perversely turned on her heel and reentered the church building. It wasn't that she hadn't expected to see him sometime or other. After all, their small town and surrounding countryside community left little room for anonymity, and really, she'd counted on seeing him and his children. But she'd planned—she'd hoped—it would be on her own terms, not in the middle of the church parking lot, with scores of onlookers. Five years was a long time not to have seen the man who'd owned her heart since she was fifteen.

And still did seventeen years later.

Meg drew a deep breath and let it go. The last five years had covered so much of life's rocky bumps, his and her own. The main one being the death of her cousin Dee Dee...his wife.

"Meg Lawrence, you sure are a welcome sight." Sandy Yoder, one of her mother's buddies greeted her in the middle of the crowded church hall. "When did you get in? Yesterday, I suppose. I just know your mama was happier'n a June bug to see you. Is she any better?"

Meg hated to be rude, but she heartily wished she had entered the building from the opposite door. She'd already said hello and exchanged news with most of the three hundred or so of the church membership this morning, and Sandy would keep her talking about nothing and everything, making her late home.

"Hi, Sandy. Yes, Mother's very glad I'm home. Excuse me, but I just want to, um, ask for this morning's sermon on tape for her." She moved to edge past her, but a bump from behind shoved her into two teenage girls trying to get through the crush going the opposite way.

"Oh, sorry, honey, I—Lissa?" The young girl stood only a few inches short of her own five foot nine inches, surprising Meg as she glanced into the girl's face.

"And Aimee." She confirmed the younger girl's identity and broke into a broad smile.

Her thoughts scrambled to remember how old they were now.

Yet with one breath, she recalled. How could she not, when she'd been around their mother so much during their births and after. Lissa had to be fourteen now and Aimee twelve.

"Hi, Aunt Meg," Lissa said eagerly. She glanced at Mrs. Yoder for a moment before meeting Meg's gaze. There was hope and hesitancy in the girl's green eyes, so like Kelsey's. "We thought we'd missed you."

"Yeah, we wanted to see you right away before you—" Aimee, dark-eyed, with her expression eager for adventure like her mother, was effectively cut off by her sister's elbow. "Um, I mean, before you go back to England. Last time you were home, we got to see you only for a few minutes."

"Oh, girls..." Meg's heart warmed immediately even though she felt a tug of guilt for neglecting them so long. She drew them into a hug. Lissa returned the embrace shyly while Aimee's was unequivocally enthusiastic. "I'm sorry about last time. But we'll definitely make time together this visit. Days and days of it, if we're lucky."

Mrs. Yoder placed a hand on her shoulder with a look of mild reproof at being ignored. "I must go. Happy you're home, Meg, dear, and I'll be by to see your mother in a day or so." The woman added portentously, "She does need you, you know."

"Yes, Mrs. Yoder," she answered soberly. "I'll look forward to seeing you then."

Meg waited until the older woman had turned away before she grinned at the two young girls. She felt suddenly happy and younger, as though the three of them shared a special understanding. They grinned back. She took their elbows and started for the door. "I hate to pull that old saw on you girls, but—"

"My goodness, how you've grown," Aimee said, laughing, her voice joining Meg's.

Lissa rolled her eyes as Meg groaned.

"Terrible, isn't it?" Meg confided with a grimace. "I used to hate it when people said that to me. Especially since I kept growing and growing, both up and out."

She'd been a large child for her age, and a big girl. The comments about her size hadn't always been kind, and Meg had had to work hard to cover her sensitive feelings. Even now she filled a size sixteen admirably, but she no longer cared that she wasn't a sprite. She exercised, ate a balanced diet and accepted herself the way she was.

Meg looked at the two girls, noting Aimee's slender resemblance to Dee Dee, and the shape of Lissa's mouth, so much like her father's.

Nostalgia turned her heart over. She and her cousin Dee Dee had met Kelsey together at a baseball game the summer she turned fifteen and Dee Dee seventeen. Both girls fell hard for the laughing young man who already studied agriculture in a leading state college; they became a threesome that summer. But two years later, Dee Dee was the girl Kelsey had married.

"I guess I haven't been a very good adopted aunt," she said with regret. "I haven't seen you for so long."

"Oh, but you send us cool Christmas presents every year," Aimee reminded. "And birthday checks."

Meg chuckled. True, she'd scoured the shops every December for just the right gifts. She'd loved these little girls of Kelsey's and her cousin's, and the boys, too. She'd indeed felt like a favorite aunt before she moved to New York, and then eventually to England. Suddenly, she realized she'd missed them more than she'd thought.

"I'd planned on coming out to see you one day this week," she assured them.

Aimee jumped on it. "When?"

"As soon as I make sure my mother is truly all right after her heart attack scare. Kathy," she said, mentioning her sister-in-law, "is sitting with her this morning. Which reminds me. I'd better go."

As they swung through the door, a young, dark-eyed boy broke from a knot of youngsters milling on the sidewalk, tugging a little girl behind him.

"There you are, Lissa. Where've you been?" he demanded, scarcely giving Meg a glance.

Meg stopped, a tiny disappointment running through her. Eleven-year-old Thad hadn't recognized her.

But then, why should he? He and his brother, Phillip, nine, had been left home with Kelsey when Dee Dee came with the girls to visit her the last time she was home. Dee Dee had invited her out to the farm to see Kelsey and the boys, but her time had been so short, she hadn't been able to. She hadn't seen either of the boys for five years. Or their father.

"Thad," Lissa complained, "I told you I'd be a little late getting out today."

"Well, I got Heather like you told me. Now take her." He shoved the child forward. "She's yammering for you, anyway."

"Couldn't you have waited with her over by the spot where Dad usually parks? I just wanted—"

"Dad's already here."

"Already?" Lissa scanned the parking lot, spotted the old truck and groaned. "I wanted to talk with Aunt Meg for a little longer."

"Well, take Heather, will ya? I have ta see Cort before—" He dashed away.

"Thad!" Lissa protested. "Come back here."

"Dad'll wait for a little bit," insisted Aimee. "We don't have to go just yet."

"Where's Phillip?" Lissa wondered out loud as Thad disappeared around a corner.

"Lissa, I'm hungry," Heather complained, tugging at her sister's hand.

"In a little while, Heather," Lissa said. "We have to find Phillip."

"I'll go find him," Aimee offered on a long-suffering note.

"Can we have McDonald's today?" Heather asked.

"We might if you ask Dad. But don't count on it," Aimee said. "We're s'posed to go to Linda's house to eat dinner."

Meg caught a quick look of disgust pass between the two older girls as Aimee took off after Thad.

"Linda?" she asked Lissa.

"You know. Linda Burroughs."

Ah, yes. Another of the old crowd, another woman who had once vied for Kelsey's attention. Now widowed, Linda would be a natural choice for another mate, she supposed, from Kelsey's viewpoint.

Lissa pulled her little sister forward. "Heather, this is Aunt Meg. Say hello."

Meg dropped to her haunches. Heather was Dee Dee's last child, with the same gamin face and great dark eyes as Aimee. As Dee Dee.

Heather was only a toddler the last time Meg had seen her...the last time she'd seen Dee Dee.

"Hello, Heather. I'm Meg, your mother's cousin."

"I thought you're an aunt."

"Not really. Your sisters just call me aunt because I'm so much older than they. But I am family, you know, and I've known your sisters and brothers ever since they were babies."

"Did you know me when I was a baby?"

"No, I'm sorry to say."

"Why not?"

"I've been living over in England for a long time."

"Oh. Why didn't you come to see me?" The little girl's gaze was puzzled and a bit plaintive.

Why hadn't she returned more than once in five years?

She hadn't come home for the very reason she hadn't been ready to see Kelsey again three years before and just moments ago. Not even when Dee Dee died.

She'd been so in love with Kelsey that she'd been on the verge of declaring herself; instead she'd chosen to put half a country and an ocean between them rather than to either embarrass Kelsey and Dee Dee or make a fool of herself. She'd taken a new job with a leading New York investment firm, and from there, to England. She'd hoped to get over him with time.

"Well...I'm here now," she answered the little girl.

"Hello, Meg," Kelsey's deep voice interrupted, sending waves of remembered yearning through her, bridging the years as though they were mere minutes.

Time hadn't been her friend.

Slowly, Meg stood, noting once again that he topped her by several inches even when she wore heels. Staring up at him, she felt the impact of his gaze like a brick had socked her in the middle. Yet she couldn't help but notice that the gentle, laughing face she remembered had taken on worry lines and those wonderful mossy eyes appeared tired.

He smiled warmly, showing even white teeth. As always, her heart jumped as though ready to turn somersaults.

"Kelsey..." Her mouth went dry. She tried not to gape at him, tried to return the smile, knew it was tremulous. She was thirty-two, and yet this man could still reduce her to a giddy sixteen-year-old.

"Expected you home when I heard your mother was ill."

"Yes, I came as quickly as possible."

"How is she?"

"Much better, thank you."

"She's home from the hospital, now, isn't she?"

"Yes."

Her mind had taken a coffee break, she supposed, because she could think of little more to say. All the sophistication she'd gained over the years dealing with wealthy investment clients, with dating a variety of men, all her business and social poise, waved bye-bye as it winged past his head.

"Daddy, I'm hungry," Heather said, wedging herself against her father's legs. "Can we go for hamburgers?"

"We'll go in a minute, honey. But we're due at Mrs. Burroughs's house at one. Lissa, go round up your brothers."

"Dad..." Lissa protested.

"Lissa," he responded in a firm voice.

"Okay." Lissa threw her a pleading look. "Don't go away before we can make a plan, will you Aunt Meg?"

"No, honey, I promise," she told the girl, regaining some of her usual easiness. "Perhaps I can take you girls out to lunch one day next week. Even some shopping."

"Oh, that would be super. I'll be right back, okay?"

"I'll stay right here till we have a day fixed." She turned back to find that Kelsey was studying her face.

"Been a long time."

"Yes, it has."

"You didn't marry that Frenchman, after all."

"No. Our lives were too...dissimilar." Her mother had kept the rumor circuit busy, as always, no matter how tenuous. Henri had been history almost before the proposal.

"What about that English fellow your mom was all excited about a few months back?"

His question was asked seriously, but a glint of amusement made his eyes dance. Her nerves settled down; this was the Kelsey she treasured.

"Clive. Mmm, yeah." She chuckled and shrugged, jiggling

her keys. "Actually, I still like Clive quite a lot. Mother certainly wouldn't mind him for a son-in-law at all, but..."

Aimee and Phillip rounded a corner of the rapidly clearing parking lot, noisily arguing with Thad. Lissa trailed behind.

"Why didn't you come home for Dee Dee's funeral, Meg?" Kelsey asked out of the blue, snapping her attention back to his face.

His gaze had grown still.

Why? She'd been vacationing in Italy, thinking about marrying Clive when she'd heard of Dee Dee's death. Being thousands of miles away, she could never have reached home in time for the funeral.

She hadn't tried, sent condolences and white roses, Dee Dee's favorites, and simply grieved on her own for the cousin she'd counted more like a sister.

But she'd said no to Clive, too.

Now she swallowed hard against the lump in her throat, offering simply, "I...couldn't. I'm sorry, Kels. I loved Dee Dee quite a lot, you know."

His voice deepened with emotion. "Yeah, I know...."

"Can't we have hamburgers today, Daddy?" Heather begged again as the other children arrived.

"Not today, Heather," he replied staunchly, finally dropping his gaze. "Maybe next week."

"Hi, Thad," Meg greeted. "Hi, Phillip. Remember me?"

Phillip shook his head, looking curiously puzzled from one to the other as Aimee cozied up to her. Thad simply gave her a suspicious stare.

"It's Aunt Meg," Lissa told the boys. "Say hello."

Thad's frown deepened. Phillip continued to stare.

"Boys," Kelsey said in an uncompromising tone. "It's polite to answer when someone says hello."

"Hi," Phillip answered directly while Thad dutifully mumbled a greeting. "You're the lady that likes us. Lissa says—"

"We should go, Dad," Lissa cut in hurriedly. "You know Mrs. Burroughs wants us to be on time."

"True enough. Okay, elbows and knees, pile in."

"Da-a-ad," Lissa protested his teasing description.

Meg fixed it with the girls to pick them up on Thursday for their outing if her mother's health continued to improve, and with quick goodbyes, turned to go.

Kelsey's voice stopped her. "Glad you're home, Meg," he said softly, his gaze intently speculative. "Missed you."

"I missed you...all of you...too." She stumbled through her reply as her stomach turned to jelly.

Had he missed her? Really as much as all that?

Chapter Two

"Meg, don't use that Spode bowl for the corn. Take down the ironstone, the green ivy leaf pattern," Meg's mother, Audrey, directed from the living room the following Wednesday night. "Kathy's kids are just too rambunctious when they help clean up."

Meg ignored the way her mother always referred to her brother's children as "Kathy's kids" instead of her own grandchildren. Audrey Lawrence didn't quite approve of the girl her son, Jack, had married, even after nearly ten years of marriage, and some of that distaste fell on the children.

Privately, Meg sometimes wondered if her mother would've quite approved of anyone her brother might have chosen. With Meg, Audrey seemed content enough with the men she dated and was even hopeful over Clive. But then, she'd never really come close to actually marrying one of them, she reminded herself.

"At least they help, Mom, and don't grumble when they do," Meg remarked as she dutifully took down the ivy leaf bowl and set it on the kitchen counter before taking the stainless flatware into the dining room to finish the table setting. The good silver only came out for special occasions, preferably without children.

"I'd think you'd just be happy to see Andy and Sara at all,

since you usually complain Jack and the family don't come to see you very often.''

"Jack could manage more than he does,'' Audrey said with a sniff. "St. Louis isn't that far.''

"Jack has a busy schedule, Mom,'' she said, refraining from mentioning that her brother might come more frequently if their mother were more gracious toward his wife. "He came as fast as he could when you needed him, didn't he? And Kathy has been wonderful to park Andy and Sara with her mother this last week to come and help take care of you.''

At the moment, Kathy was out getting milk.

"Yes, but it took a heart attack for Jack to make the first trip in three months.''

Meg closed her mouth on the suggestion that her mother could've made the three-hour trip to St. Louis just as easily. The truth was, before the heart attack scare, Audrey was so busy with church activities, her women's clubs and social engagements, she'd scarcely had time for her children. They'd teasingly called her the "merry widow'' more than once.

"It wasn't a full-blown heart attack, Mom. You're lucky that way, because now maybe you'll pay more attention to taking care of yourself properly.''

"It was real enough!''

Meg hid a sigh. Her mother had always been a hard woman to please, but since her illness, she was more disgruntled than usual.

Even though the doctor had assured Audrey that her attack had been slight, and she was recovering nicely, her mother hadn't regained her self-confidence in the things she could do.

Meg decided to turn the subject.

"Why don't you come into the kitchen and supervise icing the cake. Jack and the kids will be here any min—''

Andy and Sara swung through the back screen at that moment, and the phone rang. Meg picked up the kitchen extension just as Jack, following the children in, called, "We're here. Hi, sis.''

She glanced up to smile a welcome at her brother and nearly dropped the phone when she heard Kelsey's deep voice.

"Sounds like I called at a busy time. Am I interrupting dinner?"

"Oh, Kels."

Jack looked up, raising his brows. She turned her back on him. He knew her too well, and she didn't want to risk his reading anything into her expression while her heart pounded into her throat at the very sound of Kelsey's voice. Her face had always given her away where Kelsey was concerned, anyway.

"No, we haven't begun yet," she said.

"Good." He paused. "About tomorrow..."

Kathy came in with the milk, and joyous shrieks followed when Andy and Sara threw themselves at their mother.

"Hi, munchkins." Kathy laughed, hugging them close.

"Hmm...a few days absence makes Mommy popular, huh?"

"Definitely does with Daddy," Jack replied with a wicked grin over his children's heads, then leaned to kiss his wife.

Meg's heart always warmed at the love she saw between her brother and his wife, and she even owned up to a bit of envy of it. But now she plugged her ear with a finger against the happy noise.

"I hope my plans with Lissa and Aimee are still on," she said into the phone.

"Jack," her mother called from the other room.

"No problem there, Meg," Kelsey assured. "The girls are so excited, they've talked about it all week. They're trying to make up their minds what to wear."

"Oh, tell them nothing formal," she said as Jack landed a kiss on her forehead, leaned into the phone to give a "Hi, Kelsey" before going on his way into the living room. "Shorts, T-shirts and sandals are fine."

"Okay." Another pause ensued from his end while a brief knock sounded on the back door.

"May I pop in for just a minute?" Sandy Yoder called through the screen. "I'm not here to stay."

"Sounds like you're really busy," Kelsey said, turning her attention. "Tell old Jack and all hello, and my best to your mother. I'll, uh...I'll see you tomorrow, Meg. Bye."

"Yeah, Kels." She hung up the phone feeling like Kelsey hadn't given her the real reason for his call.

The plump woman set a huge cherry pie on the kitchen table. "I just knew you'd have need of a little extra something with Jack and the children in the house for a few days."

"That's really nice of you, Mrs. Yoder." Meg picked up the big ivy leaf platter and dished up the pot roast, her mind only half engaged in what she was doing. What had Kelsey really wanted? "Shall we set a plate for you at the dinner table?"

"Oh, no, dear. I've had my supper. Don't like to eat so late, y'know, and I'm on my way to meet with the church building committee."

"Why don't you go on in and say hello to Mom, then," Meg suggested. The next few minutes bustled by as she made gravy from the pan drippings while Kathy finished getting the other food on the table.

"Well, I've got to go," her mother's friend said, walking back through the kitchen a few minutes later as Meg filled the iced tea glasses. "The committee is meeting at seven-thirty. Was that Kelsey on the phone a moment ago?"

"Mmm..." Meg answered, concentrating.

"Poor man. He hasn't been the same since Dee Dee died, y'know," Mrs. Yoder continued, shaking her head. "Too bad he hasn't any folks to help with that brood he's got. They need a mother."

"I suppose so," Meg answered automatically.

"He should get on with marrying Linda Burroughs and be done with it. Linda's good at managing a household, y'know, and she'd put some discipline back into those children."

Kathy made a quick pass through the kitchen, picked up the bowl of corn and basket of bread rolls, slanted Meg a speaking glance and headed once more for the dining room.

"Oh?" Meg murmured. "I didn't think they were so badly behaved. Just kids."

"And Linda's girl—can't think of the child's name—but she's Lissa's age. They make a matched pair, I'm thinking."

Meg had forgotten that Linda had a girl Lissa's age, and she wondered why Lissa hadn't bothered to mention it on Sunday.

If she and the girl were friends, wouldn't she have said so? But Lissa hadn't appeared at all eager to go to the Burroughs's house, Meg thought.

"I hear you're taking Lissa and Aimee for a day out tomorrow."

"Yes, I am." Now how did Sandy Yoder hear that? From her mother, no doubt.

"That's very sweet of you, Meg. I'm sure Kelsey will appreciate it as much as the girls. But do you...well, do you honestly think it the best thing? You came home to take care of your mother, after all, and you've been home only a week."

Meg almost laughed aloud at both the sweet patronizing and the gentle reproof. Her mother's friend meant well, but she still thought of Meg as a youngster who needed a guiding hand. Meg guessed that in the face of her mother's illness, Sandy Yoder thought she should be the one to offer it.

"Thanks for worrying about Mom, Mrs. Yoder." She went back to stir the bubbling gravy, then turned off the stove. "But Kathy and Jack are staying till Saturday. Mom won't miss me tomorrow."

"Well, if you really think so, I suppose. But Meg, dear, don't let yourself get too, y'know...involved with Kelsey Jamison. He...well, he's the kind of man who's totally self-involved, if you know what I mean. And that farm of his needs so much—"

"Mrs. Yoder..." Meg drew a long breath to keep her temper from rising like the simmering gravy. Her thought of Sandy Yoder being sweet in giving her unsolicited advice just burned to a crisp. The woman wasn't sweet at all, Meg decided—she was just an old-fashioned busybody.

"Sis, we're ready." Jack stuck his head around the old-fashioned swinging kitchen door and threw an unrepentant, pointed grin toward Mrs. Yoder. "Are you?"

"Yes. Yes. Everything's done in here," Meg answered in gratitude; another moment and she'd have been very rude indeed. Everyone accepted Jack's occasional mild rudeness with a shrug, but if *she'd* cut the woman short, her mother never would've heard the end of it, and then Meg in turn would've had to hear about it for days.

"Oh, dear. Well, you run along. I'll pop in again in a few days."

"Sure, Mrs. Yoder. See you then." Meg decided she would be very busy the next time her mother's friend called in to say hello. It would be the truth, anyway. On Monday she had to make contact with her office in London; she'd left two clients in the air about investments. She just hoped Clive had been watching their accounts. And she'd postponed a decision on recommending a resort compound for the Neels, her firm's oldest client. Also, she'd turned over to Clive a new client, an important European hotel chain that sought investors. Another wanted her services in expanding their holdings, wanting to include a strategic piece of real estate in Hawaii.

At eight-thirty Meg tucked her tired mother into bed, and Jack and Kathy did the same for their children before sneaking off to the front porch swing. By nine-thirty Meg looked at her watch and wondered what to do with herself for the next hour. She was restless. The house was quiet.

She might as well pull out some work; she hadn't touched her briefcase since arriving home. At the very least she could review that real estate proposal and the report on the financial stability of the firm making the offer.

Instead, she walked into the kitchen and dialed Kelsey.

It rang five times. Six. He wasn't there, and neither were the children. Seven. No answering machine, even. She chewed her lip with unreasonable disappointment.

But she shouldn't feel so, she chastised herself. Kelsey was a busy man. He had a life of his own, and his children—

"Hello."

The receiver was an inch from the disconnect button when she heard his voice. She yanked it back to her ear.

"Kelsey?"

"Yeah?" He sounded preoccupied. Almost short-tempered. Maybe she shouldn't have called.

"It's Meg."

"Meg?" A curious relief entered his tone. "Oh, hello."

She relaxed "I called because..." Why had she? She couldn't very well say she'd phoned simply because she wanted to hear his voice. "I'm sorry, Kels, about earlier. About rushing you off the phone."

"That's okay, Meg. I understand. Sometimes things are in total chaos here, too. I should've picked a better time to call than suppertime, myself."

"No, you're welcome to call anytime." In the background she heard laughter and what sounded like a bleat. "Now it sounds as if you're the one who's busy."

"Not really. We're out in the barn. Thad and Phillip have a young Hereford bull they've been raising for two-year-old class in 4-H this year. Fair's coming up, and they're counting their chances at winning the Grand Champion."

"Oh. Do they really have one?"

"Mmm. They might."

"Well, I wish them luck. Did the girls raise anything?"

"Lissa didn't seem to want to do it this year. Aimee has a lamb she's babying, but I don't think she's put her best into the effort. Too impatient, I guess." His voice suddenly grew quiet.

Too impatient. Like Dee Dee. Quick, vivacious, passionate-about-life Dee Dee.

Nostalgia waved over Meg, and she wondered if Kelsey's thoughts centered on remembering, too.

It was almost her undoing.

"I guess I'll see you in the morning."

"Yeah. I was about to shoo the kids to bed."

"No, Daddy," she heard Heather in the background. "I don't wanna."

"Lissa," she heard Kelsey order in a muffled aside. Lissa answered, but Meg couldn't hear what was said.

"I'm keeping you," she said apologetically.

"No, it's okay. I shouldn't have let them stay out this late, anyway, since tomorrow's a big day for 'em. Lissa can get Heather to bed, and the rest of the kids are on their own."

Meg frowned. It seemed to her that Lissa was doing a lot of mothering. Did Kelsey depend on her too much? Who did Lissa have to turn to?

"Kelsey, was there something else you wanted when you

called earlier? I had the feeling you were about to ask me something when we had to end our conversation."

"Um, as a matter of fact, I wanted to ask a favor."

"Ask," she prompted, when she heard the hesitation in his voice. "I can only bite your head off through the phone lines if I don't like it. Tearing you limb from limb would have to wait for personal contact. And then again, I might just say yes."

His rich, deep chuckle shot through her like a sugar high. Oh, how she'd missed hearing it. She craved more.

"You've taken to biting off heads while out in the big bad world, have you Meg? Like the Queen of Hearts?"

His amusement delighted her. "That's it. Cross me, buddy, and I'll send out my black knights. Now what's the favor?"

She heard his sigh. Kelsey didn't like to ask for anything, she recalled.

"Would it be possible for you to take Heather with you tomorrow? I know it's a lot to ask."

"No, it's not. I intended the invitation to include Heather, anyway. I'm sorry if I didn't make myself clear."

"Great!" The relief in his voice was substantial. "Really great. I have to run up to K. C. to pick up new tractor parts. I'll take the boys with me, but it's not the kind of thing the girls— well, you know. Anyway, there's no need for you to run all the way out here. I'll drop the girls off on my way, if that's all right with you?"

"Sure, Kels, that'll be fine. At ten."

They said good-night, as longtime friends would, neatly and with the warmth of long association.

She wouldn't wish for more. No…it would be foolish.

"Boys, stay in the car," Kelsey instructed as they pulled up in front of the Lawrences' white two-story house. "We'll only be a minute."

Aimee was out of the car before he'd opened his own door, and Lissa quickly followed.

"C'mon, Heather," Lissa urged.

"I wanna go with Daddy."

Kelsey held his impatience down. Heather, even though excited to be going on the shopping trip just five minutes before, liked to indulge in possessive streaks. This one had been brewing all morning. He didn't always know what to do about them; he didn't remember the other kids acting so dependently. But the other four'd had their mother, too.

"No games this morning, little sprout," Kelsey said, holding her door wide, insistently. Heather reluctantly unbuckled her seat belt and slid out of the car.

"Why can't I go with you?"

"You'd be bored in two min—"

Meg stepped out onto the front porch dressed in a black-and-white swingy-skirted outfit that stopped inches above her knees. Kelsey couldn't help himself. His attention was caught in how attractive her long legs looked—and he looked all the way down her well-shaped calves to her feet, elegantly encased in black sandals, and back up again. The sight of those long limbs hit him squarely in the middle and with a force to equal a tight-fisted punch.

It surprised him. A lot.

He yanked his gaze back to her face. Meg's skirt wasn't any shorter than most women's shorts, so it must be the sophisticated combination of garments, he guessed. Meg always did have pretty legs—he just hadn't imagined those curves would ever cause him such a disturbance.

"All ready?" Meg sang out, aiming her comment toward the girls as she came toward them.

"Oh, yes," Lissa said, enraptured.

"Uh-huh," Aimee agreed, already three steps up the drive.

"I wanna go with Daddy," Heather began again, her eyes tearing.

"Don't be such a baby," Lissa said with a long sigh.

"I'm *not* a baby," Heather protested, the pooling in her eyes growing by the second. She edged against Kelsey's leg, locking her knees as though she didn't plan to budge.

"Heather, we don't have time for this." Kelsey held his impatience under a tight lid. He gave in to his youngest child too often, according to Linda, but it was easier sometimes to make life run smoother. "If you don't want to go with the girls, then just get back into the car. But I don't want any gripes later. Understand?''

"Troubles?" Meg asked as she came up to them.

"Only the usual kind," he told her in a resigned tone.

"Hmm," she acknowledged in sympathy.

As Meg crouched down to look into the little girl's face, her chin-length hair swung forward. Kelsey noticed the honey streaks mingling with the sunny gold and light brown, all shiny like a shampoo ad.

"I'm sorry you don't want to go with us today, Heather," Meg said with sincerity. "We're going to shop and have lunch and shop some more. Who knows, maybe we'll find the latest Disney video somewhere to bring home."

Meg glanced up at him, gave him a lightning grin, then pushed a strand of hair behind an ear as she turned back to his youngest child. He thought her actions were designed to lift Heather's mood. Her smile certainly lightened his own.

"But that's okay," Meg continued. "We can pick it out without you."

Meg rose and turned her back. "C'mon, girls." She hung an arm around each of the older girls' shoulders as she steered them toward a late-model brown compact car. "Lissa, I think you'd look fabulous in something green to match your eyes."

Lissa looked back at him as though to ask, Is it okay to leave Heather? He nodded her on.

Meg captured the exchange, then turned a quizzical gaze his way. The expression smote his conscience; he guessed he did ask too much of his oldest girl. She'd been stuck taking care of Heather for most of the summer.

Meg resumed her escort. "And, Aimee, you'd look darling in one of those denim outfits. The boys, now— What'll we get the boys?"

Meg tossed her hair and looked at him over her shoulder with a conspiratorial smile. "See you whenever, Kels. Don't expect us early."

"Bye, Dad," Lissa barely remembered to say. Aimee didn't bother to look back at all.

"No-o-o..." Heather cried. "Lissa...don't leave me." Heather launched herself forward.

Lissa stopped and turned just in time to catch her little sister. "Dad?"

Her gaze entreated him to do something. Kelsey thrust out his chin in guilt. He'd really been careless to let too much responsibility land on Lissa's shoulders. She was losing her childhood altogether too soon. "Don't worry, Lissa. Heather can go with me."

"I wanna go with Lissa," Heather protested.

"Does that mean you want to go shopping with us?" Meg asked, emphasizing *us* so the child would understand who was in charge of the outing.

"Uh-huh."

"All right. We'd love for you to join us." Meg tipped her head, engaging the child's full attention. "But, Heather, this is a grown-up girls day. We're going to have lots of fun, but not the kind of fun that babies like. So what do you think?"

Heather considered her for a long moment. "I'm not a baby!"

"Oh, I'm so glad to hear that. You had me worried there for a minute. I really *didn't* want to leave you behind. Shall we go now?"

The girls scrambled to get into the brown compact. Meg gave him a last wave. And a wink.

She'd handled his daughter very well—certainly better than he did sometimes. Linda Burroughs would have advocated a spanking with tight-lipped disapproval.

"Okay, I reckon that's settled," Kelsey said, hoping his relief was well hidden. Somehow, though, he expected Meg knew all about it. Her smile was too angelic.

Chapter Three

"Where are we going, Aunt Meg?" Lissa asked from the adjoining front seat as they left the outskirts of Sedalia. Heather had been remarkably quiet next to Aimee in the back.

"Well, I hear there's an outlet mall near Odessa now. Ever been there?"

"Uh-uh," Lissa replied.

"Let's check it out, then. Okay?"

"Whoopee," squealed Aimee. "Sydney Burroughs thinks she's so cool 'cause she's been there *three times* this year."

The Burroughs family again. Meg wondered just how close Linda and Kelsey had grown. But if they were, why hadn't Linda taken Lissa and Aimee along with her sometime?

"Some people like shopping a lot more than others," Meg commented. "It's like a hobby. And with only two people in the family, they probably have more time for it. Perhaps Sydney and her mom shop because they haven't much else to do. Did you ever think that maybe Sydney is really lonely without her Dad? I'm sure her mother is."

"Yeah, but that's no excuse for Sydney to act so dorky. We lost our mom...." Lissa's voice held a well of sadness. "That's just as bad."

Meg felt her throat clog, and she reached out to pat Lissa's hand. "Yes...yes, it is. But Sydney has only herself and her mother. The five of you children are so lucky, so blessed—you have each other. And your dad is super special."

"D'you really think Dad's special, Aunt Meg?"

Meg glanced at Lissa. Lissa's bright gaze held hope and a subdued excitement, wiping out the sadness Meg'd heard in her voice a moment before.

"I certainly do." Meg was so used to hiding behind a friend-ship-only facade where Kelsey was concerned that the words came naturally. "Why, we've been friends for eons, and I missed both your parents a whole bunch when I moved abroad."

That was the unvarnished truth. Meg had missed both Dee Dee and Kelsey like crazy, yet she'd missed Kelsey more. Much, much more. But she'd never confessed her deepest feel-ings to anyone but God, trusting Him to help her through her heartbreak, and in those first months alone in a foreign country she'd done so regularly. Slowly, she'd felt better knowing she'd made the right choice in leaving her hometown. Leaving behind a love she could never see fulfilled.

Yet even while content that she'd done what she must, the idea of never seeing Kelsey again, even as a friend, had left a hole in her the size of the Grand Canyon. She'd filled that hole with long hours of study and hard work. Her business success had been very rewarding. Still, it had taken her a long time not to yearn after Kelsey daily.

After all this time she felt as though she might be suffering a setback. A huge one. She was in the strange position of com-forting Kelsey's children, and she found the exercise satisfying. Very happily satisfying.

"Anyway, I suspect your friend Sydney is very lonely being an only child," she told the girls.

"Yeah, and Sydney was really jealous last Christmas when we got your package from England, Aunt Meg," Aimee said with a touch of glee.

Meg cleared her throat of the laughter that threatened. "Aimee, I don't think we're aiming to put Sydney's nose out of joint, are we?"

"I guess not. It's just that I get tired of Sydney being a pest about how much she gets to do," Aimee said with a sigh. "Shopping, movies, doing stuff in Kansas City. The lake, too. Her uncle owns a place and invites them down all the time."

"Well, after today, you can tell her you've been to the shopping mall, as well," Meg remarked by way of consolation.

"What's a nose out of—that word—what do you mean?" Heather asked, at last indicating she didn't plan to sulk all day. Thank goodness, Meg thought.

"Oh, it's just an old expression my grandmother used to use." Meg glanced into the rearview mirror at the back seat, but all she could see was the top of the child's curly hair. "Heather, did you know your mom and I had the same grandmother?"

"You did?"

"Yep. Grandma Hicks. She and Grandpa had a farm, too, when I was little. Dee Dee and I loved visiting her. She always made us laugh."

During the rest of the drive, Meg told the girls stories about Dee Dee and herself at their age, painting pictures of their mother and other family members long gone. They shopped until very late before driving home, happily tired.

A field of black walnut trees came almost to the edge of the long gravel drive to the farmhouse. Meg recalled that Kelsey had planted them the year Lissa was born, claiming they'd help to pay for college one day. Soybeans occupied the opposite field.

They passed the once-white weathered barn before they reached the old cottage-style house in a small, grassy clearing. Separate garages lined up in the rear, having been built at different times and connected by a roofed enclosure which held the lawn tractor and other tools.

Two dogs ran up barking, as Meg shut off the engine.

"Hush, Charlie Brown," Lissa instructed what appeared to be a mixed breed as she got out of the car, scolding and pushing the brown nose away. The small golden spaniel investigated Meg's door.

At the commotion, Thad and Phillip spilled out of the house with Kelsey right behind them.

"Daddy," Heather called. "See my new sneakers? And I got Sunday shoes, too."

"Phillip. Thad. Wait till you see what we brought you," Aimee crowed. "Royal's shirts and caps. Aunt Meg spent a fortune."

Lissa gathered two big shopping bags from the back seat. "I'll take these in and be right back, Aunt Meg."

"All right, hon."

Following Aimee into the house, Lissa called, "Heather, come on and put your stuff away right now and change out of your new things. I don't want to see them all stained."

"Meg, tell me you didn't!" Kelsey both laughed and protested as he hung an arm over the half-opened driver's door. "You'll spoil them for sure."

"Occasional spoiling won't hurt them, Kels. Besides, I think the girls were long overdue for a little shopping spree." She didn't mention how awed Lissa and Aimee had been at her letting them pick out a whole outfit apiece, including shoes and under things, or that she'd bought Lissa a few cosmetics.

"Well, I hope you didn't deplete your savings."

"Hardly." She smiled into his green eyes and wanted to melt. "And I loved every minute of it."

"Generous as always." He straightened, bringing the door completely open, and dropped into a falsely aggrieved tone. "Get out and come in, ma'am. We fellahs cooked up a mess of beans and hot dogs out in the backyard while you girls have been rompin' through the stores. We're hot and starved, waitin' for our women folk to wander on home."

Meg climbed out, laughing, and matched his tone. "You mean you men folk've been slavin' all day while we was out galavantin'?"

"You got the picture, lady," he said, in a mock growl. "You'll stay, won't you?"

"Please, Aunt Meg," Lissa urged, returning to the car for the last shopping bag. Then in a near whisper, she said, "I need to talk to you, anyway."

Kelsey raised a brow at his oldest daughter. "Seems to me

you girls have had Meg to yourselves all day. Aren't you all talked out?''

"But, Dad, that's different. I wanted...oh, never mind."

As Lissa turned away, Meg noted the shy mixture of emotions shining from her lowered eyes, her lashes blinking as though to keep sudden tears at bay.

"What is it, Lissa?"

"I just wanted a chance to talk to you alone, Aunt Meg. You know, *girl* talk. Not *kid* talk."

Hadn't there been anyone at all for the child to share her feelings with? A woman with whom she felt comfortable? Meg remembered all too well her own emotional roller-coaster adolescence and imagined Lissa was facing the usual uncertainties. Without a mother.

Meg glanced at Kelsey and caught an expression of arrested curiosity, a glimmer of pain and guilt. And a touch of helplessness.

It was a different side of Kelsey; she'd never seen him helpless before. He glanced her way, drew a deep breath and held it, his lips pursed, before saying low, "Stay...please."

Meg's heartstrings definitely felt a tug. More than one, actually, and more like sharp little jerks. "I think we can manage that. Let me call Mom and Kathy and see how things are at home, all right?"

"Super. I'll be back in a sec, okay, Aunt Meg?"

"Sure, honey. Take your time."

Kelsey watched Lissa walk away, his eyes thoughtful. "Are you sure you want to, Meg? Get more involved, I mean. My youngsters are a demanding lot."

"Girl talk is a favorite indulgence for the females of the species, don't you remember, Kels?" she said, making light of the situation. "I don't mind."

"All right. At least you've been warned. Now come on round back."

Meg had been to the small farmhouse many times, but it seemed a lifetime ago now—when Dee Dee had been a part of it all. The old house had taken on a personality of its own, she decided, and lost some of Dee Dee's precise touch. Children's clutter decorated the tiny front porch and straggly ivy and begonias peeked from a huge overgrown pot on the step. Beyond the screen door, she spotted the edge of a TV set crowding the opened living room door.

Kelsey, however, guided her to the backyard. An old charcoal grill smoked gently near the weathered picnic table under the oak tree; the smell of wieners and beans permeated the air.

The back screen opened and all five kids ran out.

"Dad, Thad's hogging the last of the dill pickles," Aimee complained. "Make him share."

"I called 'em the other day." Thad hugged a jar close against his chest.

"That's enough, Thad. Put the pickles on the table and get the cordless phone for Meg."

"Dad, that's not fair. I called—"

"No arguments tonight, and do as I asked. We have a guest," Kelsey reminded.

Thad opened his mouth to protest; at his Dad's expression, he changed his mind. But not before he sent Meg a silent glance of resentment. It hurt just a little. Meg wondered what she'd done to trouble the boy. But how could he be upset with her when they barely knew each other?

Maybe that was it; she'd made a fuss over the girls but not the boys. Something she'd have to remedy.

Meg made her call and relaxed when Kathy told her that Audrey had a couple of friends visiting and assured her she wasn't needed at home. Audrey, though a little petulant, accepted her explanation, and Meg promised to look in on her mother before retiring.

The children urged her to the barn to see the 4-H projects.

Meg oohed over the boys' bull, Fred, and listened to all his finer points and did the same for the girls' sheep, Betsy Ross, dutifully patting and admiring.

"I'll be the first to admit I don't know much about farm animals," Meg said for Kelsey's ears only as they trooped back to the house.

Kelsey chuckled. "And you actually admit to such shame after growing up in America's heartland?"

"Well, I have only a cat. Besides, I'm a town girl. I didn't grow up with farm animals if you recall."

Meg's father had been an unassuming man content to be a small-town lawyer, never expanding his practice beyond himself and one clerk. But when he died just after she'd graduated college, he surprisingly left her mother well enough provided for, and she and her brother Jack each had a small nest egg for their futures.

"What of those visits to your grandparents' farm you and Dee Dee used to talk about? They had animals, surely. And all those state fairs you attended with Dee Dee and me, visiting the animal exhibits? I seem to remember you loved the fair."

"Oh, I did. It was one of summer's highlights. But then, it would be, in a small town, wouldn't it?"

"Big-city girl now, huh? Only a cat?"

"Umm-hmm. Jasper. The only four-legged animal in my life."

"Well, back then, you sure made the rounds of the animal pens and sat through endless hours of judging as if you knew a thing or two."

"Fooled you, didn't we?"

"We?"

"Dee Dee and I only sat through all that to please you. We really liked the carnival rides best. And the lop-eared rabbits. They always resembled story book creatures from Winnie the Pooh."

"You insult me, Meggie! How could you lead me on so?"

Meg couldn't help it. She giggled as though she were Lissa's age.

"It was easy. You were always so excited about everything to do with farming and working the land. The newest animal breeds, the newest machinery, the latest methods."

"Now wait a minute. Didn't you even like the homemaking stuff? The cooking and sewing and all that? You won something or other one year, didn't you?"

Meg grinned. "You got me there. Yes, I did get a blue ribbon for my fudge. Grandma Hicks's recipe. But I haven't made it in years."

"The big city has ruined you!" he said in mock horror.

"That's right. I've forgotten any rural connections I once might've yearned for."

"Poor baby!" He threw an arm around her shoulders, hugging her to his side in a display of fondness she'd long missed. Funny...no other man had ever affected her the way Kelsey did. She loved his banter, felt young and appreciated under his big-brother attitude. Yet she'd always hungered to know what his lips felt like in a lover's embrace.

"Did you hear that, kids?" he called as they reached the back porch, letting his arm drop. "Aunt Meg is suffering from malnutrition."

"What's that?" Heather asked, piling chips on her plate.

"It's starving till you die," replied Phillip, already munching on a hot dog. "Dad, can we get the marshmallows?"

"Lissa's getting them," said Aimee, handing Meg a paper plate filled with a hot dog and beans. "C'mon, Aunt Meg. After we eat, we'll teach you how to roast marshmallows on the grill."

"Starving? Didn't anybody feed you supper before?" Heather asked, her feathery brows drawn with perplexity.

"Your Dad's just teasing, honey. I've been taking care of myself perfectly well." Meg slid onto the picnic bench, and Kelsey followed.

"Uh-huh," Kelsey said with a snort as he squirted mustard from a squeeze bottle onto her wiener before doing his own. "Taking care of yourself? All you've had for nurturing are tall buildings, harsh concrete and high fashion with nothing to keep you company but that dry, lifeless stuff of crunching numbers. You've been deprived of your roots, Meggie. How have you survived without a little earthy visit now and again to feel alive?"

"Oh... I've managed." She bit into her dog. More than managed, if he only knew. She had a side to her that he'd never known.

True, Meg had missed considerably Missouri's rolling hills, Ozark Mountains, the rivers and easy accessibility to green open spaces, but she'd discovered in herself a rare talent for growing a different kind of crop than what Kelsey produced. Money. Lots of it. Heaps of it.

As she silently munched, listening to the children's exchanges, observing Kelsey's gentle rule over the table, she thought about her career. It did surprise her....

Meg had a gift for investment banking. She understood it, the industry talked to her. Her ability to recognize good—even fabulous—investments could only have come from the good Lord, Himself, she thought, because she seemed to be the only one in her family to have it. Jack, following their father's lead, had gone into law, but rather than settle for a small-town existence, he'd taken his degree into the St. Louis corporate world. He did fine for himself and his family, but Meg knew her brother wasn't into making a fortune.

No one knew just how large her own investment portfolio and bank accounts had grown, either. It wasn't something her family discussed as a rule, other than her mother occasionally asking if she was making ends meet all right. Meg hadn't flaunted her ability; Clive knew, but only because they worked so closely together.

But as for a connection with the land, the kind her grandparents had known, and as Kelsey did...no, that hadn't been her path. It might have been if Kelsey—

Meg drew a sharp breath and let it out slowly. It was time to go home! Spending time with Kelsey and the kids was making her loopy. Wonderful and miserable at the same time.

Meg stared at the children, now shuffling for a space around the charcoal embers, with marshmallows stuck onto the long ends of their sticks. It would be so easy to become too attached to them. To suffer heartbreak all over again when she had to leave.

"Lissa," she said suddenly, "why don't you walk me to the car. I really need to get going."

"Sure, Aunt Meg."

"So soon?" Kelsey said. "I'd hoped we could talk after the kids went to bed."

"Some other time, Kelsey. I promised I'd be home to tuck Mom in."

"Of course." Did she detect real disappointment in her refusal to stay longer?

"Well, thanks," he said. "Thanks for spending the day hauling my daughters around—and for all the clothes and things. Kids?"

Five young voices made a chorus of various responses.

"You're very welcome. We did have fun, didn't we, girls?" Meg said, smiling. "We shall do it again sometime."

She said good-night, and Lissa fell into step as they walked to her car. The fourteen-year-old was quiet.

"Was there something in particular you wanted to discuss with me, Lissa?"

"No, not really..."

"Mmm..."

"It's just that I don't have anyone to talk to about grown-up stuff."

The night sounds had begun; crickets chirped and mosquitos buzzed. A soft breeze whispered through the oaks by the house.

"There's always your Dad."

"Yeah, I know. But sometimes he's too busy and he doesn't...well, he tries, but—"

"A girl needs another woman, I suppose. Is that it?"

"Uh-huh. But not just any woman! Once he suggested I should talk to Sydney's mom, can you imagine?"

Meg hesitated a moment before answering. If Kelsey were thinking of Linda in those terms, it wouldn't help matters if she fostered more dissatisfaction in the girls. "Lissa, I don't remember Linda Burroughs very well. What is it you don't like about her?"

"Only everything!"

"Oh-oh. That bad, huh?"

"Yeah. She criticizes all the time and thinks she knows all about how I feel when she doesn't. And she thinks I should wear the same kind of dorky clothes Sydney wears. I couldn't stand it if Dad got, you know, *seriously* serious about her."

"Well, perhaps you should tell your dad how you feel about Linda."

"I 'spose so, but it's hard to find time without the other kids around. And sometimes Dad's just not in the mood, you know? Then there's always so much to do! I mean—'' Lissa bit her lip. "I'm sorry, Aunt Meg. I don't mean to complain so much, but—''

Meg made a shocked sound. "Oh, my, my, *my!* Here I thought I'd met the perfect teenager.''

Lissa erupted in the desired giggles, and Meg joined her.

"I'm serious, Aunt Meg.''

"It's all right, Lissa. I'm not kidding, either. No one expects you to be perfect. Even though I thought you were when you were little.''

"Maybe that's why I'm so glad you're home. I always remember good times with you. And Mom and Dad always talked about you with lots of love and stuff—you know?''

"Yeah...'' Meg's heart turned over. She remembered, all right.

"So, Aunt Meg, I was wondering if—that is, Aimee and I talked it over, and we thought maybe you might be tired of—of living on your own?''

"What do you mean, on my own?''

"Well, maybe you've come home to stay?''

"Oh, I don't know about that, Lissa. I have a great job that I like very much, and I don't think my mother will need me after a few weeks. I'd just get in her way and make her nervous.''

"Not that. I mean...Aimee and I thought...we'd hoped—''

Lissa stood very still and held her breath, a peculiar expression fluttering over her face.

"Lissa? What is it, hon?''

"Aunt Meg, would you marry my dad?''

Chapter Four

Meg sucked in air, wondering if the fragrance of the honey-suckle vines resting against the old board fence next to her car could cause hallucinations. Surely she hadn't heard right.

"Um, Lissa..."

"Please, Aunt Meg, just listen. Please? I'm seriously serious."

"Well, I—" She swallowed hard.

"You said you like Daddy, didn't you? You did say it! You think he's really special, remember?"

"Yes, I do think he's special, and yes, I like him very much." Meg's heart raced at the vast understatement. If only Lissa knew.... "But, Lissa, there's a lot more to marriage than merely liking each other."

"But that's a start, isn't it? Dad likes you, too. He was all excited when he found out you were coming home. I could tell."

Kelsey excited about her homecoming? Her mouth went dry as her mind whirled with the thought.

"And you like us kids, don't you?" Lissa nudged.

"Oh, I do...yes, indeed I do. But Lissa—" Her mind tumbled over what to say. "I think Thad and Phillip might not return the regard. And Heather..."

"Don't worry about Thad and Phillip, Aunt Meg. They'll love you just as much as Aimee and I do, once they get to know you better."

Aimee skidded to a stop in front of them, out of breath and flushed. "Did you ask her?"

"Aimee! What are you doing here?" Lissa questioned in an urgent whisper. "I told you to keep the rest of the family busy. Where's Dad?"

"Keep your shorts on, will ya?" Aimee hissed back. "The boys went to the barn, and Dad said he had some calls to make. Heather's playing with her new doll we bought today. That'll keep her busy till bedtime. Anyway, how about it, Aunt Meg?"

Meg studied the eager young faces in the growing dusk. She had the silliest feeling of wanting to laugh and cry at the same time, remembering her own earnestness at their age. But sometimes a girl of a certain age could be just as earnest about something completely different a week later. "You girls can't be, um—"

"Uh-huh, yes, we are. Majorly serious," Aimee insisted.

"You don't want to marry anybody else, do you?" Lissa asked in a suddenly alarmed tone. "I mean, Aunt Audrey said you were dating that English guy, but—"

"Well, no. No, I don't plan on marrying anyone."

"Whew! I thought for a minute—" Lissa sighed.

"Well?" Aimee pushed. "What do you think? Isn't it a great idea?"

"I don't think you know what you're asking," Meg began slowly, staving off hysterical laughter with gritty determination. "You can't just ask someone to marry your dad out of the blue. He has to do that for himself."

"But we want you to be our new mother, Aunt Meg," Aimee pleaded. "And it isn't out of the blue. We've been thinking about it for a long time. You were Mom's best friend and she wouldn't mind. Honestly. And Dad needs you, too."

"Aunt Meg doesn't think the boys like her," Lissa said.

"But they just don't know you very well, not like we do. And I know Heather can be a pain sometimes." Aimee made a face, admitting, "She's spoiled."

Then Aimee's face brightened, her brown eyes glimmered with a new thought. "That should tell you how much we all need you, Aunt Meg. You can unspoil Heather for us. And if you marry Dad, you can move back to Missouri! You want to, don't you?"

Meg nearly gurgled her laughter. "I'm not so sure about that one."

"Aunt Meg, you're absolutely, positively the only right woman to marry Dad," Lissa said in a no-nonsense tone. "Please, please, just think about it."

"Why do you say that, Lissa? What makes you think I'd make your dad a good wife? And mother for you all?"

"Because Aimee and I prayed for you, don't you see? The minute we heard you were coming home, we went to The Boss. We asked Him for you. I mean…Aimee and I don't want that Linda Burroughs, for heaven's sake. If Dad married her, everybody would be seriously miserable." She tucked in her chin and shook her head. "I mean *seriously* miserable."

"Your dad might not think so." Meg suddenly felt exhausted. Her emotions had run amok all day and in the last few moments they'd been through hoops. She didn't know whether to laugh or cry.

She had to consider that Kelsey might be in love with Linda. Though he hadn't said anything or even hinted at it. But then why would he? And when would he have had time?

"Dad doesn't want her either, really," Lissa assured. "It's just that she keeps calling him and stuff like that."

"Besides," Aimee airily enthused, "now you're home, there's no reason for him to go out with her anymore."

From the house's open windows she heard a telephone ring. Insistently. Where was Kelsey? He'd gone inside to make calls, Aimee had said. Yet no one answered, and although Meg couldn't hear what the answering machine said, she heard the low murmur of Kelsey's recorded voice.

Her nerves went on overload. Perhaps one of his calls was to Linda. Just maybe he'd waited for her to leave to speak to the woman who was now in his life.

"I really have to go, girls." Opening the car door, she slid into the seat. "My mother will be in a tizzy if I'm not there soon."

"You'll think about it, won't you, Aunt Meg?" Lissa begged. "Please?" asked Aimee.

"Umm..." was all she could manage. How could she *not* think about Lissa and Aimee's wild, improbable proposal?

Think? Or dream? And wonder what Kelsey wanted, or who?

Meg made her escape quickly, feeling if she remained one minute longer she'd be signed on the dotted line of a marriage contract—even a motherhood contract—before she could breathe out the words *I love you.*

She just wished Kelsey's daughters weren't so completely charming. Her enchantment with the kids only added to the fanciful possibilities her overworked longings had already created. Never mind the drawback of needing to win over the boys; it wouldn't keep her dreams from soaring.

Sleep? Not much of it tonight, Meg suspected.

As the compact's taillights disappeared down the drive, Kelsey remained still as a statue near the dark living room window. He hadn't meant to eavesdrop, hadn't intended to horn in on his daughters' adolescent desire to talk with a mother figure.

He just hadn't figured on his children asking Meg to *be* their mother.

He felt caught between sheer dumb shock and the need for bellyaching laughter. He'd had no idea his children wanted another woman in their lives so much. But not just any woman, he reminded himself. Meg.

He did know they didn't much care for Linda, though. But how had they become so desperate about it all?

Had he been so casual in accepting Linda's invitations that he hadn't given the entire matter his proper attention? He'd only thought of Linda as another lonely adult looking beyond their children for occasional company. He'd never felt romantic toward Linda, never indicated he had anything but friendship on his mind. The question of marriage had never come up. Or even hinted at, from his end of things.

His two oldest children astonished him. Imagine, suggesting

to Meg...! Telling her not only of their own need, but his. Asking...

And then he did imagine. *Meg!*

His Meg, cousin by marriage, pretty and sweet-tempered in a way that was seldom seen in this day and age. Yet a nineties woman for all that, smartly intelligent, efficient and seemingly tireless.

It hit him somewhere between his heart and his gut.

How impossible was it? His kids needed a mother, all right, all five of them. A full-time ever-present big-hearted woman. Who better than Meg? Meg, whom he knew, liked—even loved as a friend.

He wouldn't give a thought to how badly *he* needed a wife. Someone to offer warmth and love. Some nights— Well, it was just as well he didn't dwell on how empty he sometimes felt, how lonely his bed. But he wasn't about to marry just anyone in order to fill it.

As needy as his body sometimes felt, Kelsey couldn't bring himself to engage in a casual affair, either. He didn't want to, couldn't think of making love in a careless, meaningless fashion with someone who meant little to him—something he'd be ashamed for his kids to know.

But Meg Lawrence wasn't just anybody. She was...

Well, she was Meg!

Kelsey made a turn around the darkened room before finally lowering himself into the big chair. He leaned his head back, his thoughts and emotions in a swirl.

Dee Dee had been the love of his youth, and he wasn't ready to leave her memory behind yet. Or ever.

Besides that, any woman who came into his life would have to realize he was already on overflow as he tried to balance his and his children's lives right now. Who—what woman in her right mind—would want to marry him with five little rowdies to curtail?

And what would she get out of it? His affection? He wasn't sure, other than his own physical needs, if he had any love left to offer a woman.

But Meg would know all that without any explanation, his

heart murmured. She had been so much a part of them all those first years. Asking Meg to marry him would be like asking a part of himself to come home.

Stunned at that sudden thought, he rose to pace the room once more. The children's voices drifted to him through the open windows; he should call them in to bed. Instead, he leaned on the window sash and listened to the night sounds, wondering about the new thoughts and growing excitement rioting through his system.

Slow down, he told himself. Just because Lissa and Aimee want it to happen doesn't mean it will. Or should.

He had to think about this logically. Why would Meg even consider giving up her career? A highly successful one, according to Audrey Lawrence. If Audrey could be entirely believed, Meg was the star player in her firm. Audrey exaggerated sometimes, but still—

Could he ask Meg to give that up? Where would he find the unmitigated gall?

He circled the room again, picking up and putting down an industry magazine on raising beef cattle, finally turned on the corner lamp over his computer, knowing he had to update his files, stared at the pile of unfolded laundry on the couch and once more listened to the distant voices of his children. He should urge them to bed soon.

Yet he couldn't bring himself to rob them of all their childhood; he'd let them stay up a little longer and sleep late tomorrow. Even though he couldn't.

He'd have to leave Lissa in charge again while he worked. He'd tried part-time housekeepers, which was all he could afford. At the beginning of the summer he'd let go of the last one.

Yes, and the house showed constant neglect, with the laundry always behind, and too many meals of hot dogs, macaroni and cheese, and frozen pizza. And Lissa and Aimee had less freedom to be teens all the time. Though he thought he could hold off his worry about Aimee a little while longer, Lissa already talked of the school's homecoming dance this fall, and he hadn't a clue how to parent a girl child who'd reached the age of raging hormones and daily temptations.

Furthermore the house needed a coat of paint, his south fence should've been replaced last year, and Thad had barely passed fifth grade math. He hadn't the time to coach him no matter how he stretched his day. Phillip...he felt decidedly guilty about his second son; Phillip was so quiet most of the time he was scarcely noticed. That couldn't be good.

The children cried out for a mother. He wanted a wife.

The more Kelsey tried to shake the idea of asking Meg to marry him, to come and make harmony from his chaotic days, to share with him the raising of his needful children, the more the idea mushroomed.

And he knew he'd likely get little rest until he had an answer from Meg.

He finally rang the back door cowbell, three shakes, signaling the kids that it was bedtime, and set his mind to catch up with his accounting before midnight.

But he knew he was going to do it. Ask Meg.

Lord, where do I find the courage? he prayed.

He laughed, suddenly, a little harshly. Why he even bothered the Lord, Kelsey didn't know. God had better things to do than to listen to Kelsey's grumbles or hopes and desires. He'd found that out a long time ago. He'd have to figure out where to find courage on his own.

But where?

On Saturday, Jack, Kathy and their kids left. Meg had enjoyed their company, enjoyed her brother's banter and her sister-in-law's practical approach to Audrey's sometimes unreasonable demands, but she understood their need to return home.

Audrey saved her obvious relief at their leaving until the last goodbye had been waved.

"How wonderful to have a little peace and quiet restored," she uttered, sinking into her favorite wing chair. "I just don't know how much longer I could have stood the daily racket."

"Now, Mom, you said yourself you enjoyed teaching Sara and Andy how to play those simple piano songs. And you liked having Jack hovering about."

"Yes, but children are so tiring nonetheless."

Meg grinned at her mother as she fluffed up a cross-stitched pillow. "And you thrive on telling them stories of when you were their age, and about Jack and me."

"I suppose. But they're so hard on my antiques."

"Think of it as giving your furniture more character," Meg teased, picking up a dust cloth. "Three generations on Grandma Hicks's dining chairs becoming four."

"Sara did show a remarkable interest in my old china, didn't she? And the cut glass bowls from Aunt Katherine."

"Yep." Meg held one of her mother's favorite china figurines up to the light, dusting it lightly. She'd seen dozens of collections in England and had added to her mother's each Christmas. "You might just have found your next heir to the family treasures, Mom."

"I guess I should think about it." Audrey rose and gazed tenderly at the things in her curio cabinet. "What with my weak heart, I should think about a will, too. To decide what Sara might want and little Andrew. I don't suppose you'll ever have children now."

A quick sharp jab invaded Meg's dreamy state. Why couldn't she? Thirty-two wasn't too old.

Thirty-two. How long was she going to wait before putting that dream forever on the shelf? If she'd wanted only a child, she could've married Clive.

She'd been steadfastly refusing to think about the discussion with Lissa and Aimee the whole morning. Refusing to want what they'd offered. Or rather, overriding the surge of hope it gave her. It wasn't...wise...to entertain such hope. Her heart might prove to be more fragile than her mother's.

Meg carefully replaced all the figurines in the curio cabinet, closed the door, folded the dust cloth and turned her teasing back on high.

"Weak heart, phooey. Dr. Collins says you're stronger than you know, if you'll only give up the invalid act. You just need to eat properly and get more exercise."

"Oh, Dr. Collins. He doesn't know everything," Audrey said with a sniff. She pointed to a figurine on a corner table. "Don't miss that one, Meg."

"Don't avoid the issue, Mom."

"Oh, exercise." Her mother dismissed the thought with a wave of her hand. "I can't imagine myself joining one of those public gym clubs."

"Well, think of joining the walking club, then. I hear there's a group of older people from the various churches that make the half-mile circle around the downtown shops every morning," she said, reminding her mother of the growing popularity of the activity. "Then they have morning coffee together.

"Some of those people even make the round four or five times. Paul Lumbar—" Meg casually threw in the name of the handsome older man all the single church women over fifty had been buzzing about lately "—mentioned it the other day when he called."

"Mmm... Well, yes, it was nice of Paul to call. Perhaps I might give it some thought when I regain my strength."

"You do that, Mom." Meg changed the subject. "I have to go into town and find a fax machine to send Clive some information before tomorrow. Can I call Sandy to come spend the afternoon with you?"

"I suppose. I might even enjoy a little quiet bridge game if the circumstances were right."

A smile caught up with Meg. If her mother wanted to play bridge, she couldn't deny her own improvement any longer.

"I'll call Sandy before I change clothes," Meg told her mother as she sailed from the room. "I'll leave it to her to call whomever else you want."

In old downtown twenty minutes later, Meg found a small store front that listed "Computer, Postal and Office Assistance" on the door just below the name "Justine's," and parked in the curb-front parking. A moment later she stood at the counter waiting for the pretty brunette, the only clerk in sight, to finish her phone conversation, and glanced about. Two copy machines, three computer booths, a counter holding a fax machine and weighing equipment, all drastically contrasted with the high ceilinged, brick-walled old building.

"Can I help?" The brunette broke into a welcoming smile. "Oh, Meg! I heard you were home. How are you?"

"Fine, Justine. When I saw the name on your door, I just knew the business had to be yours. You're the only Justine in town."

They'd been classmates from the first grade, although never more than casual friends. Still, Meg enjoyed renewing the friendship every time she was home. "So when did you open?"

"A couple of years back, after my youngest entered first grade. Since Dad owned the building, but couldn't keep paying tenants for long, I decided to give my idea a try. Don't make much here in the old part of town, but—" she shrugged and laughed "—it keeps me off the streets. And I fill a few business needs."

"That's great, Justine. You're just the person I need."

"You mean you came in for something besides to say hello?"

"You bet. I've got several faxes to send, and—" Meg glanced at the computer booths. A nearby sign gave a list of services and prices, including the hourly charge for computer use. "You wouldn't by any chance be on the web, would you?"

Justine raised her eyebrows in mock insult. "Sure am, missy. No backward little town or lack of the latest equipment for us."

"Wonderful. Terrific. Where do I plunk my money?" Meg responded, laughing.

At Justine's invitation, Meg moved behind the front counter and sent her faxes. Then she inspected the computer booths, screened to give privacy, and decided on which one she would use.

As usual whenever she immersed herself in whatever was happening around the banking and investment world, Meg was lost to her surroundings for long moments of time. An occasional bell, signaling a customer, or a ringing phone didn't even register with Meg for the following hour. Finally, though, three noisy kids made their presence felt and Meg looked up.

"Sorry, Meg," Justine said apologetically. "My kid, Mark, and his buddies usually hit me two or three afternoons a week for the computer games. At least I know where they are, you know? And summer hours are hard to fill."

"It's okay, Justine. I'm about to wrap up here, anyway, and I imagine Mom is wondering where I've got to."

Meg hit the Print keys on something she wanted to save and stacked papers back into her briefcase neatly while waiting for the printout.

The door swung wide, and she heard Justine greet someone, then move to one of the copy machines. Meg collected her printout and walked from behind the booth.

Fashionably dressed in a blue summer suit, Linda Burroughs stood on the customer side of the counter. She didn't look as though she'd gained a pound over a size eight, and her blond hair was highlighted perfectly.

"Why if it isn't our globe-hopping traveler," Linda said. "My, my, Meg, you do look wonderful."

"Doesn't she, though?" Justine chimed.

"Thanks, Linda." She could kick herself for wearing her old cutoff jeans she'd found in the back of her closet. She hadn't taken time to change as she'd wanted to do. "You, too."

"Kelsey's children were full of you being back home when they came to dinner the other day. They could hardly talk of anything else."

Meg smiled, murmuring, "Lissa and Aimee remember me from the old days."

"So Kelsey said," Linda commented a little dryly. Her dark blue eyes studied Meg with curiosity. "You've been home for a couple of weeks, now, haven't you? I heard your mother is doing just fine.

"She is, and thank you for asking."

"From what Kelsey tells me, Meg, you have a very demanding job. When do you go back?"

"Oh, I left my return open," Meg answered smoothly. Small towns always wanted to know everything; they thought of themselves as extended family, entitled to the truth about everyone. "I didn't know how long Mom would need me."

"And your boss is okay with that? My, my, aren't you lucky? I couldn't leave my real estate business for so long without a substantial loss."

"Yes, I am lucky. But thank goodness I've discovered Justine's business. She's a find." Meg searched the bottom of her purse for her wallet, then pulled out her credit card. "I've arranged to use her computers part-time for the rest of my stay."

"Ah, yes," Linda agreed as she accepted her copy work from Justine and collected her purse from the counter. "This girl keeps us all in the nineties. She sometimes saves my hide, actually. Like today when our copy machine is on the blink."

"Please, please. You'll have me blushing," Justine protested with a preen. "And I plan on taking you all into the next millennium. Maybe I should take my bow now."

They chuckled at Justine's sally before Linda said, "Well, good to see you, Meg. I imagine you're eager to get back to England soon. Hope I see you again before you leave. I'll tell Kelsey I ran into you when I see him tonight."

Linda breezed out of the door without looking back, her proprietary air floating behind her.

Kelsey and Linda had a date tonight? Startled, Meg simply murmured, "You do that."

"Hmm," Justine said, gazing at the retreating woman with a puzzled frown. "It's a little like saying 'here's your hat, what's your hurry' isn't it? Didn't you hang out a lot with Kelsey and Dee Dee a long time ago?"

Meg drew a deep breath. Whatever had possessed her to even think of the possibilities of marrying Kelsey? Or that he might want her when Linda was available? The girls were simply living in a dream.

"Yes. We were all close, once," she answered slowly.

Stuffing her wallet back in her purse, she handed over her credit card.

"How much do I owe you, Justine?" she asked, willing the other woman to hurry the transaction. She had to leave before she gave away her crumbling heart. How foolish of her to once again pin her hopes in a childish dream. Lissa and Aimee were entitled to their dreams. However, she was a grown woman. She knew the difference between dreams and reality.

Kelsey, of all people, did as well. She could only hope the girls hadn't mentioned their idea to their dad.

Chapter Five

$\mathbf{T}$he two unknown cars in the drive told Meg her mother's bridge game was most likely still in progress. But who of Audrey's friends owned that cherry red fifties Ford Thunderbird?

Meg glanced at her watch. Four-thirty. Surely they couldn't mean to stay much longer. Perhaps she could hurry her mother's friends out with a mention that Audrey's strength wasn't up for marathons yet. She really didn't relish the idea of making polite conversation.

All the way home she'd had Kelsey on her mind, but there seemed no way around what Linda had implied; Linda wanted everyone to think she and Kelsey were a set. And in spite of what the girls had said or wanted to believe, Meg thought things might be rather serious between Kelsey and Linda.

Well, why not? Why wouldn't Kelsey have moved on to a new love after Dee Dee died? Meg'd been gone from her hometown for a long time. Long enough not to know exactly whom Kelsey might be interested in anymore. But her heart sank with the thought of it being supercilious Linda Burroughs.

Oh, my! That was small-minded of her. She sounded as bad as Lissa and Aimee. And to even fret over it meant she'd allowed too much hope from the girls' proposal into her thinking.

Meg let the screen door slap shut behind her as she entered

the kitchen with her arms full of groceries and her thoughts swirling. How could she have let herself in for this kind of hurt all over again? Her heart shrank a little more with each passing moment, until she thought it no bigger than a lemon.

"Meg, is that you?" Audrey called, out of the murmuring voices from the living room, as Meg stepped through the back door. "What kept you? I thought you'd be back long before now."

"Yes, Mom, it's me." Meg set her bag of groceries down on the kitchen counter. Spotting several of her mother's best iced tea goblets beside the fridge, she wondered about how much bother Audrey had gone to in entertaining the bridge set. Probably, though, Sandy Yoder had taken care of serving the tea and cookies. "We needed a few things from the grocery store, and I picked up the cleaning."

"Well, come along in, dear. I'd like you to meet someone."

"Be right there, Mom." The phone rang. Automatically Meg lifted the kitchen extension. "Hello."

"Meg?"

Her heart lurched into her ribs as she recognized the low voice. Maybe it hadn't shrunk so much after all.

"Hi, Kelsey." She made a huge effort at keeping her tone casual.

"Hi." Hesitation followed.

"Everything all right with the kids?"

"Yeah. They're fine. In fact, I wanted to thank you again for all the clothes and stuff you bought 'em. The girls have preened over them every day since you took them shopping."

"You don't object to the makeup for Lissa, do you?"

"Uh, well, yes and no." Humor laced his voice. "I guess I'm a typical daddy. If you'd asked me beforehand, I would've said she's way too young yet. But then, since I know you wouldn't have bought it if that were true, I guess I have to face the fact that she's no longer Heather's age."

"Well, get your boots out, Kels. Lissa will be knee-deep in boys before another year passes."

"That's what scares the daylights out of me." He paused, and Meg could hear him breathe for a moment. She wasn't used to an uncertain Kelsey, and her senses sharpened. What was it?

"Meg, I'm in town and I thought maybe—"

"Who is it, Meg?" Audrey called. "Can't you hurry it along?"

He was in town before meeting Linda, Meg assumed. Linda had said—strongly implied, anyway—they had a date tonight. Yet he'd called her. Something was on his mind. She put her hand over the receiver and called, "I'll be there in a sec, Mom."

A sudden girlish giggle trilled out from the living room, followed by a masculine chuckle. She turned toward the sound, wondering who was there besides the usual card-playing crowd.

"I'm sorry," Kelsey murmured. "Have I called at a bad time again?"

"Not for me, Kelsey." Never. "But Mom's bridge group is here, so I suspect she needs me to fetch something for her. I just came in five minutes ago from errands and things."

"Oh." He honestly sounded disappointed. "Ah, that's good, then. I mean that she's up to that much excitement. Audrey must be feeling more herself."

"Yes, she is." What had he been about to say? "She's even considering taking up walking for exercise."

"I hear walking is great. And she won't need you around much longer." A sudden lighthearted note entered his voice. Now why would he be especially happy about that?

"No, I suppose not." But while the thought seemed to brighten his outlook, it suddenly depressed her more than she would have imagined. If her mother no longer needed her, there went her excuse to delay her return to England. And until that moment she hadn't realized she'd wanted one.

"Meg—" Her mother stood in the kitchen door frame.

"Be right there, Mom. Sorry, Kels, but—"

"It's all right, Meg, I heard. You need to go. Just tell me something."

"Uh-huh?"

"Can you meet me for coffee at Betty Jean's Café before church in the morning? I can drop off the kids early for Sunday school and there's something...um, ah, a matter I'd really like to discuss with you."

"Sure, Kelsey. What—oh, never mind. I'll see you tomorrow."

She hung up the phone and headed toward the living room, ready with a smile for her mother's friends. To her surprise, Sandy Yoder, Ginny Hames and Babs Dunning acknowledged her presence with all the eagerness one might a piece of used furniture. Instead, their attention focused on the tall slender man who rose with old-fashioned politeness, pushing his glasses onto the top of his thick gray hair.

"Meg," her mother spoke with a gentle warmth in her voice, "I'd like you to meet Paul Lumbar."

So this was the new man in town who was currently turning all the over-fifty feminine heads. "Hello." She offered her hand. "It's nice to meet you."

"It's nice meeting you at last, Meg. Your mother speaks of you so often." He proved to be as charming as rumor had claimed, Meg thought thirty minutes later as she saw the collected company out. And he'd invited them to dinner after church the next day. Her mother had accepted for both of them before Meg could make an excuse.

"Mom, are you sure you're up to a long day tomorrow?" Meg asked as she carried the remains of the snack tray back to the kitchen. "Church and dinner out?"

"Oh, I think I'll be all right. Especially if I have an early night tonight."

"Okay, just checking. But don't plan on doing anything else afterward but coming right back home."

"All right, dear. Just as you say. Now I think I'll rest a bit before supper if you don't mind."

Meg turned to stare after her mother. What was in that charm potion Paul dished out, anyway? Audrey had been all sweetness and light the whole afternoon.

At ten minutes to ten, Clive called, catching Meg just after she'd finished her shower. Her mother had dutifully gone to bed at around nine.

"Clive, what are you doing calling on a Saturday night?" she said as she pushed her wet hair from her face. "It must be—"

she glanced at the clock on her bedside table "—nearly five in the morning there. Sunday. Is there an emergency?"

"It's lovely to hear your voice, too, Meg, luv." Clive's teasing chuckle rippled over the line "No, it's not an emergency. Why can't I call you on a Saturday night? You weren't planning to be out, were you?"

"No, but you usually are. I'm surprised you're still awake, but I am glad to hear from you. I don't suppose you went into the office today—er, yesterday—did you? I faxed you with some thoughts on the Half Moon connection."

"Well, as it happens, I'm not up before dawn. I'm not even in London. I'm still in the Virgin Islands."

"You are?" She sat on the bed and reached for her comb. "I thought you planned to fly home yesterday."

"I did, but I changed my mind. Thought I might fly to New York to have a meeting with Lansing and Jonas." He mentioned another of their clients. "Just wanted to touch base with you before morning."

"I see." She plumped another pillow behind her back. "What's wrong, Clive? Isn't Serenity as nice as the photos?" She spoke of the private resort property on an outer island that Clive had gone to investigate for the Neels Corporation, one of their oldest clients. She'd planned make the trip a month ago before her mother's illness had sprung up.

"Nothing like that, Meg. The place is even lovelier, though it's a little overpriced and needs a bit of updating."

"No hidden swamps, sink holes, big-time hotels falling over the property line or anything?"

"No, that isn't it." He laughed at her penchant for looking for the worst possible feature of a location before working up to the best. "Serenity passes muster on all the check points. Flowers, sun and sea from all sides, just as promised."

He launched into a discussion of the finer points of the conference resort he and Meg were recommending to the Neels corporation. "The only problem is the place is really too large for their needs at present and Lazarus Neels is jumpy about the price being over their heads. You know how he hates long-term debt."

"Old Lazarus putting on the breaks, is he?"

"A bit. Wish you'd talk to him, Meg. He seems to listen more closely to the positives when you do the presenting."

"Did you remind him of the climb their company has made over the past three years?"

"Yes. And his daughter Jane did, too. She's excited about buying Serenity and sees all the possibilities. But the old man remains overcautious. I tell you, Meg, if we don't wrap this baby up in the next month, Lazarus will back out of the buy altogether."

"But if they continue to go forward at their current rate, they'll grow into it within the next three to five years without breaking a sweat. In which case, they'll be very grateful to us for finding it for them."

"I know, I know. Said all that. Sounds better coming from you."

"Hmm. Perhaps we could suggest offering something to ease him into it."

"Like what?"

"Like a time share for the first five years."

"You're kidding."

Meg didn't answer as she thought rapidly, tapping a pencil against a discarded magazine.

"You are kidding, aren't you Meg? He'd never go for it. Times shares..." He sounded as though she'd said something disreputable with a nasty smell to it.

"Not the old kind where a corporation holds the strings, Clive. I'm thinking of time shares with another company—one, or at most, two other companies. Neels would retain control over the property."

"Something more like a lease?"

"Something in between, I think. If we find someone Lazarus respects, someone reliable, of course, with whom he'll be comfortable. A mid-sized company, though smaller than Neels, would do it. It would give Neels all the right buttons. Prestige and all that."

A long silence followed. "Just might work. Jane understands the potential of owning Serenity," Clive enthused. "The idea of having their own conference and training center located where there's sun, sand and water in a continually warm climate makes her feel they'll have something, a place for learning and for holidays to entice their employees and clients alike to stay loyal to them.''

"Her instincts are right. Overall, a good choice I should think," Meg agreed.

"But we have to convince the old man...."

Meg sighed. "All right. Will a phone call do it?"

"It may. But Lazarus plans to be in New York for the Lansing and Jonas meeting, and I thought— You know he likes you, Meg. Thinks you're a 'fine piece of womanhood.''"

"That old flirt," Meg responded with a laugh. Then she pursed her mouth in thought while her usual excitement rose. This had been her package from the beginning, and she wanted to see it through. The best part of any deal was tracking it to a successful conclusion. Besides, it was unfair to put the Neels off any longer, or Clive, for that matter. He had his own accounts to see to.

Clive was still talking. "And since your mother is so much better, I'd hoped you might fly in for a face-to-face. It would only take a couple of days, Meg. I'm convinced you're the one to cinch the deal."

Meg rolled off her bed, reaching for a pad of paper from the side table, already thinking of a company in the north of England that might be interested in joining Neels in an island venture. "Well, give me a day to make some arrangements here, okay? I'll call you when I know I'll be coming."

Meg hung up, wondering how her mother would react to her leaving for a few days after promising her a whole month. Perhaps Sandy or one of her mother's other friends would spend a few days with Audrey while she was gone. Two days should do it. Three at the most.

But there was a larger problem looming than what a mere two days could cover, and Meg hadn't yet given much thought to the answers. She couldn't stretch her leave of absence from work much longer than the month she'd asked for, yet the idea of leaving her mother to live entirely on her own again concerned her. She and Jack were Audrey's only living relatives, and neither of them were within easy distance. Besides friends, who would be close by for her mother when she returned to England?

Perhaps it was time they found someone to share her mother's house or else suggest her mother move in with Jack or Meg. Although Audrey wouldn't welcome either suggestion, Meg was sure. Audrey loved her independence.

She made a note to talk with Jack and Kathy about the matter and closed her notebook.

But it wasn't the problems surrounding her mother's care or the usual excitement of finding all the components necessary to complete a business agreement that crowded her mind as she fell asleep later. No, she had no doubt those solutions would work themselves out with a little extra finesse on her part. What made her heart flutter was the knowledge she would see Kelsey again in only a few hours. She wondered why that was still true after all these years, why she hadn't fallen out of love with him. Or why she'd never found a man to supplant Kelsey's place in her heart.

But she hadn't, and that was that. Now she wondered what bothered him, what was on his mind. What did Kelsey need from her?

What if Lissa and Aimee had told him of their proposal?

She sat straight up in bed, wide-eyed, suddenly feeling overwhelmed with—not anxiety. Of course not. She was a grown woman and experienced in worldly attitudes. Such a small thing to cause a tizzy.

Her hands flew to her flushed cheeks, and she jerked them away, then dropped them into her lap.

Oh, what if they had. How mortifying! For her and for Kelsey.

Oh, Father, please, please don't let either of us be embarrassed in this situation. The girls are so young and they haven't a clue as to how I've felt all these years. Or Kelsey, either. Please, Lord, help me to think clearly in the morning and not hope for the impossible or...anything at all...or make an utter fool of myself.

She lay back down, curled on her side, with the sheet pulled up to her chin. Well, she'd just have to laugh it off. Surely she and Kelsey could share the joke together like the old friends they were.

They didn't have to let it create a mountain of embarrassment.

Turning over, she punched her pillow. She'd wear her new buttercup yellow dress with the high waistline. It didn't make her figure look much slimmer, but it went well with her coloring.

No—she'd wear the navy linen. She looked slimmer in it.

By eight the next morning, Meg had settled for a casual soft blue print skirt with a solid blue knit top to match her eyes. Betty Jean's Café sat on a corner in the old part of town only two blocks from church. It boasted an old-fashioned family menu in a sixties setting. Most of its customers came from long habit and loyalty. Meg slipped into the booth opposite Kelsey at exactly the appointed time.

Without his usual straw cowboy hat or his sometimes baseball cap, his gleaming auburn hair lay smoothly brushed against his head. He had dressed in a suit and tie, attire he seldom wore. He had little requirement for it, she knew; few farmers did. Granted, the outdated brown suit and solid green tie could never pass as anything more than very conservative, but he'd dressed up, just the same.

She'd caught him a second before he looked up. His downcast gaze appeared thoughtful, and his mouth had settled into a solemn expression. She blinked, wondering if he planned on going to a funeral.

Then he smiled at her, and her heart went on its leapfrog game.

"Morning, Meg."

"Hi, Kelsey." She glanced at his almost empty coffee cup. "Have I kept you long?"

"No, not really. Lissa and Aimee needed to be at church early because the junior choir is singing for this morning's service."

"Oh, that's nice." She owned up to a tiny bite of disappointment. He hadn't dressed up for her; he planned to attend church to hear his girls sing. "Where are the boys? And Heather?"

He signaled for the waitress to bring coffee. "Heather was

invited to Miss Maybelle's, her Bible teacher, for Sunday morning breakfast along with three other children entering kindergarten next year."

"Ah, yes. I remember Miss Maybelle. She coached me in every Bible verse-and-fact contest while I was in grade school. I'm amazed at her faithfulness and tenacity." She chuckled. "And longevity. Does she still own that property to the south of you?"

"Uh-huh. I've asked her if she wants to sell it several times, but she isn't ready to let go of it yet. Been in her family too long. But she lives in town now." He picked up his spoon, set it down again and glanced away. "The boys had pancakes already and now are riding their bikes in the park. I told them to check in with us in thirty minutes." He glanced at his watch. "Twenty-five now."

"With strict instructions not to get dirty before church, too, I bet."

"You got it. I guess that kind of parenting never changes, does it?"

"No, I suspect not."

The harried waitress finally came to their table, filled their coffee cups, left containers of fresh cream and rushed away. Kelsey stared after her with impatience. "Did you want something to eat? A donut or something?"

"No. I ate breakfast with Mom before I left."

"It's okay to leave her alone now?"

"Yes, she'll do fine for a short period of time. In spite of her protests to the contrary, she likes her time alone. Anyway, she plans to attend church this morning."

He nodded and stirred two creams into his cup and two sugars.

"My goodness, Kelsey," she teased, trying to ease his unusual tension. "If I put all that in my coffee I'd be a butterball in no time at all. I have to watch all my calories as it is."

"I wouldn't worry too much about that, if I were you. You look good, Meg. Really good." His expression remained earnest, though he tried for a smile, as though making fun of his own effort at complimenting her. "Didn't I mention that the other day?"

"Um, I don't recall hearing it. Thank you." He'd paid her a few offhand compliments when they were younger, but she'd always thought them in the nature of a big brother. This was of another kind altogether.

"Well, you look very nice this morning. All the time, really."

She tipped her head and stared at him over her coffee cup.

"Thank you, Kelsey."

"This is no good." He set his cup down suddenly, letting the liquid slosh over its rim. "If I drink any more of this stuff I'll be so jittery with caffeine the kids'll think they have a snapdragon for a dad."

She laughed, the sound bubbling out of her spontaneously. He joined her, his lips spreading in a genuine smile, while his eyes took on their mossy look.

"What is it, what's the matter, Kelsey? I've never seen you so...jittery. It's not like you. Can I help?"

"Actually, you can. I mean..." He brushed back the neatly trimmed hair above his left ear, sighed and leaned back. His expression turned determined. "We've been friends for a long time, Meg. Good friends, I like to think. I'm just going to shoot straight, okay?"

"Sure, Kels. Fire away."

"I overheard what Lissa and Aimee said to you the other night. Out on the drive. I've been thinking about it. About Linda..."

"Oh." She swallowed hard and put down her cup, willing the rising blush to abate quickly, or better yet, wishing to hide it altogether. But it was no use, so she rushed into a response. "Oh, Kelsey, I wish— Don't be angry with the girls. They mean well, you know, and they'll get used to Linda in time. She's really a good person, and she'll make a wonderful effort to..."

She lost her momentum as he staunchly shook his head.

"No. Linda's a nice woman, Meg, but she's all wrong for the kids. She has no patience for them, and they don't get along with her girl. Besides—" he looked at her with a growing realization, a frown puckering his brow "—I'd make her a lousy husband. No real respect between us, you see. While with you—''

"With me?'' she squeaked out.

"Meg—'' he held her gaze ''—why haven't you married by now?''

"I don't know.'' Clasping her cup hard to keep her hands still, she felt mesmerized with the intimacy of this conversation. "Just never found anyone I wanted to spend the rest of my life with when it came down to the nuts and bolts of a commitment, I guess.''

"Are you ever sorry?''

Dropping her gaze, she hesitated for a long moment.

"Sometimes.''

"Don't you want to?''

How could she answer that? "Well, I always thought I would. Like most women, I suppose.''

"Would you consider it, Meg? Marrying me?''

Looking up, she could only blink at him, wondering if she'd hear her morning alarm go off at any moment.

"The thing is, Meg—'' he straightened and reached across the table to pry her fingers from her cup ''—I think the girls are on to something. We could make a go at marriage. You and I.''

Meg looked at his callused hand holding hers, his fingers strong and steady, his nails clean and neatly pared. Her own hand trembled.

"The way I see it,'' he continued, "we could form a kind of partnership. I haven't much to give you but myself, but I'd be a faithful husband. And you'd be close to your mom, that's something to consider.''

"Yes, I've been thinking about that,'' she murmured absently.

"We have a lot of advantages on our side, Meg—we've known each other for years, respect each other. I don't have to tell you anything about Dee Dee or question the fact you'll be good to my children. You're fond of them, and they love you.''

"I'm not sure about the boys. Or Heather.'' She made her

comment in jest because she didn't know as yet how else to respond. But for once he answered seriously.

"They'll love you when they know you better. As much as the rest of us do. In God's own time, you'll see. As you said a moment ago, they'll adjust to a mother's hand. And you understand how to handle Heather." He grinned his old teasing grin. "As Aimee said, she need's unspoiling. Maybe we all do."

The boys would love her as much as the rest of them? Did that include him?

Even if it did, that didn't necessarily mean Kelsey was *in love* with anyone but Dee Dee's memory. Could he ever fall in love with another woman?

A sudden rapping on the window beside their booth brought their faces about like puppets, startling them from their concentrated attention on each other. Thad and Phillip. They beckoned eagerly, their muffled voices telling them to come see the old cars driving through town on their way to a car rally.

Meg's usual sharp mental switches eluded her as she tried to take in what the boys wanted while a long-held breath whooshed from her lungs. Kelsey had just asked her to marry him. She'd heard the very words that had filled her thoughts and fueled her longings for days. Would it be wrong to marry Kelsey for her own selfish desires?

Oh, but she wasn't kidding herself. He'd never have thought of asking without the kids' prompting, and he wasn't offering anything like a romance.

But did that matter? They were two rational adults who looked at life's practical needs first. Kelsey thought they had a shot at building a good marriage. At a fulfilling, long-lasting relationship based on friendship.

Now it was up to her. Now she had to discover if she had the courage to chance getting her heart broken. Because if she married Kelsey and he never fell in love with her, that's exactly what would happen.

Chapter Six

The moment Meg stepped into the church foyer where she'd promised to meet her mother, Sandy stood ready, waiting to pounce. Audrey was coming with Babs Dunning.

"Meg, dear, really! You should have a little talk with Aimee."

"Aimee?" Meg blinked rapidly to bring her cloud-raptured thoughts back to the moment at hand. She'd barely been able to think in a straight line since leaving the café. Stalling, she tucked a strand of hair behind her ear. "Why? What's wrong with Aimee?"

"Why, she's making outrageous statements which are bound to upset your mother. You should put a stop to it right away." Sandy pursed her lips. "That's how rumors get started, y'know."

A sinking feeling started in Meg's middle. "What statements?"

"My dear," Sandy stepped closer, her blue eyes purposeful, and lowered her voice as church attendees streamed by, "she's saying you are going to be her new mother. That you are going to marry Kelsey. Imagine!"

"Yes..." Meg swallowed hard. Was that so hard to believe? "Imagine."

Was it so hard for Sandy to think the handsome Kelsey would be interested in her? And whatever had gotten into Aimee to announce such news before knowing whether it was true or not? Before she and Kelsey had a chance to think it through as he'd suggested earlier as they left the restaurant? And if Sandy had heard of the possibility...

Her unformed question was speedily answered when at that moment a long-established church couple smiled at her, the woman saying, "Congratulations, Meg."

Meg silently acknowledged the woman's good intentions with a vague smile, but inwardly groaned when Sandy gasped, "Meg, don't tell me that it's true! You and Kelsey—"

Unwilling to indulge Sandy's curiosity a moment longer, Meg muttered, "Excuse me," and turned against the stream of people pouring forth from Sunday morning Bible classes and heading toward the sanctuary. Three minutes later as she attempted to hide in the church library just off the main hall, Miss Maybelle waved her down. Usually only a few people were there so close to the worship hour. Just her luck to find Miss Maybelle.

She'd known and loved Miss Maybelle all her life. She hadn't the heart to avoid her now, and reached out to place a kiss on the tiny woman's cheek.

"Meg, how happy I am to hear your big news," the seventy-five-year-old said upon greeting, her brown eyes lit with youthful vigor. "I hope you don't mind. The girls told me, of course. They are so excited they just couldn't keep it to themselves."

Meg was happy that *somebody* thought she wasn't diving off the deep end by considering marrying Kelsey. Besides two fanciful young girls, anyway.

"Nothing has been decided yet, Miss Maybelle."

"No, no. Of course not. But you and Kelsey will make a wonderful match." Miss Maybelle had never quite lost her Georgia accent, and her voice became dreamy as she bobbed her cottony white head and patted Meg's hand. "I almost wish I still lived nearby, now that you'll be out that way."

"How sweet of you to say that, Miss Maybelle."

"I was fast friends with your grandma long ago. Still got that twenty-acre piece of ground next to Kelsey's house. He's been after me to sell it to him, but I haven't wanted to let it go just yet. Sentimental and foolish, I guess."

"Oh, not necessarily. Kelsey feels strongly about his own place."

"Well, I've been renting it out for pasture to the Millers. They're the people who bought my old place, you recall. Always wanted Bennie to take it over, but he wasn't of a mind to then, and wanted to see something of the world, he said." She patted Meg's hand. "Oh, never mind, dear. I'm just ramblin'. Now I realize it hasn't been widely announced about you and Kelsey yet, so I'll keep mum. Just so happy for you."

"How kind of you to say, Miss Maybelle," Meg murmured, hardly knowing what to think of this turn of events.

Had the girls told the whole church she and Kelsey were thinking of getting married? She wished she could find out exactly what had been said before encountering anyone else, but there was no way she could get to the girls now. They were already preparing for choir. Thankfully, she could trust Miss Maybelle to keep her word.

The organ, the piano, two guitars and one trumpet sounded the start of the service with a rousing chorus intended to rev up everyone's stay-awake buttons. The new senior minister who had become pastor two years previous never allowed anyone to take the service for granted. Meg looked at her watch. Time to meet her mother.

Her heart sank with a galvanizing realization. What if her mother heard the rumors before she had a chance to smooth the way? She must get to Audrey before anyone else did. Kelsey had never quite measured up to Audrey's idea of success, even when Dee Dee was alive; she certainly wouldn't be overwhelmed with joy when Meg told her she wanted to marry him.

And she did. She truly did, no matter if she took a year to think about it or truly faced whatever changes and challenges that would require of her. Yet all the practical ramifications hadn't even hit her yet, she knew.

She didn't care. At the moment she simply wanted to bask in the joy of Kelsey's proposal. And dream the same dreams of a young girl—to hear Kelsey say he loved her. That she meant the world to him. That he might wither and waste away without her.

Meg's dreams hit the reality floor with a thud only moments later when she reentered the church foyer. She spotted her mother immediately, huddled near the main door with Babs and Sandy. She hesitated to intrude; Audrey didn't look happy, and it didn't take three guesses to figure out who and what they whispered about when Sandy's glance flew at her like a hawk after its prey.

Audrey's blue eyes narrowed, one brow raised. Meg nearly groaned aloud. Her chances of having that private conversation with her mother to gently explain her news before someone else told her just dissolved into zero, she guessed.

"Mom—"

"We'll discuss the matter later, Meg," Audrey said, her mouth tight as she took Meg's arm, leaving her friends behind. Meg suppressed a sudden urge to giggle, feeling like a ten-year-old again.

Without another word, they entered the main sanctuary where the congregation stood for the opening song. Several people nodded in greeting, letting their smiles welcome Audrey back after her absence. A number of glances included a knowing sparkle for Meg. Paul Lumbar gave her a half-hidden thumbs-up and beckoned them to sit beside him. Had he heard, too?

Sandy and Babs accepted Paul's silent offer while Audrey ignored it. Instead, she angled Meg toward an empty space across the center aisle. Meg gave Paul a slight lift of her shoulder in apology, to which he answered with a knowing grin. Obviously, he already knew of her mother's unpredictable moods.

Meg felt a quick tug on her skirt. Looking up at her, wide brown eyes shining, Heather whispered loudly, "C'mon. We saved a place for you."

"You did?"

"C'mon, Aunt Meg," the child insisted as she grabbed her hand. She had on the denim jumper and red knit shirt Meg had bought her. "C'mon, Aunt Audrey. Down front where we can see Lissa and Aimee."

The child's eagerness caught at her heartstrings. Meg let herself be led down the aisle. Toward a third-row seat.

"Meg!" Audrey's outraged protest followed. Heads turned. Eyes stared.

Meg tucked her smile out of sight and pretended not to hear it. Audrey hesitated for only a moment. She sniffed and slid into the wooden pew next to Meg, looking straight ahead.

"Lissa and Aimee's gonna sing," Heather told Meg proudly, her gaze full of excitement.

"Yes, I know," Meg whispered, then glanced toward Kelsey. He gave her a slanting look that clearly said "This is the way it is" while a smile tugged at his mouth. Her own smile spread in answer, her heart lifting with pure joy as her attention returned to the service.

Could he possibly feel her love leaping the small distance between them? How strong was his affection for her, right now at this moment? Or was he simply recalling the many times she'd shared a pew with him and Dee Dee during their youth? Did he long for a return to those times? Was his proposal an effort on his part to recapture something they'd all lost?

He leaned past her to hand Audrey a song book, his sleeve brushing her arm. Momentarily his gaze held a vulnerability, swiftly contained. Kelsey rarely allowed anyone to see that inner core; the times she'd noted it could be counted on one hand. It pulled at her the same way it always had. Whatever the bond between them meant, it was there.

When they sat down after the song, Heather snuggled against her side. The boys sat beyond their father. Automatically, Kelsey stretched his arm along the pew back, his fingers almost touching Meg's shoulder. They must look like a family.

It gave Meg a warm feeling of anticipation. But—she thought in wry amusement—so much for Kelsey's suggestion to quietly give themselves a week or two to think about all the possibilities and consequences of marrying before making their final decision. Now positively everyone they knew would be waiting with baited breath to see what would happen next. They'd expect to be entertained with enough details to fill a hundred-page notebook.

Especially her mother. Yet Meg didn't think her mother found the sudden situation a happy entertainment. Not at all. But beyond the momentary irritation of the whole church knowing their family drama, something about the whole situation tickled Meg's funny bone and she had to drop her gaze to hide her thoughts.

The challenge of keeping a young child reasonably quiet for the duration of the service was a new one for Meg, but she didn't mind it. Kelsey impressed her with his patience and ease in monitoring the boys. When the junior choir stood to sing, Heather waved excitedly at her sisters. Lissa answered from her front-row position with a dazzling smile before locking her gaze on the choir leader. The music began. Meg's heart swelled with pride, and her pulse kept time with a steady *yes, yes, yes.* This was what she wanted from life.

Then a sobering, wayward thought crept in. Dee Dee should've been here sitting next to Kelsey to hear Lissa sing her first solo. This was Dee Dee's family. Dee Dee's husband. Was it wrong of Meg to want them so much?

"Meg, you've been home only a few weeks," her mother lamented three hours later, after they'd reached home and the long-awaited privacy. As promised, they'd joined Paul for Sunday dinner, but excused themselves shortly afterward. "Please just think! Surely you haven't forgotten how people talk?"

"People always talk, Mom, no matter where you live. Tomorrow something else will claim their attention." Meg reached for a hanger from her mother's bedroom closet, accepted her mother's rose print dress as Audrey slipped out of it, then hung it up.

"Well, what I want to know is if there's any truth to it. Are you going to marry Kelsey?"

Meg didn't answer immediately while she smoothed back the flowered spread and fluffed the perfectly fluffed pillows. She'd hoped her mother would have a rest before they tackled the inevitable discussion. Obviously Audrey wasn't going to postpone it another minute.

"Possibly," she began brightly, then straightened and looked at her mother. Lines of displeasure bracketed Audrey's tight mouth, something Meg had expected to see. But for the first time, Meg noticed a light of real concern in the older woman's eyes which gave her pause.

She might as well hit the subject straight on, Meg decided. Her mother would fret until they hashed it out, and fretting would do none of them any good.

"I haven't made a definite decision, but...probably," she admitted.

"Meg, you can't be serious."

"Seriously serious," she returned with a chuckle, recalling one of Lissa and Aimee's favorite expressions.

"Meg, how can you? After all these years of hard work and dedication to your career, how can you possibly consider giving it up? You are doing so well. And with Kelsey of all people?"

"Considering it is the easy part, Mom." Meg continued in her light vein, hoping to deflect her mother's earnest intent. She pulled the shade against the bright afternoon sun. "And why wouldn't I want Kelsey?"

"Surely you can't mean that."

Meg did, but she knew her mother wouldn't, didn't understand. Or didn't want to. She'd never quite figured out why her mother didn't like Kelsey. Her father had, she felt certain. And Jack liked him.

"It's inconceivable to me how you can take such a huge step without further thought," Audrey continued, her eyes troubled. "You love doing what you do. I thought you were happy in England. And what about Clive?"

"I do, I am, and I don't know yet, Mom."

"Don't be flip, Meg."

"I'm sorry...." Meg sighed, biting her lip. She sat down next to Audrey on the bed and took her mother's hand, stroking the long fingers. These fingers had offered many a tender touch when Meg was little and a help when she needed it, even an occasional swat if Meg had warranted it. They weren't as straight as they once were, or as graceful, but they would still give whatever Meg asked if they could.

"I don't intend to brush you off, Mom," she said gently,

continuing to stroke her mother's hand. "It's only that I don't have all the answers yet. You're right, I am happy in London. Reasonably, anyway. And when I'm in the middle of a negotiation for an unusual property or putting together a great investment package for a client that I know will fly—well, I'm on an all-natural high as tall as Mount Everest."

"Well, then? Are you really ready to give all that up?"

"I don't know, but— It's no longer enough, Mom. I'm thirty-two years old, and I want to get married, have a family."

"Then why haven't you? You could have married any one of two or three eligible men over these last few years. What about Clive Jordan?"

"I'm not in love with Clive, Mom." Although she'd been attracted to him, she must admit. She'd definitely considered his offer of marriage—until Dee died. "And I don't think Clive is really in love with me. We do very well together in business—great, actually. But that simply isn't enough for marriage."

"But, Meg, lots of business marriages are successful."

"Oh, Mom, that's not for me. Those alliances... Something is just missing."

"Something missing? You mean love? And you think Kelsey Jamison is in love with you? Meg, Kelsey doesn't love you! He only wants a baby-sitter and a housekeeper."

"Mom—"

"Oh, Kelsey's all right in his own way, I suppose. Dee Dee thought so. But, Meg, he has no ambition to be anything more than a small-time farmer, while Clive..."

Clive Jordan lived and worked on a world-wide stage. He lived at an expensive London address, drove the best cars, entertained lavishly, spoke knowledgeably of the arts and theater. Something her mother admired. He'd turned on his charm for Audrey last year, when she'd spent a month with Meg in London and he'd taken them to a show and late supper.

Meg sighed and rose, wandering to the window. This was the house in which she'd grown up. Looking out, she viewed the small side yard where long ago her father had planted rose and peony bushes, spring bulbs and summer day lilies. The backyard contained an intricately bricked patio and barbecue pit he'd taken pride in building with his own hands. John Lawrence had been content to be a small-town lawyer, a big frog in a small pond, and had never wanted to live anywhere larger or more sophisticated. He loved knowing and being called by his first name by almost everyone in the community. He'd loved being of service to his town. When he'd died the year before Meg moved away, it seemed the whole county attended his funeral.

"Mom, I know how impressed you were with Clive and England when you came to visit me in London last year...."

A new thought drifted across her mind. All at once it occurred to Meg that perhaps her mother hadn't been as content with small-town life as her father. Fragments of memories began to surface. Her mother's love of fine things, expensive restaurants, art galleries and theater. She'd chosen her wardrobe with care and style, never appearing in public without makeup. And the way Audrey had pushed for vacations in large cities—St. Louis, Chicago, Washington, D.C., Los Angeles and San Francisco. She hauled them all over each attraction and later enthused for weeks after visiting those locations.

What had Audrey wanted from her own life? More, obviously, than her husband, John. And while he'd admired Audrey and he didn't mind the travel, he never appreciated her push to emulate a life-style so different from his own. Meg wondered— had her dad's contentment been a great disappointment to her mother?

Meg turned and stared at her mother. Audrey, though growing older, was still a pretty woman, with fine blue eyes and few wrinkles. And in spite of her recent brush with heart problems, she had many years left if she was mindful of her health. Why couldn't she still pursue something exciting? Something of her very own?

"Mom, what did you dream of doing as a young girl?" She changed the subject completely. "You know, what did you want to be when you grew up?"

Audrey glanced up in surprise. "Why, I don't know. The same thing any girl dreams of, I guess. I went through the normal stages of wanting to be a nurse or teacher or a ballerina. I don't know."

"But wasn't there something special? Something that excited you and made you happy to think about, that you never tired of doing?"

"Oh, I suppose so. Art. I had one teacher who encouraged me in it. I loved to draw and paint and took a few sketching lessons in high school and then I wanted to go to Paris to study the great painters."

"Did you? I never knew you ever wanted to do more than those few sketches hanging in the dining room. They're really very good. Why didn't you continue your studies?"

"Oh, my parents discouraged anything impractical. They thought I should take a degree in teaching. Then I met your father my freshman year in college and—" she shrugged, lifting her palms "—after that I guess nothing else was as important as getting married."

"You loved Dad deeply, didn't you?"

"Well, I just suppose I did." Audrey stretched out on the bed, moistened her lips and smiled, a softness stealing over her features. "Yes, I loved him more than I loved life."

Meg nodded her understanding. Love had been known to change many a girl's direction, but she saw no need to let her mother's talent die altogether. She'd look into finding a good art class for her mother next week. It could only help her recovery, besides allowing her less time to be lonely.

"I know you miss Daddy," she said gently. "I do, too. But, Mom, that's how I love Kelsey. I've always loved Kelsey."

Saying it aloud gave her goose bumps. And from her very pores, an old wash of guilt; the understanding that Kelsey belonged to someone else still hung over her. Was it right for her to want him? Were her motives in the right place?

Meg brushed those ancient guilt feelings aside. She wouldn't think of that now. Her feelings had nothing to do with logical thinking. They just were. And Kelsey and his children needed her. So what if it was for just a housekeeper at first and for taking on a mother's job?

She took a deep breath and continued. "And I love those kids and I think I can do a good job of raising them. I think Dee Dee would want me to. I know it's chancy to marry Kelsey

before he thinks of me with anything more than friendship—''
in God's own time, Kelsey had said ''—and there's no guar-
antee he ever will, but don't you see? If I don't try, I'll never
know.''

And maybe my love for him will have to be enough....

Chapter Seven

Meg didn't have to ask one of her mother's friends to stay, after all. Jack took a week's vacation so that he, Kathy, and the kids could come again while Meg flew to New York on Tuesday. He promised the children some fishing to help keep them occupied. When they arrived, Sara and Andy made a game of vying for Audrey's attention, and for once she seemed pleased to spend time with them.

In New York, Meg slipped into her professional manner as easily as putting on her aqua summer suit and sensible heels, and presented her proposal for Serenity to Lazarus, David and Jane Neels with her usual mixture of enthusiasm and detail. Clive sat in on the meeting, but was content to let Meg carry the show.

Jane clearly thought Meg's idea quite brilliant. By time sharing Serenity for the first five years, their organization's immediate investment outlay would be significantly reduced. Lazarus was tentative, but he finally approved the plan, providing Meg could come up with firms he liked, to share the resort-conference center. Lazarus insisted on a personal, hands-on approach, though; he stipulated that Meg herself oversee the complete transaction.

Meg was torn; she wasn't quite ready to return to work full-time; still felt needed at home. But she must balance at least part of the next month between work and personal needs if this complicated transaction was to see a successful conclusion. A hidden sigh of relief caught her almost unaware when Lazarus seemed happy enough to allow Clive to get the ball rolling by making the initial approach toward the firms she suggested.

Later Meg went to dinner with Clive, the Neels and another business associate, but her concentration on their company kept getting sidetracked by thoughts of Kelsey and home. Of Audrey and her unvoiced loneliness. And Kelsey's. Of the art teacher Meg'd sought out for her mother…and Kelsey. Of the children and their different personalities, what life might be like on the small farm away from the bustling cities…and Kelsey.

When old Lazarus excused himself before dessert, she relaxed against the high-backed booth and grew even quieter, letting the others carry the conversation.

The day had been long and demanding, quite like many she'd put into her work over the years. She'd enjoyed it. She felt at the height of her abilities when putting the right spin on any investment. Today she'd given her best, happily confident of her advice for the Neels. But what would she have answered if old Lazarus had stubbornly insisted she jump back into negotiations without delay?

How could she simply go back to filling her life with only work when Kelsey's intriguing proposal still dangled enticingly?

Her very eagerness to accept him scared her right down to her fingertips—so much of her wanted to leap without looking. Yet why hadn't she snapped up Kelsey's suggestion of marriage immediately? Why was she hesitating over the answer, when she wanted Kelsey with all of her heart?

Did she want to marry Kelsey for the right reasons? Wasn't love the right reason?

She tried to figure it out. Five years before she'd put her love in a box, tied it up tightly and turned her back on it. It was not an obtainable thing.

Or even honorable, the way things were. "Thou shalt not commit adultery" was a commandment Meg could never ignore however much her heart hurt or yearned. She believed wholeheartedly in the sacredness of marriage, and Kelsey belonged to Dee Dee.

Besides that, she'd loved Dee Dee, as well. Meg would never have knowingly brought grief to her cousin.

*You did not choose the wrong path...*came the gentle prompting.

That was true, she hadn't. And now Kelsey was free.

Meg made an involuntary move, her hand almost upsetting her water glass. She *had* chosen the correct path when she'd needed to, and she had nothing to regret. But with that same thought she suddenly realized she'd built such a high, protective wall against that "unwise loving" that it still staunchly remained. Now she could let it crumble. Indeed, she could. Her mouth curved as she grasped new understanding.

Thank you, Lord...thank you!

Loving Kelsey hadn't been a sin, but she could easily have entered into sin if she had acted out on that love. Now Kelsey was free and so was she! Free to love him without restraint, without guilt. Dee Dee wouldn't mind.

No, Dee Dee had always known of her love for Kelsey. To her cousin's credit, she'd tried to ease Meg over her infatuation when she married Kelsey. Later, by mutual consent, they'd never discussed Meg's feelings. Though she always suspected Dee Dee of knowing why Meg moved so far away from home.

And as for her future with Kelsey?

Meg didn't think she'd try on any rose-colored glasses anytime soon. She had a strong feeling that taking on a ready-made, fully blossomed family might be like handling a three-ring circus. Even so she felt full of eagerness to brush up on her juggling skills.

As for loving Kelsey—she didn't know if she could trust herself not to blow her chances, but she'd pray for wisdom and direction as she always had. She didn't know any other way.

"Are you all right, Meg?" Clive asked, setting her glass out of harm's way and then looking at her with a curiosity and speculation he didn't try to hide. "You haven't been quite yourself since old Lazarus left us."

"Sorry, Clive. I guess my thoughts were wandering."

"I'll say. You didn't even notice when Jane and David excused themselves."

"Oh!" Meg stared at the empty space opposite her and Clive, white napkins thrown on the table. She wanted to giggle, but she contented herself with a smile. "Have I been rude?"

"Not really. Jane and David scarcely paid you any mind. And I'll excuse you if you have breakfast with me in the morning. Do you have to go back to Missouri right away?"

"'Fraid so."

Clive groaned and leaned toward her with his chin in his palm, resting on his elbow. His large blue eyes turned winsome, a charming tactic he wasn't above using to gain his own way. "Wish you were coming back to England with me instead. I can't get along much longer without you."

"Oh, stuff and nonsense," she teased, then pointed out, "Elizabeth is there, and Blake."

"But they're not you," he insisted on a slightly petulant note. Then he sighed and said, "What time is your flight?"

She had reserved an early flight into Kansas City for the next morning and already wondered how her mom had fared with Jack, Kathy, Sara and Andy. Then her heart lifted at how soon she might see all of the Jamisons...the kids...

Kelsey.

She jerked her mind back to the kids. Lissa was to try out for a solo in the next church production—had she made it?

Aimee had been invited to go along on a long bike ride and camping on the Katy Trail with a friend's family; the planned trip would take three days, and Kelsey wasn't sure if she was old enough to go. He'd been mulling over his decision.

The boys still talked of the old cars they found interesting that Sunday morning of Kelsey's proposal and Paul Lumbar's old car collection, especially the model-T Ford, hoping to finagle a ride during the July Fourth celebration. And the coming state fair where they planned to show Fred.

Heather had meticulously explained about the fair's carnival rides as though Meg had never heard of them, and exacted a promise from Meg to take her. Especially on the Ferris wheel.

Amazing, Meg thought, how swiftly her heart had become entangled again. With all of them.

"Has your return to your hometown become troublesome, my dear Meg?" Clive asked, scanning her face thoughtfully. "I thought your mother's health to be improving."

"Oh, Mom is recovering quite nicely, thank you."

"That's good. But something is pulling your mind away," he remarked. "It's unlike you."

"Mmm... I suppose it is." Gazing at his sophisticated good looks, Meg wondered why she hadn't fallen in love with Clive. Most women crossing his path did. His golden streaked hair and thick eyelashes, his strong jaw and plummy English accent left a huge trail of sighs in his wake.

He'd really only asked her to marry him that once, half kiddingly after they'd gained an important client. Yet he'd insisted he was sincere. And she'd given it some thought before turning him down. Clive led a full urban life-style with world travel and exciting business challenges thrown in, and she had to admit she found some of that tempting.

But her heart didn't sing when she was in his company.

"Let's call it a night, Clive. Will you walk me to the elevator?"

At his nod, they rose. Meg led the way out of the hotel coffee shop and toward the elevators. Clive punched the buttons and gave her a searching look.

"Clive, I do need to discuss something with you," she told him, deciding she might as well prepare him now for her leaving. They'd worked together so well, he'd come to depend on her for any last-minute fill-ins or secondary opinions he might need. He didn't worry about calling on her anytime day or night. He'd once told her if she could bottle all her instinct for investing, he'd buy it all. Now she'd no longer be available at the drop of a pin.

"Aha!" His brows shot up as though making their own accusations. "Thought so. Okay, give over. What's been going on?"

"I, um..." She hesitated, sucking in her bottom lip. "I'm not going to return to England, Clive."

"What? You're quitting the firm?" His mouth dropped in shock. "How can you do that to me? Who's made you an offer? Is it Mannings? Swallows? I'll top it, Meg, just tell me."

"No, nothing like that, Clive," she said, grinning at his ferocious glare. "I'm going to get married."

"Oh!" He gazed at her, blinking in puzzlement, then relief and then sudden consternation and suspicion, grasping her total intent. "What's that got to do with your work?"

She chuckled and leaned back against the door frame. No one had ever accused Clive of being slow. "Everything. I'll have a family to take care of in Missouri, Clive—five children as well as a husband, to be exact. I hardly think you'll want me to make the commute to London at the ring of the phone."

"Well, no, but—five children?"

"Yes."

"Good grief! You can't be serious?"

"Oh, I am. Quite."

"But...wouldn't you rather start out in the normal way with only a husband to begin with? Me, for instance?"

Meg maintained her smile but shook her head.

"What's this chap, whatever his name is, got, to pull you back to the wilds of Missouri? How could you have lost your heart in so short a time?"

"It isn't the wilds at all," she teasingly pointed out. "As I've told you before, we have all the desired arts and questionable delights of modern civilization anyone would want. Even indoor plumbing. But where I'll be *is* a *bit* country—" her voice softened, giving her away "—and I've known Kelsey Jamison for a very long time."

Clive studied her for an extended moment through narrowed eyes.

"Well I don't see the need for you to throw in the towel completely, Meg." He shoved his hands in his pockets. "I can't replace you that easily. In fact, I'm sure I can't replace you at all."

Her smile widened. "Oh, Clive. You will. You can move Elizabeth and Blake along in the field. And you needn't worry that I'll leave you high-and-dry altogether. I'll finish the projects I've started or turn over the ones that someone else can handle.''

He was silent, rocking back on his heels. Finally he drew a long-suffering breath. "When do you plan on deserting me?"

"Rather soon. In a month, I think."

"That's impossible. I can't give you up that quickly."

"Oh, it will be easier than you think. With daily communication via the web and faxes and phones, I can wrap up a lot of work from Missouri."

"But why do you have to quit entirely, Meg? This is the nineties. Women have been known to balance career and family just fine, you know. If you insist you must have this fellow, tell him I won't let you go entirely. I need your particular brand of expertise, my dear, especially on the real estate projects. Like this one with the Neels. How about on a consulting basis?"

"Hmm... Consulting part-time might work out." She brightened. It might be the very thing to both appease her odd moments of need to engage her career and ease her mother into less concern for her future. "I'll give it some thought."

When Meg returned home the next day, her mother had a list of things she wanted Meg to do. Meg thought them mostly stalling tactics to keep her from seeing Kelsey.

First, Audrey demanded they sort through the things stored in the attic, a long-overdue task. Meg wondered why Audrey suddenly found it necessary to do so without delay, but she and Kathy took on the job willingly. They laughed over old school pictures of Jack and Meg, and murmured sentimentally over clothing and toys. They sorted through boxes filled with old letters, the remains of her father's law office, records of long-closed cases, odds and ends of outdated furniture and many of Meg's own mementoes from school.

Meg felt it all worthwhile when she found Grandma Hicks's well-used Bible. Tucked away in many of the pages, Meg found favorite recipes she remembered her grandmother making, including the fudge recipe, and self-directed notes written in her grandmother's hand. She took it down to her own bedroom, carefully cleaned its old leather cover, and read that night and the next from its many marked passages.

"I can do all things through Him who strengthens me..." and "Trust in the Lord and He will direct thy path." Meg felt a warm link with someone whom she'd adored as a child.

On Friday Audrey insisted Meg go with her to the doctor and then to shop for a new dress. Meg happily accepted the outing as another sign of her mother's recovery.

Her mother hadn't mentioned their discussion of Kelsey's proposal again, and Meg thought it a good opportunity to bring up the subject of her future plans. She wanted—hoped for—her mother's approval, but she'd settle for acceptance. However, Meg knew she was the one who had to bring the families together.

After they'd each found a new dress from a local store, Meg suggested they have a cooling soft drink to refresh them against the heat and the drive home. Meg pulled up to a drive-through window. As they waited for their order, she took a deep breath.

"Mom, I'd like to invite Kelsey and the children over for dinner the day after tomorrow. Since it's the Fourth of July, I think it would be nice to have an old-fashioned family cookout. Is that all right with you?"

"Oh, I don't know, Meg. With Sara and Andy here, that will be a lot of squally children around. You know..."

"No, Mom, I don't know." Meg glanced at her mother. "It used to be that you never found that a problem. You liked kids—why don't you anymore?"

"Oh," Audrey said and gestured defensively, "I've grown used to life alone, I suppose. I like my peace and quiet these days."

"Well, the doctor thinks you can return to life in the golden fast lane any day now and you did fine with your bridge club last week. Jack and Kathy are going home Sunday evening. Wouldn't it be fun to have a family picnic before they go? A real old-fashioned July Fourth celebration?"

"I suppose," Audrey gave in grudgingly. "But I hope you're not planning to make a habit of this, Meg."

Undaunted, Meg asked the Jamisons to dinner for the holiday, asking them to come at four when the heat of the day began to wane, and she and Kathy spent the day before preparing a huge meal.

They served it outside on the brick patio. Sara and Andy mixed well with the younger Jamisons; Sara was only a few months older than Heather and the girls took to each other like two chicks from the same nest. Jack and Kelsey joked and teasingly sparred as they had long ago. Jack dragged out the battered old croquet set their dad had been fond of, and he and Kelsey taught the children how to play.

"Did you and Mom play this when you were kids, Dad?" Thad asked with an "in the olden days" tone as he whopped his wooden ball hard enough to send it into the oak and maple trees that bordered the backyard.

"Cool," Phillip remarked in awe, his gaze following the ball.

"Yeah, cool," Andy seconded.

Meg could almost see the idea forming in the two younger boys to follow Thad's play with ones like it.

"Not often," Kelsey replied to Thad's question with a quick laugh. "Mostly I was into baseball and the old swimming hole." He bent to line up his ball and said without looking at his son, "Now go chase your ball, and the next time you hit it that hard you'll take a penalty. Remember the object of the game."

Phillip's and Andy's expressions fell. "You mean we can't—" Phillip started.

"Nope."

"Aw, Dad!" Thad objected. Yet he ran to get his ball without further protest.

"Oh, that muddy old spot down on the river bend is awful." Lissa ignored her brothers' byplay to scoff at Kelsey's love of the old river spot. "I'm glad we get invited to swim in a clean pool sometimes."

"Yeah. And the lake is mostly clean," came from Aimee.

"If we ever get to go."

"Dee Dee and I played croquet when we were youngsters," Meg put in, addressing Thad. The boy glanced at her curiously, but didn't reply. "And we went swimming in the old mud hole, or the lake. In fact, Dee Dee and I were best chums and did lots of things together when we were little. She even lived with us for a year after her parents died. Before she married your dad.''

"Who was her mommy and daddy?'' Heather asked. "Did they know me when I was little?''

Meg smiled, a lump rising in her throat. "Actually, Heather, your mom's mommy and my dad were brother and sister, so we had lots of family picnics and things together. But your Gardner grandparents died while your mom was a teenager. I'm sorry you didn't have a chance to know them. They were lovely people.''

The lump in her throat grew larger. Heather would never know Dee Dee, either. She glanced at Kelsey, his eyes mistily acknowledging her unvoiced sadness over the loss.

It occurred to Meg for the first time that the Jamison children had lost a lot of people from their lives even before they were born. Kelsey's mother was gone, too, leaving them with only one grandparent alive, Kelsey's father. But his father lived in California now and seldom visited Missouri.

Meg glanced at her mother, sitting in the shade of a maple. Thankfully, she felt sure Audrey had many years yet. Meg recalled happy memories from her own childhood, and her mother's sense of fun, a zest for life. When had she lost that gift, Meg wondered.

With a dawning idea, she beckoned to Sara and Heather. Glancing over her shoulder, she bent to whisper in their ears. "See those red hollyhocks on the back edge of the flower bed?'' She waited for their nods. "I bet if you asked very nicely, Grandma will teach you how to make hollyhock dolls.''

In open delight, Sara and Heather took off in a run, calling eagerly for Audrey's attention.

"That was a neat trick,'' Kathy murmured next to her as they attended putting the finishing touches to the picnic table.

Meg merely chuckled. "Mom loves hollyhock dolls.''

Moments later when she dared glance their way, Meg felt her heart lift. Three heads bent together, one graying, one sunny bright and one with chestnut curls, sharing the delight of the old-as-the-hills pastime. Her mother's voice drifted to her in instruction, folding in a gentle love along with the colorful flower dolls.

Kelsey gravitated to Meg's side as dusk fell. They sat companionably watching the children while they chased fireflies at the earliest sign of dusk. Kathy and Jack joined them, calling encouragement. Even Audrey seemed to relax, more her old self, Meg thought.

As they served second rounds of peach cobbler, Kathy, who had never known Kelsey well, whispered "Kelsey's a peach" into Meg's ear, and grinned her pun and approval. Later, they all walked to watch the firework display in a nearby park. When the excitement ended, they returned to the Lawrence house, and Kelsey mentioned it was time for them to leave.

"No, not yet," Heather complained. "Can Sara come home with me?"

Sara looked hopefully at her mother. "Not this time, honey," Kathy told the little girls. "We'll be going home in a few days."

"C'mon, gang. Time to go," Kelsey called into the dark reaches of the yard. "Give your thanks for a nice evening."

Heather hugged Meg tightly, then Audrey. She fussed about leaving her new friend, Sara, but was consoled with the promise they would come again soon. Lissa and Aimee thanked Meg and Audrey effusively for the "coolest family get-together," Thad perfunctorily, and lastly, Kelsey murmured his in real gratitude for a great time. Audrey rose to the sincerity in his tone and graciously indicated they would repeat the evening soon.

"Phillip," Kelsey called, counting heads as he headed toward the car and found one missing. "Come on, time to go."

When no answer followed, Kelsey turned to Thad. "Where's your brother?"

"I dunno."

"Lissa?"

"He was around a little while ago."

Jack rose lazily from his lawn chair and wandered over. "He's probably with Andy and Kathy in the house. I'll go fetch 'em."

A few moments later Jack returned, his attention sharpened.

"Kathy hasn't seen 'em. Neither of the boys are there. Reckon they could've taken off somewhere on their own?"

"That's not like Phillip, but—" Kelsey turned away and called again.

"I'll try the other direction," Jack said as he strode down the street.

"Maybe they're hiding," Meg offered. "I'll check the backyard."

Lissa and Aimee followed behind as Meg rounded the corner of the house. "Phillip? Andy?"

From a distance she could hear Jack's call, and Kelsey's. Then Thad's. She checked the hedge border that ran the property line, but nothing appeared unusual. Beside her, Lissa called her brother's name again, and Aimee checked the hidden nooks between house and yard.

Above her, Meg heard a muffled sound. She came to a halt and listened. Something light landed on her head. A twig.

"Phillip? Andy?" she called, her gaze searching the trees above her head. A branch shook slightly. "Boys! Come down, right now."

"Aw, you found us." Andy's disembodied voice drifted down. "We wanted to stay up here all night."

Phillip didn't protest, but swung down, hanging a moment, his feet dangling near Meg's shoulders. Meg grabbed his legs, wondering if she could take his weight without it tumbling both of them. Then she felt Kelsey at her shoulder, bolstering her but reaching past with one hand to grab Phillip under his ribs. Phillip let go. She felt Kelsey's arm go round her, his feet braced. His strength added to hers, they caught the child together, and for an instant Kelsey's arms circled them both.

A moment later he swung his youngest son to the ground, then reached for Andy.

"You little scallywags," Audrey scolded as she came up. "I'd have another heart attack, except—"

"There you are, Flip," Aimee said, running to stand beside Meg. "You scared us half to death. Why'd you do that?"

Phillip answered with a shrug.

Lissa called the searchers back, and moments after the boys

had been gathered up, Jack herded his two children into the house while Kelsey stood sentry until he'd counted five noses firmly packed into his old blue car.

"What were you about to say earlier, Mom?" Meg asked curiously. "About why you wouldn't have another heart attack?"

"Oh, don't you remember?" Audrey chuckled, surprising Meg with her light humor. "You and Jack did something very similar once. I almost called out the police before we found you. The two of you caused me palpitations."

Once again they said their goodbyes. Kelsey glanced at Meg with a fleeting regret, but in the end, merely muttered, "See you soon, Meg?"

"Sure, Kelsey. Soon."

All in all the evening had gone quite well, Meg thought later as she prepared for bed. None of the children got into a fight. Her mother actually enjoyed everyone's company, and, after overcoming their brief fright over the boys hiding, even hunting them down seemed fun, reminiscent of an earlier, more innocent time.

Meg was more sure of her heart than ever. Was Kelsey? They had never once found a moment alone and she'd felt only the strength of friendship between them throughout the evening. She hoped fervently he hadn't thought better of his proposal and that he still wanted her to marry him.

Chapter Eight

❧

On Tuesday Meg drove out to the Jamison farm. Lissa had promised to baby-sit for a morning church function and had taken Heather with her, Aimee was on the Katy Trail outing with her friend, and the boys had gone on a fishing overnight with another church family. A whole morning had been cleared for her and Kelsey to talk, and oh boy, did she plan to chatter up a storm. She sincerely hoped he did too; a lot of ground needed covering. Meg had packed a basket of goodies for a lovely lunch.

Her heart felt light as air, and a smile hovered on her lips for most of the drive. She couldn't remember the last time she'd spent any time alone with Kelsey, asked him what he thought of local politics or world events, what his philosophy about child discipline was or how his cattle and wheat prospered. At least three hours loomed ahead without family members or kids or anyone to interrupt....

And she and Kelsey would make a firm decision about their future.

When she parked her car, she at least expected to hear the dogs barking, but in the farmyard quiet reigned. In seconds Kelsey, dressed in cutoff denims and a bright blue baseball cap,

88 In God's Own Time

stepped out of the front door. He must have been watching for her. Or listening to the crunch of tires on gravel.

"Hi, Meg. Hot day."

"Hello, Kels. Yes, it'll be stifling by noon." All at once she was struck with shyness, something totally foreign to her personality. No one else on earth ever affected her that way. No one but this man. To cover her momentary confusion, she turned to reach for her picnic basket and her straw sun hat.

"Let me help you with that. What did you bring, anyway?"

"Oh, I know you told me we'd run into town for lunch, but I thought it might be better...um, nicer, that is, if we didn't have to waste time."

"That's thoughtful of you, Meg. Miss Maybelle is going to give the girls lunch before bringing them home, and the boys are gone till tomorrow. Aimee, till tomorrow night. So we have no one to please besides ourselves." He laughed. "Feels strange after all these years. A little awesome, in fact."

He took the basket and fell into step beside her. "I hope it's something that can wait a bit. I have to stick close to the house till eleven or so because I'm expecting a call. But afterward we could go down to that spot near the river to eat."

"The place where we used to picnic sometimes?"

"Yeah. That won't bother you, will it, Meg? Because you and Dee Dee and I used to go there together when the kids were little?"

Meg remembered very well the beauty they'd all found there. Shade trees overhanging the gurgling stream bed in summer, mixed woods nearby that burst with redbud and dogwood in spring and vivid color in the fall. A patch of wild gooseberry bushes stood within yards of where they always threw down their picnic things. In the middle of summer, she and Dee Dee had sometimes picked berries for pies while Kelsey taught a progressing three-, then four-year-old Lissa to fish, and later, Aimee, Thad and Phillip.

A quick, unexpected stab of poignancy shot through her and she wondered if Kelsey felt it, too. They'd spent some happy times there. Would the place remind him too much of what he'd lost with Dee Dee?

Yet Meg thought he'd asked a deeper question. Would this place, this house he'd shared with Dee Dee call up too many memories for her? Could she live here?

His gaze softened when she glanced at him, reflecting some of what she felt; he couldn't prevent his own memories from crowding in, but he no longer seemed to draw pain from them. Either he'd gone beyond associating places with too much emotion or he'd grown comfortable with them.

At any rate, this was his home, and his children's.

"The river spot sounds lovely, Kelsey. I'd like to see it again."

Kelsey led her through the back door into the kitchen, and Meg spent a few moments putting the cold chicken, cheese, fruit, pickles and potato salad to wait in the refrigerator. The made-from-scratch brownies and rolls she left in the basket.

She straightened and looked around the old, outdated kitchen. It still retained Dee Dee's personality. Although basically clean, the room looked tired. The countertops were worn, and the faded yellow walls held a slap-dash display of children's art and kitcheny wall plaques from a bygone time. A green-painted wooden picnic table and benches in the corner served as a dining area. She'd helped Dee Dee paint it. Dee Dee had often talked of redoing what she felt was the main hub of her family, but they'd never had the money for it.

Surely, if anyplace reminded Kelsey of Dee Dee it would be this small farmhouse. He must feel memories of his wife everywhere. She certainly did.

"Want some coffee?" Kelsey asked.

"Not right now, thanks."

"Then come on through, if you don't mind." He led her into the crowded living room where his computer corner took up a full quarter of the room; his screen's wallpaper fluttered with flying geese. "I'm waiting on a call from the man who owned Fred's sire," he explained. "He lost the bull this year and wants to buy Fred. Say's Fred's the best of his progeny."

"Will the boys sell him?"

He scooted a basket of clean laundry to one side with his foot. She sat down where he indicated on the scruffy sofa. This room looked very little like it did the last time she'd seen it, she noted. Only the brown couch, a little more faded, and a few wall pictures had been there five years before.

Used to working with the latest technology, she examined his office corner with a brief glance. The computer was fairly new, she noted, but the office furniture and two bookcases had seen better days. Obviously, Kelsey had bought them used. There wasn't an inch that didn't overflow with papers and books. She idly wondered if the old house had decent enough wiring to handle anything more. Certainly, the room was stretched to the max.

"Don't think so," he answered as he sat in his office chair and leaned back. "At least not before the fair. They've put in too much work on the animal and we spent a bundle for stud fees to get him in the first place. But after, they probably will. Especially since they'll like the idea of Fred beating the beef houses to live a long life as a stud. But then, if we already have one buyer who wants Fred for that purpose and he comes in well in the judging, there might be more than one person who'll want him for the same reasons."

"The boys're learning about business early, aren't they? The law of supply and demand."

"Farm kids do," he reminded her, his tone a little nostalgic. "About some things, anyway. But the world is by turns so much bigger and so much smaller than what we knew growing up, or our parents. I'm not sure—" he sighed deeply and shook his head "—small-time farming or raising livestock will be either boy's choice for a life, or the girls'. Nor should it, necessarily. Though I'd like to have enough to leave them should one of them want it. But even good farm managers find it hard to make ends meet these days."

"True," she nodded. "Are you sorry you chose it?"

"Nope." He swung his chair to stare out the window, and laced his fingers against the back of his head. "No, I could never imagine doing anything else that would bring me so much contentment." He paused. "Though I could always find a job that pays better, I suppose. And I might have to take an outside job for the kids' college money, anyway."

He swung back to look at her directly, dropping his hands against his thighs. "Probably, in fact. Does all that—any of it—scare you, Meg?"

"Mmm... In what way?"

"Oh, that I'll never have much money. That getting the kids raised will be a struggle in itself and take most of my life for the next fifteen years." He smiled, his mouth slanting crookedly and went straight to the point. "I can't offer you much beyond what you see, Meg. A rather unequal partnership. Hard work and countless hours. It isn't much..."

He'd referred to his proposal as offering a partnership for the second time. Yet she didn't find the term displeasing, although a little lacking, to say the least. After all, he wouldn't think of a second marriage in the same way as he probably had thought about his union with Dee Dee—not wildly romantic. But she wasn't a starry-eyed crazy-in-love kid any longer, either. Just in love.

She chose to lighten the pitch of their conversation.

"Oh, I don't know about that, Kelsey," she said and grinned. "Don't downplay the sweet appeal of being personally chosen by Lissa and Aimee, and I think I can now count Heather in, to be their new mother. Having a hand in raising them will offer its own reward. That's quite a bit in your favor, and don't you forget it."

"How could I?" He eyes lit up in amusement. "They did make quite a case for it, didn't they?"

"I have to admit they did."

"I heard the whole thing, you know. After I got over the shock—" He broke up in mirth and shook his head.

"I know," she agreed, and joined his laughter. "They seemed to have planned it for a long time."

"Ever since they heard you were coming home for a time," he replied through his chuckles.

"Yes," she nodded, her growing laughter interspersing her speech. "It's a *majorly* serious matter. Schemed the whole thing."

"I had no idea they—" Kelsey let his laughter roar "—they—"

Meg nodded, unable to voice anything but side-splitting amusement.

"Um...," He tried again after he wiped the heel of his hand against his tearing eyes and—almost—containing his laughter. "One thing I can promise, Meg, if you decide to say yes. With five kids to deal with, you'll never have time to get bored."

"No, I wouldn't expect to. Especially if I have to swing from the trees with Phillip." She, too, quieted and tipped her head, her hair swinging against her neck. She wondered if this was the right time to mention something she'd been thinking of for days, but whether it was or not she had to know.

"Kelsey, you have five lovely children, and you're right—I love them very much and they'll be both fun and a challenge as well as a handful. But when you asked the other day why I hadn't married, you didn't ask whether I wanted children of my own or not."

He looked a bit startled, but glanced quickly away as though wanting to cover his reaction. "Do you?"

"Yes, I think I do. One, at least. But you have a basketful, and I couldn't fault you for not wanting more."

He was quiet for a long moment. "I had thought five enough, Meg. But I wouldn't mind making it a half dozen. After that, I must admit I might find fathering more of a stretch than I could comfortably cope with. Could you be happy with only one child of your own?"

"Yes, I think so. Especially with the others." Especially if the only child she would bear from her own body was his, too.

"Agreed, then. One child of our own."

One child of their own making. Meg felt warmed by his expression, his inclusion and understanding. If they entered into this partnership, it would be on equal recognition of each other's needs.

"Kels—"

The phone rang and Kelsey swung round, scooping up the receiver in a swift move. "Hello."

With a nod, he indicated it to be the call he'd been waiting for. Meg gave him an understanding return nod and rose to look at the family photos lining the wall beside the front door. Snapshots of the children, each as toddlers, and one of Dee Dee's parents. One Meg had taken. She remembered the occasion well. It was an enlarged snap of Kelsey and Dee Dee holding hands right after they became engaged.

She stopped to gaze at the last picture. The three of them, taken just before a summer baseball game, their smiles broad and happy and very young. While tiny, slender Dee Dee was glued to his side, Kelsey and she stood almost shoulder to shoulder, a brotherly arm draped carelessly across Meg's. Leaning closer, Meg wondered how she'd had the ability to cover her confused emotions, those desperate yearnings of her teen years. Yet she saw nothing beyond the obvious in her youthful expression.

Those were the days she'd learned adeptness at concealing her self-doubts over her Amazon size, her envy of Dee Dee. Yet Dee Dee had always known. One of the reasons she'd remained so fond of her cousin was that Dee Dee had never betrayed her, never made Meg feel awkward over the fact that Kelsey was hers.

"Ready, Meg?"

"Yes..." She turned to see him waiting, a curious questioning light in his gaze, almost smiling. He must have strong memories every time he looked at those photos, as well.

Yet he asked her nothing of her impressions, merely saying, "Let's go, then. Before anything else crops up to interfere."

They gathered the food, the cooler and an old patchwork quilt made from worn denim to throw in the back of Kelsey's old black pickup. The two-mile drive along a rutted dirt road off the highway jounced them along while they spoke of mundane things like who still used the creek and the crops or animals they saw along the way and the inevitable topic—the weather and its effect on the current growing year.

After Kelsey parked under an oak tree for shade, he took the cooler and blanket while she carried the basket. Meg glanced about, assessing the changes to the spot—the added growth. And the sameness. Others had used the location, but not often. It seemed their own, still.

As they spread out the food, Meg examined the quilt's sturdy design and uneven, cherry red stitches. It looked like one the girls might have made. Thankfully, Meg didn't recall ever seeing it before. Just as well, she mused. Although she'd loved Dee Dee dearly, in all honesty, she didn't think she could wade through another sentimentally heavy attachment to something that had once belonged to her cousin. Selfish of her, she supposed.

Then it occurred to her—she'd grown to womanhood envying Dee Dee, although she'd left that eroding emotion behind a very long time ago. She'd made the emotional separation that one does in adulthood, carved out a life of her own, a place where she shone on her own merits, and her self-confidence had grown apace. She was her own person.

Now a new thought bubbled up. She'd said she wouldn't be put off by memories, and she vowed not to be. She understood the need to never forget nor underestimate the children's desire to remember their mother, nor Kelsey's. Yet she wasn't ashamed to admit wanting to make her own imprint, her own place with Kelsey. They shared memories of Dee Dee, but...she didn't want to live in Dee Dee's shadow.

She wanted to start fresh. If they were to have a real partnership, Kelsey needed to, as well. Could he?

They ate for a few moments in silence.

"Kelsey," she said, putting down her half-finished chicken leg and picking up a sweet pickle. "You talked of our marriage as a partnership."

"Mmm..."

"How do you mean that? What do you need from me?"

"Oh," he said, and chewed a moment. "I guess the usual things—adult companionship at night after the young'uns are asleep, someone to share a late-night bowl of popcorn with, plan out the next day's needs, and the next week's. Someone willing to listen to me when I'm frustrated at day's end or happily speculating on a new idea in breeding. And, of course, as we've mentioned—share holidays and seasons and the joys and sorrows of child rearing. Meg," he said, reaching for his iced tea, "I hate being a single father. I want someone to sit beside me listening when Lissa sings a solo in the church choir, or the boys play ball, or—'' he chuckled ''—when Aimee makes the debate team.''

''Is that what Aimee wants to do in school? Debate?''

''She doesn't know it exists yet, but I can see her heading it up the moment she hits high school, can't you?''

''As a matter of fact—'' she narrowed her eyes, conjuring up Aimee's animated features in dramatic pose ''—I can.''

They both chuckled, thinking of Aimee's penchant to argue her point in any given family debate until Kelsey simply commanded, ''Enough.''

''What about Heather?''

''I think Heather might turn out to be the princess of drama.'' He waggled his brows, making Meg laugh again.

''Well, it's a little early for Heather,'' she returned, still smiling. ''We'll see.''

''What were you like as a little girl, Meg?''

The question caught her unaware. It seemed they'd known each other forever, yet she knew little of Kelsey's early childhood. He and his father had moved to Missouri from Illinois shortly before he started college. Looking back, it seemed Kelsey had seldom mentioned his home or his parents.

''Awkward and shy,'' she said. ''Somewhat like Phillip, I guess. Never trusting myself enough to say much in a crowd.''

''Oh, I can't believe that. Well, if you were, you'd outgrown it by the time I met you and Dee Dee. You and she kept me running hard just to stay in place—I sometimes felt like a tennis ball between the two of you. And you always had something for us to do or someplace to go, and a quip or a joke.''

''Hmm...'' She'd worked hard at maintaining that image.

''Remember when we toilet-papered the youth pastor's new car on his birthday? Joe Sanders, right?''

''And that rascal got back at us by turning the water hose on us during the next youth picnic.'' They chuckled with the shared memory. ''Do you know what Joe's doing now?''

''Yeah. He's a pastor down in Springfield. Anyway, I don't recall the time when you were ever awkward or shy, Meg.''

''I suppose not. But those kinds of high jinks blossom from the fermenting minds of idle youth. Or at least youth with little responsibility and can-you-top-this smugness.'' She shrugged and grinned. ''I think I've lost the knack.''

He returned her smile and shook his head in disbelief. ''You'll have to prove it. Besides, your knack for being pleasant company remains intact.''

Pleasant company, pleasant company! Would he never see her as *exciting* company?

''What else should we talk about, Meg?''

She let her lashes drop and picked up the pickle jar and tightened the lid. ''Oh, I don't know. You and Dee Dee, I suppose.... Do you, um, still think of yourself in those terms, Kels? 'Me and Dee Dee'? or 'Kelsey and Dee Dee'?''

Stealing a swift glance at him, she saw the gathering pain in his eyes before he turned to look at the river. He hadn't expected her question.

''Yeah, Meg, I do sometimes.'' His voice was low and gravelly with gut level emotion. ''Sometimes at night I dream I hear her calling from another room. Twice I've even leapt out of bed from it, running to the kitchen to find her. The first time I was so shook up I—I couldn't...''

''Stop crying for the rest of the night?''

''Yeah.''

She rose to her knees, reaching out to touch his shoulder, her heart swelling with her need to comfort him. She longed to fill his emptiness with her own love. He slid his arms around her waist, pressing his face against her chest, seeking her generous warmth, seeking relief, she thought, from pain.

''I guess I'll never stop dreaming I'll find her again some day,'' he mumbled, then swallowed hard. After a moment, he pulled away and stood, hands in his pockets, as he stared at the river while he regained his composure.

Meg kept her gaze on the crazy quilt, running her fingers against the mixed texture while she fought her own confused senses. She'd loved Dee Dee, too. Would Kelsey really never stop dreaming of her, longing for her?

The hurt that gnawed at Meg's confidence so long ago rose again like Lazarus. Would she always run second to Dee Dee?

''But I can't live in the past,'' he stated with quiet determination, seeming to let it go. "Or wish for what can never be again. My children need too much."

He turned back to drop once more on the quilt, picking up his plate again. Meg remained quiet, pretending to eat while she silently prayed for hope to resurrect in both of them. For Kelsey, hope to replace his underlying despair with God's love. Hope that he could once more draw from God's grace. For herself....

A flock of geese flew overhead, squawking, before passing.

"Sounds as loud as my kids, don't they?" Kelsey remarked, his tone letting her know he wanted to move away from their overemotional exchange. "Okay, Meg. What else does this partnership need?"

"Oh, let's see," she said, following his lead. "We don't have to choose where to live or work. How do you see us dividing up household responsibilities?"

Kelsey groaned and lay back, his hands behind his head. "Now there's one to shake the dew off the morning."

He glanced at her from beneath half-closed lids. She raised a brow, not giving an inch.

"All right. Okay. I know modern marriage counselors say a guy should do his share of the household stuff and cooking, but honestly, Meg, I've got enough to do with everything outside. I've let repairs go because I haven't had either the time to do them myself or the extra money to hire it done. And I'm a lousy cook. Haven't you noticed how I'm pigging out?"

"I did, rather. You seemed to enjoy supper the other night quite well, too."

"You bet. Me and the kids together. We're all so dog tired of no cooking or my cooking we might start barking any day now. Lissa and Aimee do some of it, but there's a lot they don't know how to do. I've eaten so many burned or half-raw dinners these past two years I'm shocked I still know what a good meal is. And you can sure make a tasty meal, Meg."

"Don't try that flattery, Kels."

"What is it our grandmothers used to say? The way to a man's heart is through his stomach?"

"Better not say that too loudly in public or too widely, Kels."

She wadded up and flung her napkin at him. "It might reap a crop you'd rather leave buried."

"True." He ducked, sat up and grabbed the pan of brownies. "Mmm... You put nuts in 'em. Heaven. Ya wanna marry me, Meg?"

"I'm thinking it over."

"Can you bake a cherry pie? How 'bout a lemon or pecan?"

"Kels—"

"Woof! Woof!" he managed between bites.

"You—" she launched a second napkin wad.

"Marry me, Meg. The kids and I *need* you."

His face alight with playfulness, his eyes nevertheless held real hope of her affirmative answer. How could any woman resist such appeal? Particularly when she didn't want to?

"Help to raise my children and bring a little order into my house, and I'll never ask you to take on anything outside, Meg. Not even a kitchen garden, unless you particularly wanted one. 'Specially since I've learned you might get the lop-eared rabbits mixed up with the cottontails or mistake a bull for a cow or...something," he teased.

"So help me, I'm—" Hands on her hips, she rose to her knees, threatening another paper napkin wad.

"So, will you?"

"Yes, but—"

"Yippee!"

Jumping to his feet, he grabbed her hands and pulled her up to swing her round, much like one of his kids might. His laughing eyes grew quieter, the color mossier. "Oh, Meg. This makes me so happy. I know we can make a go of it. We'll be teammates like we used to be."

He'd been captain of the church baseball team, she his first pick.

He leaned toward her, lowering his lips to hers. His mouth was warm and gentle, but without undue demand. Meg allowed her eyelids to close as she savored the sweet touch, wonder filling her at the knowledge that this man wanted her to be his wife. Then he drew back, his gaze searching and totally solemn. "Thank you, my dear. Thank you for saying yes."

Meg could only nod, hiding an unreasonable hurt. He hadn't offered a false pretense at love, and gratitude wasn't even close to what she'd hoped for. Didn't he find her attractive even a little? But until he truly felt something stronger for her, Meg would have to settle for the simple affection of friendship. As she always had. Yet she feared it might leave no opportunity, no opening for him to fall in love with her at all.

Chapter Nine

"You wouldn't mind if I...um, changed the house around or anything?" Meg asked on their drive home, giving a lot of attention to smoothing the wrinkles from her cotton shorts. Kelsey glanced at her, wondering about her unusual hesitancy.

"Not at all," he assured as they jounced over a particularly bad rut, "if you think it'll do any good."

"It's pretty crowded," she said carefully. With diplomacy.

"Yep. It sure is."

Meg had put on a lot of polish over the years. He'd been noticing little things ever since she'd come home. Like not wanting to insult him over how tight the space was in his house, or how cluttered. He couldn't seem to stay on top of things, no use denying that.

He'd lived single for two years now, and he'd given little thought to where they'd put another person in their small house, much less find somewhere for the two of them together. He should've gone ahead and added a room last year when he realized the girls needed more space.

"Whatever you want to do in the house is fine with me, Meg. I said you'd be in charge of it. But I'll tell you," he said, shaking his head, "there's no way that I can see to stretch any more room out of that small frame house. After Dee Dee died, I turned the largest bedroom—and that's not much, you know—over to the girls. Lissa's worked it around several times, but no matter how you slice it, having three girls in there makes it crowded. The boys are tight, too.''

''Mmm... And you?''

''Oh, well...'' He lifted his baseball cap and brushed back his sweat-dampened hair. ''I took that little room off the kitchen.''

Meg nodded, sucking at her lower lip. Then as she thought that over, she eyed him sideways.

''As I recall, that room barely accommodated a baby crib and a small chest. The last baby I remember in that room was Phillip, and even then Dee Dee complained over the lack of space. It certainly wouldn't take a full-sized bed.'' Meg let her glance slide down his long frame. ''How do you manage?''

''With a narrow cot.'' He half shrugged, his hand spreading in a helpless gesture against the wheel. It told Meg more than he knew about the way he'd approached life these past years, the loneliness he'd faced. The tiny room wouldn't invite spending any more time in it than necessary—someplace merely to sleep or change clothes. She thought of all the times she'd used her own bedroom as a retreat, a comfort zone. A narrow cot had about as much appeal as a bed of eggshells and certainly wouldn't allow room to even think of another person sharing it. Unless she wanted to hang from the ceiling.

Yet it did give Meg a better understanding of how alone Kelsey must feel sometimes as the only parent of his brood. He'd said he wanted an adult companion. Kelsey had always been so outgoing, so strong, she hadn't thought of him in that kind of need. In her teen years when she'd viewed him through star-studded gazes, Meg had thought him capable of anything and perfectly self-sufficient and contained. A quick intake of feeling rushed over her as she realized just how deeply he buried his vulnerability, his loneliness.

Meg knew Kelsey well enough to understand he treasured his children. He wouldn't change his life. But the active fathering of five children, or having a demanding occupation, working dawn to dusk and beyond—*things to do*—couldn't take the place of a mate or satisfy that deep hunger for an equal partner. Or a heavenly one.

Oh, she knew that one all right.

Father, please let Kelsey open his heart to your love, to be filled with your fellowship.

The prayer flowed from her thoughts along with a flooding desire to once more put her own arms around him and hold him, to babble out her love if only he would recognize it. Yet a gentle caution calmed her.

Don't, Meg...don't rush in too soon. Wait...your time will come.

Taking a long, steadying breath, she kept her hands in her lap. After a moment Kelsey sighed, and a tenseness that she hadn't even noticed before seemed to ooze out of him.

"A single bed doesn't take up much space. But now—" He glanced at her thoughtfully, leaving the unspoken words to hang. Now that they'd made a firm decision to marry, they had to find a room big enough for the two of them.

"I've thought about enclosing the front porch to extend the living room, and rearranging the dining room—" he shook his head, his expression glum "—but a Band-Aid solution isn't the answer. I should seriously think about adding a room, I guess."

"*Seriously* serious?" she teased.

"Yes, I think that's the expression of the day," he agreed with a quick laugh. "Or majorly serious."

They both grew quiet for a moment.

"There's that old sleeping porch above the back bedrooms," Meg reminded him, the idea coming out of nowhere. The narrow, crooked stairs led off the biggest bedroom, the one the girls now shared. She recalled Grandma Hicks telling of hot summer nights spent on a similar sleeping porch when she'd been a girl.

"That's all it is, though, Meg. An old screened-in sleeping porch. It was never enclosed against heavy weather and would have no heat in winter."

"But it might do for the remainder of summer."

"For who?"

"For us."

"You'd be willing to use that?" His brows shot up almost to his hat brim, yet his voice took on a hopeful tone.

"What's the alternative? When we marry, what then?"

He was quiet again, thinking. "I don't know. It needs lots of repair and it's piled with storage boxes and discards."

"Couldn't you find space in the barn?"

"Mmm..." Kelsey felt a sense of fun rise, a lightness of spirit he'd had glimpses of all afternoon. No other woman but Meg ever gave him this feeling of having the ability to solve any problem that came across his path.

"That's an idea. Maybe we should leave the house to the kids and bed down in the barn," he said, flashing her a teasing grin as he pulled up and parked near the back door. "Take over the hayloft."

She took a mock punch at him with a loosely curled fist. "No, silly—you know what I meant."

He made a face that could compete with any his children made, then conceded. "Yeah, I guess we could use a corner of the barn for storage."

Swinging out of the truck, he came around to open her door.

"Or better yet, make more space in the garage," he said as he took her arm to help her out of the truck. "In fact, I'll start rearranging some of that junk in the garage today, and as soon as the girls get home, I'll start them on sorting through all that holiday stuff in the sleeping porch."

"Let's look at it."

"Now?" Again she'd surprised him.

"If you have other things to do, I can do it myself."

"No, no. Let's go. We've got about—" he glanced at his watch "—if we're lucky, at least twenty to thirty minutes before Lissa and Heather get back."

The heat in the house nearly stifling, Kelsey took a moment to check the window air-conditioning unit. "It's working, but on days like this it's just not enough," he commented, tossing his hat aside. Sweat gleamed along his forehead and darkened his hair to almost a mahogany shade. "Thank God for those shade trees on the west. They help."

They climbed the stairs single file, Kelsey leading the way, swiping at cobwebs as he went. Meg followed him over the upstairs threshold and stopped, uncertain of her step in the dim light. The stuffy, hot air smelled of old boxes and mold, indicating it had been some time since anyone had come this way.

"Wait a minute," Kelsey told her, a hand protectively on her arm.

He moved toward a far corner, and Meg heard a scratching, a metallic click, then shutters suddenly unfolded to open a complete expanse of wall-to-wall, framed screens. Sunlight poured in, showing streams of dust motes, along with a rush of cooler air. Outside, the leaves rustled in the breeze from the nearby oaks, giving her the feeling of being high in the trees.

She waited while he opened all three sides. A sweet fragrance of honeysuckle came with a waft of air. And roses. She hadn't remembered what grew on that side of the house, so she made a mental note to go and look.

The narrow room spread across the back of the house, the lower half enclosed with beaded board, the upper half fully screened. Old forest green paint, bubbled from the heat and peeling, went unrelieved by any decorative touch. In several places, the screening curled loose from its frame, leaving ample opening for mosquitoes and flies and other insects to invade. And plenty of evidence showed they already had.

"What do you think?" he asked, uncertain, fingers hanging on his hips.

She hesitated as she assessed the possibilities. "That it's as you described."

"Uh-huh." His face lost its happy expectation. "Pretty hopeless."

"Oh, not entirely."

"I don't know.... I can't ask you to sleep here."

He sounded so dispirited, she asked, "Well, what do you want to do, Kelsey?"

"Well, for starters..."

"Uh-huh?"

He studied her from where he stood in the corner, a dozen boxes between them, the shaded light making patterns around them and across his face. A look of raw yearning flashed in his eyes, tightening his wide mouth, and for the first time ever Meg knew she saw the core of his soul.

"I want to get married, Meg," he said very low. "I didn't know how much until this minute."

Unexpectedly, she found she had to moisten her lips to answer. Even then, her words felt dry. "All right. We've agreed on that."

"But I mean right away, Meg, if that suits you." He took a step toward her. "As soon as we can. Before the fair, even."

"Why the rush?"

He glanced at her briefly, then away. "It would give us the rest of the summer to settle into being a family before school starts again, for one thing. And—it isn't like we don't know each other—but I thought maybe we should wait awhile, a month or so before we, um...share a bed. Give ourselves time to see each other every day. There were times when everything was easy, but—"

"That was a long time ago and there were three of us then," she said, completing his thought.

"Yes."

"A month?"

"Will that give you enough time? Did you want a big wedding? Oh, Meg, I'm sorry. I wasn't even thinking of that. It wouldn't be fair to rob you of all the things a girl wants."

He'd called her a girl, making her smile. But before she could respond, the sound of a car reached them, and then slamming doors.

"Well, back to reality, Meg. We didn't even get twenty minutes."

"That's all right, Kels. After all, this is what we're getting into, isn't it?"

"Dad...Meg...we're home," Lissa's voice echoed up to them.

"Where are you, Daddy?" Heather called.

"Upstairs," he responded with a shout, then, grinning at Meg, he lowered his voice. "You're a glutton for togetherness."

"Just call me tribe leader," she returned.

A resounding clomping on the bare wooden stairs preceded

the girls. "What're you doing up here, Daddy?" came from Heather.

"We've got a project, kids. We're going to clean this place up."

"We are?" Heather asked, her feathery brows puckered. "What for?"

Lissa's eyes grew wide as she gazed at her father. Then she flashed a questioning glance at Meg. A shy smile blossomed into an exuberant one.

"Oh, I think it would look much nicer up here if we cleaned the place up, don't you?" Meg answered Heather, her mouth trembling with laughter, while she silently acknowledged Lissa's knowing gaze. Kelsey stood, hands shoved into his back pockets, and smiled, too.

"Heather," Kelsey spoke, "can you go get the wagon?"

"Okay," the child answered uncertainly. "If Lissa comes with me."

"No, I have something else for Lissa to do right now."

"But, Daddy—"

"The unspoiling begins," Meg murmured under her breath.

She bent low and looked Heather square in the eye. "This is a family project, Heather. Aren't you a part of this family?"

"Uh-huh."

"Well, then. We can't leave you out, can we?"

"Uh-uh."

"And do you know where the wagon is?"

"Out in the yard."

"Okay. You're getting to be a pretty big girl, aren't you? You're going to be five just before fall and go to school?"

"Uh-huh."

"Well, then you can do it. Go and get it and bring it to the back door, please. We'll need it to haul some of these things to storage."

Heather swung around and started to run down the stairs. "Walk on the stairs, Heather," Kelsey cautioned. "Don't run."

"Okay."

A second later they heard a thump. Meg caught her breath

and made a start toward the stairs, but Kelsey held up his hand and merely listened. Then they heard running feet.

"She's all right," Kelsey remarked. "She jumped those last steps." Together they let out their sighs of relief.

"I suppose I'll have to get used to it," Meg said. "I'll have to learn when to react and when not to where it concerns children."

"Is it true, Aunt Meg? You're really going to marry Dad?"

"Yes, honey. We decided today."

"*Yes!* Oh, yes! Wait till Aimee hears. Oh, this is so-o-o cool! How soon, Aunt Meg?"

"In about a month." She couldn't keep her glance from swinging to Kelsey, watching a slow, wide smile spread while he held her gaze. As usual, she felt like melting right down to a puddle. It was a good thing Kelsey would be out of the house every day. Else how would she ever manage to get any work done or take care of five kids when that smile tugged at her?

"Just before the fair," he pronounced.

The following weeks were the wildest scramble of Meg's life. Through Justine, she ordered a new computer system, the latest technology on the market. She'd been making do with her laptop while she'd been home, but it wasn't enough.

"Although, I don't know where I'm going to put it," she confessed as she and Justine talked. "I'll have to rent an office, I suppose. I'd rather have a home office to be more accessible to the kids, but Kelsey simply has no unused corner left in his house."

"Yeah, I remember how small that house is," Justine replied. "Well, there's several good office properties around with space for rent, but, ah, I have that loft space upstairs I'd be willing to rent," she said, gesturing to the wide wooden stairs against the brick sidewall. "I've been working on it as I could and right now it's full of storage, but—"

"Wow! Talk about the Lord providing. Let's go look at it." Meg pivoted and headed toward the stairs. Reaching the top, she walked around the open space with growing enthusiasm. "This'll work, Justine. And I like the idea that you'll be here all day, just downstairs. I can run in and out as I please. I'll need some office furniture and..."

Thirty minutes later, she was stuffing her checkbook back into her purse when she glanced at her friend with a grin. "Now, if you could wave your magic wand and find someone reliable to help with Mom's housework and run errands a couple of mornings a week for her, I'd call you blessed forever."

"Oh, is that guaranteed?" Justine raised her brow, looking smug. "Are you willing to put it in writing?"

"What do you mean?"

"You may begin this minute. I'll be addressed as Blessed Justine, if you please. I know a woman named Mary Claire who's looking for something very much like you describe. But she's looking for more than two days a week."

It didn't take much thought to figure that one out. "Set up an interview pronto, Blessed Justine. If she's good, I'll have her out to Kelsey's for the other three days, and she can start right away while I'm in London closing my flat and wrapping up loose ends with Clive."

To her mother's credit, Audrey rose to the occasion and accepted Meg's decision, although she did protest the speed with which Meg and Kelsey wanted to marry and the fact they wanted a simple ceremony without undue fuss.

Meg was trying to sort through a business proposal Clive had faxed to her at the little desk in the corner of the living room while her mother flipped through a magazine in which she clearly wasn't interested.

"But, Meg, you're my only daughter. I always dreamed of you walking down the aisle wearing a lovely white traditional dress. I've kept my veil, you know. Wouldn't you like to wear it?"

"It's a lovely veil, Mom. Save it for Sara." Meg heard her mother's dramatic sigh, but refused to turn around.

"Well, it doesn't have to be a *big* affair."

"I know, Mom, but I don't need a formal wedding gown and half a dozen bridesmaids to have a nice wedding. Those are for very young brides, anyway."

"Well, thirty-two isn't too old for a formal wedding," Audrey protested. "I would think you'd want to invite all your friends, and then there are many people in this town who still remember your father we should invite."

"All the people I care about are invited, Mom." She checked one figure against a second, shuffling her papers with more force than necessary, hoping to give her mother a clue that she wanted to work. "A simple ceremony doesn't mean it isn't a celebration. Besides, a formal wedding takes months to organize. Kelsey and I don't want to wait."

She'd marry Kelsey in jeans and T-shirt like the flower children of a generation back, as long as the ceremony was real, legal and binding. As long as she could love him honestly and openly.

"Why are you in such a hurry?" Meg heard her mother flipping through the magazine as if shuffling cards, a tactic she'd used when wanting her father's attention while he was choosing to be vague. This was exactly why she'd been running off to Justine's to tackle business rather than trying to work with merely her laptop at home. "If this is the right thing to do, the wedding can be just as nice six months from now. Or even next spring."

"It makes just as much sense for us to marry now, before the kids start back to school," Meg returned.

"That's another thing. You haven't time to, um, *court,* with all those children to look after."

Meg did laugh at that, turning to catch her mother's sheepish gaze. "Mom, men and women no longer courted even when you and Daddy were young. They dated."

"Well, perhaps that's so. But you know what I mean."

"Yes, I know what you mean. But, Mom, it isn't as if we've just met or didn't know each other. We're not exactly in our impetuous youth."

Her mother sighed. "I suppose not..."

Meg wondered how difficult her next round would be when she asked Audrey to allow Lissa to come stay with her for the three weeks of Meg's absence. She put it off until after supper while Meg packed her briefcase. But to her delight, her mother seemed to welcome the idea of Lissa's visit.

"You're all right with the idea, then? Kathy can't come down this time."

"Oh, my. I really don't think I'm ill enough to warrant all this concern any longer, nor am I incapable of taking care of myself, Meg. But, well, the child is a sweet little thing. And quiet. But what will Kelsey do without her for the better part of three weeks?"

"He'll just have to manage. Besides, Mary Claire, the woman who's going to come here to help you will help out at the farmhouse, as well, while I'm gone. She's also agreed to drive you around if you want her to."

"That will be quite expensive, won't it Meg? Paying someone for all that confusion? Why didn't you merely hire the woman to come here and be done with all that shuffling about?"

"Would you have wanted that, Mom? A stranger living here for three weeks?"

"No, of course you're right. I wouldn't like that. But I do think I'm well enough to live alone again—there really is no need to bother about finding someone to stay with me at all. Especially since the woman will come to clean."

Meg pursed her mouth and snapped her briefcase closed. She set it aside and turned to her mother. Crossing this bridge was bound to come. "It's just a precaution, Mom. For me. I'd feel better knowing someone was in the house with you at night. But...the truth of it is, I thought Lissa would enjoy some time out from the daily chores at home. She's had too much responsibility of late and not enough kid time. You'd be good for Lissa. She needs more woman-to-woman time with someone she trusts, and you are her great-aunt. Her only aunt."

"I hadn't thought of it like that," Audrey admitted.

"Mmm... And this will be the perfect way to give her a break without making her feel guilty for deserting Kelsey. Besides that, if you don't need Mary Claire, why don't you start driving again? The doctor said he didn't see why you shouldn't, as long as you don't pressure yourself. Take Lissa up to Kansas City to the Nelson Art Gallery, why don't you, and have a day on the Plaza?"

"That does sound nice. I haven't been there in a long time. Is Lissa interested in art, do you suppose?"

"I don't know, but you could ask her."

"I'll ask Babs to go along. She has a granddaughter about Lissa's age who lives..."

Meg let her mother plan. Asking Lissa to come and stay in her old room while she was gone had turned out to be a stroke of genius, it seemed. Meg wondered where it had come from, but then laughed at herself. She knew. She'd been touched by divine inspiration too many times not to recognize it.

Of all people, Sandy Yoder offered the most practical help. Meg and Kelsey ran into her when they were leaving the pastor's office the next afternoon. They'd arranged for an unassuming ceremony to take place at dusk following the evening church service the Sunday before the fair opened. Any church members wishing to stay would be invited to witness the vows.

Other than the children, Meg and Kelsey didn't plan on having attendants. A light reception would follow in the church fellowship hall.

"Hmm. I suppose that's the practical way to go," Sandy conceded, barely glancing at Kelsey as she addressed her concerns to Meg. "Glad to see you'll not be burdening your mother with a big wedding, Meg."

"I wouldn't dream of it," Meg murmured.

"I tried to get Meg to elope, but she wouldn't go for that idea," Kelsey offered, his face innocent of any trace of a teasing note. Meg bit her lip, but refrained from looking his way. Instead, she folded her hand into his and pinched his thumb. Sandy wouldn't appreciate his sense of humor.

"Oh, my, no. Meg never was a flibbertigibbet. At least not until...well never mind. Well, I suppose we could get the ladies' circle onto the reception. Take that worry off your mother, don't y'know."

Finding a good caterer was the next item on Meg's list, but Sandy's purposeful face gave Meg's thoughts a new direction. If the church women wanted to take on the reception job, it could involve her mother in the plans without undue work—something Meg had been a little concerned about. She hadn't wanted Audrey to feel left out of the plans, but she'd been wondering how to temper the amount of work her mother took on. And it might reduce Audrey's disappointment in losing the big wedding.

"Thanks, Mrs. Yoder, that's a fantastic idea. Mom has her own ideas, of course, but I'm sure she'd welcome your help. Why don't you run by the house this morning?"

Meg let her smile spread. With the church ladies and Lissa to keep her company, her mother would be too busy to complain much about anything. And happy as a June bug in high summer.

Chapter Ten

Two days before Meg was to fly home from England, she ran into a business snag. A longtime client of the firm died and left his affairs in a huge tangle. His heirs insisted on an accounting of their newfound investments within the week, and they wanted Clive to meet with them and their solicitors to explain each of them down to the fine print and beyond. However, Clive was away, and neither Elizabeth, who was taking over most of Meg's minor clients, nor anyone else in the office had a clue about how to handle the matter. Besides that, when contacted, Clive begged her to extend her stay long enough to cover the meeting.

"I'll make it up to you, Meg, I promise," he insisted. "I'll pass along the next big plum from the States that comes into our fold. I've already put out the word that you are our States-side associate, anyway."

"I hope you're not expecting too much from my agreement," she mentioned as a gentle reminder. "I'll work only a few hours each day and only three weekdays. Got that? Meanwhile, I have to be home no later than the fifteenth."

"Oh, you will, Meg," he returned with an I'll-promise-you-anything-if-you'll-only-do-this-one-for-me tone. Meg never quite trusted Clive when he used that overpersuasive voice.

"I'm only asking you to stay for three more days. Besides, they can't have that wedding without you."

"Oh, I don't know about that," she said on a laugh, deciding to table her concern. "*Everyone* seems to be in on this. I'm only the bride."

No one exhibited more excitement over the wedding than the girls. According to what she heard from her mother and Kelsey, Lissa and Aimee spent every waking minute planning, making notes and lists from wedding magazines, and assaulted Audrey daily with endless questions and exchanges over what would work or be acceptable to include in the ceremony or reception.

Meg, hearing about each new flight of fancy, found herself in stitches. She didn't worry about any of it though, knowing that between Kelsey and her mother, the girls couldn't go too far. And after Kelsey nixed the flock of doves idea and the bid for cupids and hearts ice sculptures, and her mother gave a "definitely not" to a rocking version of the bridal march, she breathed a sigh of relief. She did agree that, weather permitting, they could hold the ceremony in the church courtyard. The girls seemed happy enough with that and proceeded to borrow a trellised arch.

Thank goodness, there would be no surprises.

Meg wasn't above a few surprises of her own, though. Luckily the two main ones could be arranged long-distance, with Justine's help and her brother, Jack's.

"All right," she finally told Clive, admitting with a sigh, "It was going to be a pinch to get everything out of my flat by the earlier date, anyhow. At least this will give me a breathing space on this end of things."

But it very definitely tightened things on the other end. Meg had exactly six days before the wedding by the time she got back to Missouri. Six days to double-check each wedding plan that had been made in her absence, soothe her mother's fears and annoyances, spend a couple of mornings setting up her business office and still have time with Kelsey and the children.

Meg had little time to visit the farm; Kelsey assured her the sleeping porch had cleaned up nicely, he'd repaired the screens, and he'd found a few sticks of old furniture to fill it temporarily.

They'd agreed not to put anything expensive in, pending a more permanent location for them as a true married couple.

Wherever that might be. Whenever that might happen.

She refused to worry about that particular problem just now. There was enough demand on her plate at the moment, and she'd have time to tackle where she hung her clothes after she and Kelsey were married. And more than once she felt decidedly grateful she and Kelsey had opted for a simple event.

But in those six days she and Kelsey had no time to be alone. To be a couple. To talk of anything much more than what had to be done the next day or of the wedding itself.

Only late at night as she fell asleep did Meg faintly wonder if this was all too quick, too much in the realm of fairy tales, too much on the surface of life and held too little depth. Kelsey hadn't once shown much affection—but then, when did he have time? She hadn't experienced being held in his arms or noted a light of physical desire in his gaze. She soothed her doubts with the knowledge that they would have a lifetime to express love. Their time would come.

It will come, won't it, Lord?

She sighed deeply, reminding herself that faith came one day, one step at a time. Sometimes by the moment. She recalled the underlined scripture she'd read last night in Grandmother Hicks's King James Bible. "Delight thyself in the Lord and he will give thee the desires of thine heart."

She would remember....

Then it all came together with a rush. Jack, Kathy, Sara and Andy arrived. Kelsey's father sent regrets from California. Clive arrived on Saturday, driving an expensive rental car, putting up at the best motel in town.

"You didn't think you could get away without me looking over this country Lothario with a brood, did you?" Clive told her when she exhibited surprise that he actually kept his promise to attend. "Have to find out the secret of his bucolic charm and all that."

It brought the expected laugh from Jack and her mother.

Meg introduced "her brood" with pride the next morning

right before worship, coming together in front of the church doors. Lissa and Aimee developed an instant crush on the Englishman, to which Clive played with relish and extreme charm.

Kelsey hung back a moment, making his own assessment of this man who, according to Audrey last year, had hoped to marry Meg himself. He was good-looking enough, if a woman went for that polished, urbane quality, Kelsey supposed, and in addition to his obvious sophistication, he had money and wide connections. Unexpectedly, a sliver of jealousy shafted through Kelsey like a skinning knife, pulling his usually balanced thinking off-kilter; he didn't like the idea of Clive having so much of his Meg's time. Or attention. Or that he seemed to know her so well, or a side of her that he'd never witnessed. It didn't help, either, that his daughters were bowled over.

"Time to find ourselves a seat, folks," he murmured into the circle, trying to hide his uncomfortable observations. "Service will start soon."

"Yes, indeed," Audrey agreed.

Kelsey slid a hand under Meg's arm, noting with satisfaction the swift affectionate light in her blue glance as she smiled up at him. It dawned on him he'd always taken Meg's fondness for granted, that he'd missed her genuine sweetness more than he'd cared to credit. But it no longer felt enough—Meg was fond of many people in her life. He wanted more from her than mere fondness.

As their party scooted into a pew, Meg by his side with the children next, Kelsey relaxed with the knowledge they'd be married in only a few hours. He sneaked a quick glance at his watch. Less than a dozen, now.

A feeling of blessedness stole over him. Meg had chosen him, not Clive. Only God knew why, when all the advantage was on Clive's side—but he was awfully glad she had. And he'd be downright foolish to turn down this wonderful gift.

He pushed back his sleeve to view his watch again. About nine and a half hours…

The late-summer evening bloomed with perfection. Although temperatures had reached into the nineties earlier in the day, by the time the evening church service closed, the setting sun had lost some of its power. Paul Lumbar came with his 1960 Corvette Stingray two-seater to drive Meg, and later, Audrey to the church. A surprise arranged by Thad and Phillip, Paul told them. Meg's delight anchored itself in the hope Thad and Phillip wanted to give her something special.

Meg wore the creamy, lace-edged dress she'd found in London and decorated her hair with flowers instead of a veil. The children looked smart in new clothes, one of her surprises she'd brought from London. The girls were ecstatic over how pretty they looked in their new, flowered cotton dresses from a leading designer. The boys, while not thrilled with the collared shirts and pleated trousers Meg had chosen, resigned themselves to wearing them as long as they didn't have to don suits.

Wildflowers and ivy vines interwoven with florist's roses and gladioli showed off the girls' hard work on the trellised arch. Pots of geranium plants sat along an imaginary walkway leading to the arch. Against the church wall, three reception tables groaned with finger food, cake and punch.

And Kelsey sported a new navy suit. When she caught sight of him, Meg thought he could easily pose for *GQ*. Her heart swelled with pride. She didn't know whether she found him more appealing dressed formally or in his ratty old work denims, but she knew she would love him until the end of time.

True to Meg's request, Pastor Reynolds simply asked for the witnesses to gather in a circle around the bride and groom. Meg's emotions felt light and nostalgic when she took in the various faces around them; most of them had been so much a part of her childhood, her young adulthood. Justine and her family were there; Miss Maybelle and Miss Lois, Bible school teachers over the years; her mother's crowd; and Linda Burroughs and her girl Sydney. Evidently Linda had taken Kelsey's choice in stride, Meg thought.

The family stood behind them. Meg and Kelsey made their vows with simple exchanges in front of the flower-decked arch. Then just before the last pronouncement, Meg turned to draw the children closer. She'd thought about the unusual step she was about to take and had sought the approval of Pastor Reyn-

olds. The minister had encouraged her in her desire to add this
extra promise to the ceremony, but she hadn't told Kelsey about
it. Would he like it? Be put off?

"Lissa, Aimee, Thad, Phillip and Heather." She gazed into
each child's eyes as she said their names, and fought sudden
tears. Five pairs of eyes in various shades of moss, hazel and
brown stared back at her in surprise and anticipation.

"Today I am marrying your father," she glanced at Kelsey,
his gaze reflecting the same emotions of his children. Meg swallowed, almost overwhelmed with the love she'd been hiding for
all these years, and took a deep breath. "But I am also making
you—each of you—a vow as well. I promise before God and
these witnesses that I will do all in my power to be a good
mother to you. I can't promise to be perfect. There will be times
when we won't think along the same lines and, um...might have
a, um, spirited discussion over a parental decision you don't
like. But I will always respect each of you, listen to you, guide
you, correct you and love you to the best of my ability. From
this day on we will be a family."

Lissa blinked back tears, her large green eyes glowing, Aimee
grinned, her twelve-year-old self shining through, the boys
smiled uncertainly, Thad with an added look of wariness, and
Heather's eyes looked like saucers.

"Me, too?" Heather asked in wonder. "Me, too?"

Behind her, Meg heard a sniffle. She thought it was her
mother. In spite of herself, Audrey had been showing all the
signs of the sentimentality she insisted was not usual for her.

"Yes, Heather," Meg murmured, smiling gently. "You,
too."

"All of us," Kelsey agreed, his voice rough with emotion.

Pastor Reynolds nodded and cleared his throat. "All right
then. With God's blessings and by His authority I now pro-
nounce before this company that you are man—" a frog's
throaty *ribbit* punctuated his speech "—and wife, and—"

Ribbit, ribbit.

A slight shuffling indicated a loss of attention. Uncertain, the
minister paused for an instant before continuing. "And children."

Ribbit, ribbit. Mooo...

Someone tittered. Meg heard Lissa's hissed whisper. "Thad!"

"I didn't mean to."

Ribbit. Ribbit.

Several people snickered. Without moving his head, the minister searched for the source of the sound. Kelsey glanced at his children over his shoulder.

"*Sorry,* Dad!" Thad pleaded and shrugged innocently.

"Kelsey, you may kiss your bride," Pastor Reynolds said in a rush.

Kelsey turned back to Meg, sliding his hand around hers and holding tight. Her break with tradition to include his children in the vows affected him profoundly. For the first time in years, he felt his spirit soar, felt a refreshing renewal in his gratitude for God's blessings. "Thank you, Meg," he whispered next to her ear.

He placed his lips on hers, a gentle tribute bursting with a reverence he didn't know he had. When he drew back to look into her eyes, he caught a faintly puzzled disappointment. She'd expected a more husbandly kiss, one even with a little passion. He immediately wanted to kiss her again, bent to do so, but before he could, Heather pushed between them, and the older kids surrounded them.

Mooo... Ribbit...

He swiftly pivoted, pinning his oldest son with his gaze. "All right, boys, what—"

More than one of the animal imitations broke forth, and then a train whistled. *Whoo...whoo!* Kelsey's frown deepened.

"It wasn't me, Dad," Thad insisted.

"Well?" His gaze shifted to Phillip.

"I didn't mean to just now, Dad," Phillip said, pulling a small gadget from his pocket. Immediately, the thing emitted another barnyard sound. "I was saving it for later. But it won't stop."

Then a chorus of *ribbits* sounded, and more *moos.* And another train whistle. Several of the children guests doubled over in mirth. Kelsey spotted a number of the little gadgets tightly clasped in tiny hands, activating the sounds. Where had all of them come from? Who had distributed the irritating toys?

Phillip glanced over his shoulder to the row in back of him. Following his younger son's gaze, he looked at Clive, sitting beside Jack and Kathy. Clive had an innocent, interested stare. Too innocent. Too interested.

Before Kelsey could investigate the matter further, backslaps and congratulations poured forth. He had to leave it until he had more time.

Audrey stepped up to hug him in her tentative way, then his new sister-in-law, Kathy. Jack wrung his hand. When he glanced her way, he saw that Meg was also engaged in well-wishing.

He'd have to make the lack of a proper kiss up to her later, he silently promised himself. And he really wanted to kiss her properly. Very properly, now that he allowed himself to think about it—as a new husband should. He wanted them to be truly married, hoped to be a good husband to Meg. He'd held himself in a tight rein these past weeks. Yet he and Meg needed time, he reminded himself. He'd promised her that. Time to fall in love and time for loving.

A sudden crackle, hiss and pop interrupted the direction of his thoughts. Now what?

He turned to see where the noise came from and what it was. Then before he had a chance to move, firecrackers exploded all over the arch. Kids jumped and whooped and squealed. The grown-ups just jumped and groaned. The cannonading series ran from the stem on one side over the top and back down the other side. Showers of sparks shot every which way, petals with it, scattering the laughing, squealing crowd.

"Uh-oh," Kelsey muttered. He had no doubt about who was responsible for the fireworks. The firecrackers had all the earmarks of his sons. He'd have to be on the lookout for Roman candles, he suspected.

"Well, I thought we were supposed to celebrate," Thad explained as he ducked and ran from his father's reach.

Kelsey shrugged helplessly and let a slow grin spread. He hadn't been above such pranks when he was a boy.

"So we are," Meg agreed, giving Kelsey a happy nod.

Just then at least two dozen New Year's Eve horns blared out, and Meg covered her ears against the din. Every child in sight was blowing hard. At that, Jack and Kathy corralled them all and shuffled them toward the food. Meg only hoped squished finger sandwiches, cheezy crackers and cake wouldn't be spread from there to next Christmas as the kids began tagging each other.

Thirty minutes later Meg stood talking with Miss Maybelle when Jack whispered in her ear and slipped a key ring into her hand. "It's parked at the curb, Meg."

"All right. Thanks, Jack. I appreciate all that you and Kathy have done these past few weeks. And taking Mom back with you for a little while is just the greatest."

"T'aint nothin', sis," he said teasingly. "And Mom will enjoy St. Louis."

"Meg! Dad! There's the biggest blue van you ever saw parked out front with big red 'n' white ribbons and balloons all over it," Aimee sputtered as she ran up, Heather and Sara, big-eyed, dogging her heels. Across the lawn, Lissa sat in a circle of teens, including her new friend from Kansas City, Babs's granddaughter Courtney. Meg couldn't see where the boys had gone.

"It's blue, huh?" Meg asked, a smile hovering. "Who does it belong to?"

"I dunno. Mr. Lumbar said to come find you."

"I guess we're wanted in front of the church, Kels," Meg called across the few yards that separated her from her husband.

Kelsey looked up from talking with one of the church members and nodded his understanding. He gazed around the gathering.

Though many guests still milled around the food and punch tables, some of the company had thinned. Fireflies already made their flashing light against the dusk. Perhaps it was time for him to gather up his brood, he mused. Left alone for too long, one of them was bound to find more trouble.

"Where are the boys?" he asked, gravitating to Meg's side. He threaded his fingers through hers and strolled toward the front of the brick church. "Come along, girls," he called over his shoulder.

But he needn't have bothered. Aimee, Heather and Sara dashed past them at a gallop, and Lissa tagged a few paces behind them with Courtney.

The buzz must have made the rounds, Meg thought, because most of the wedding company had gravitated toward the front along with them, curious to know what the fuss was about.

At the curb sat an eight-passenger van, fitted with all the latest extras. She'd had Jack arrange for the purchase and delivery yesterday, hiding it until the right time.

Thad and Phillip had the doors open and the back end popped. Phillip sat in the driver's seat, both hands on the wheel. Thad was trying all the radio buttons.

"Boys! What are you doing there?" Kelsey asked, grabbing the back of Thad's collar to pull him out. "You know better than to invade someone else's property."

"But, Dad, it's ours," Thad pronounced.

"What are you talking about?"

"It's ours, Dad. Read the card."

Glancing toward Meg in puzzlement, he opened the card Thad handed him, read the line written there in Meg's graceful hand and felt thunderstruck.

"You bought this?"

"Yes."

"Whoopee!" Aimee shouted. "Look, Lissa. Leather seats." She tossed a grin over her shoulder at Sydney Burroughs as though to say "Can you top this?"

"I want to see," Heather exclaimed. "Let me in, too."

"But Meg—" Kelsey began.

"You made a good choice, there, Meg," Paul Lumbar said, looking the vehicle over with a professional eye. Audrey bent to smooth a hand along the dashboard with a pleased expression.

"This isn't a car, it's a bus," came from Clive. "I guess this means you're truly hooked into this country thing, huh, Meg?"

His sally brought a few laughs.

"We can all get into it, Dad," Aimee pointed out as she backed out of the interior. "We won't have to drive two cars anywhere. C'mon, Lissa. As the oldest, you 'n' me get the two middle seats.''

''Nuh-uh,'' Thad protested. ''Me 'n' Phillip get 'em sometimes.''

''But Meg—'' Kelsey tried once again.

''It's my wedding present, Kels,'' she said gently, slipping the keys into his fingers. ''To us. To the whole family.''

He glanced from her to the van and shook his head.

''Don't look so worried...'' Had she done the right thing to purchase the van before consulting him? Didn't he like it? ''I can afford it. Really.''

When he didn't appear convinced, she added, ''After all, I haven't had a new car in several years, you know. I've saved up for one. It just seemed the best choice considering there're seven of us now.''

''I suppose it does fill the need,'' he mumbled as some of the uncertainty drained from his face. ''I only hope you haven't spent every penny you've saved, Meg. It's a big-ticket item.''

''Um, Kels, I have something to confess. This isn't all...''

Chapter Eleven

❧

"**W**hat do you mean? Not all?"

"Um..." At his stunned expression over the van, Meg was hesitant to tell him of the second surprise she'd arranged. But she couldn't hold back now, and the kids would love it. "I arranged for us to have a few days in Branson."

"A few days?"

"Only three."

"Meg, I can't leave my place for three days. Who'll—"

"Miss Maybelle's son, Bennie, agreed to look after the stock and everything for us."

"Bennie?" It wasn't that he didn't like Miss Maybelle's son, but he wasn't used to leaving his responsibilities in someone else's hands, and Bennie didn't know Fred. But that wasn't the only hitch. "What about the kids?"

"We're all going, Kels. We're a team now, remember?"

While the kids broke out in renewed cheers, Kelsey studied Meg's face for a long moment, not knowing what to say. She sure was full of surprises. The van, now. He could accept the vehicle as a necessity, swift to acknowledge he hadn't given a thought to a car for Meg or the fact she might not own one after living so long in England. Mentally he calculated what the expensive vehicle had cost and wondered how large their payments would be. He hoped he could make them.

Too, he hadn't taken into account that Meg had been independent for so long a time. She was used to making decisions without the need to consult anyone but herself. He shouldn't fault her for something they hadn't had time to talk out.

Meg waited for him to say something, her blue eyes shimmering with happy anticipation. Her generosity struck him a mixed chord. He felt like a skunk for feeling no immediate enthusiasm for her gifts. An ungracious lout. But three days absence from his farm in August... He simply didn't see how he could do that.

"Bennie can manage very nicely, Kelsey," Miss Maybelle said, referring to her unmarried middle-aged son. She sometimes treated Bennie as though he were slow, but Bennie had helped Kelsey a time or two and they'd gotten along just fine. "And he'll enjoy it. He hates his city job these days. Staying on your place will be like a vacation for him. And don't worry, he'll take good care of Fred."

Kelsey nodded slowly. Miss Maybelle was right, he could trust Bennie.

Perhaps he'd merely grown too accustomed to holding the reins of control in everything that concerned him; he didn't like his mind being made up for him or surprises that made demands on him before he'd had time to think about them. It rattled him a little. But now there was another woman in his life to consider, a real-live adult who might be entitled to the expected things in life. Like an opinion of her own. Like a balanced life. Like a honeymoon.

Meg had already given up so much in agreeing to live in that ugly sleeping porch even for a little while. Could he really expect her to forgo a mere three days in a town only a couple of hours distance?

He started to grin. Whoever heard of a honeymoon with five kids in tow?

"Okay," he said, feeling instantly better that he'd capitulated. Meg's smile proved worth it, and his children's. Three days weren't that long, and he had to confess a time-out in Branson certainly would be a break. "It might be fun to see some shows. And Silver Dollar City."

That set the kids off. "Silver Dollar City!"

"When do we go?" Kelsey asked, Thad and Aimee jumping around him and Heather hanging off his arm. Phillip peered at them from where he lay spread-eagle on the van roof, his fists curled around the luggage guards.

"How about tonight? The reservations are made, and Lissa and I packed when I was out at the house the other day."

"You and Lissa?"

"Yeah, Dad," Lissa spoke from beside him. "Isn't it great to have another grown-up besides me to count on?"

Kelsey's gaze met Meg's, her blue twinkle telling him she, too, had caught Lissa's reference. He responded to her amusement, letting a smile tug at his mouth. But he felt another small regret for the fact that Lissa had more than once filled the roll of an adult before her time. She'd spent too much time taking care of the younger children. With Meg's help, he hoped to restore her to a normal teenage phase.

"Yes, it certainly is, honey," he replied. "We'll make a great team. And now it's time this team had some *fun!*"

Their three short days of time-out could've been tripled and still not been enough for Meg. Kelsey seemed to put away his daily concerns and enter a play zone. She felt as though she'd stepped backward a dozen years to their carefree youth.

She also got her first taste of true togetherness. The three-bedroom cabin she'd rented stood only yards from Table Rock Lake where they swam and used the paddle boats when they weren't taking in shows and other sights or trying a new restaurant. And she gained a new appreciation for patient parents everywhere as she discovered the joys of trying to balance the needs of seven people.

Yet she adored every bit of it. She loved playing with the kids, finding new facets of their personalities, discovering how they thought. And best of all, she never tired of looking up at odd moments to gaze at Kelsey, and she basked in knowing she could. She had a right to feel as she did without guilt.

She and Kelsey fell into their old teasing patterns. The kids soon joined, batting jokes back and forth like tennis balls, sometimes with hilarious results. A couple of times Meg caught Lissa and Aimee peeking at their father as if seeing something they hadn't before. Had Kelsey's sadness over losing Dee Dee and his struggles with making a small farm pay robbed him of all his natural exuberance? Could he find it again with her? He seemed happy enough in her company.

But at night Meg shared a bed with Heather while Kelsey pulled out the sofa bed in the living room. It was better thus. They'd agreed to wait.

Then they returned to reality with the expected thud.

Kelsey drove into the farmyard near midnight the third night. Five tired kids grumpily complained over their need to wake up long enough to stumble to their beds. Meg followed them into the house while Kelsey checked on Fred and the other barn animals.

Bennie, rumpled and wearing his T-shirt wrong side out, rubbed his eyes as he came into the kitchen. He reminded Meg of an overaged baby, with his pink plump cheeks and nearly bald head; but his blue eyes were kind and not without intelligence. As agreed on, he'd used the boys' room. "Glad to see you folks home safe and sound. Ever'thing's fine here."

Meg nodded. "Thanks, Bennie. Kelsey will be in shortly. But there's no need for you to stay up. You men can talk in the morning."

"Thanks, think I will. You want me to bed down on the sofa?"

"No," she told him. "The boys can use their sleeping bags. Don't worry about it. And don't go off in the morning before breakfast, Bennie. Stay until I can fix you something substantial."

"That's real kind of you, Meg. I will, I surely will."

After Meg settled the boys into the sleeping bags rolled out on the living room floor, she tiptoed into the girls' room. Lissa and Aimee had already returned to sleep in their bunk beds, but Heather turned over and sat up.

"Meg, I want a drinka water," the child mumbled.

Meg went to the kitchen for a clean glass, then carried the water back to Heather. She waited until the child drank it down.

"All set now?"

"Will you tell me a story?"

"Not tonight, sweetie. It's very late. But I'll save a good one for tomorrow night if you turn over now and go right back to sleep."

"Okay."

Meg tiptoed away. She almost reached the door.

"Meg, you didn't kiss me good-night."

Meg immediately made an about-face. "Well, I can't forget that, now can I?"

She leaned over to kiss the small nose. Two little arms circled her neck and hugged as tightly as they could. They didn't let go.

"Will you lie down with me?"

"All right, for a moment. But you have to close your eyes and be very still."

She settled on the narrow bunk next to the little girl, stroking her forehead. In moments the child was asleep once more. Meg thankfully rose and, yawning hugely, blundered right into Kelsey, leaning on the doorjamb.

"Been a long day," he murmured low, slinging his arm across her shoulders. He walked her to the door that led to the sleeping porch, out of immediate sight should the girls awake, but not out of hearing.

"Mmm," she answered in a whisper. The nightlight plugged into the wall near their feet shed little illumination on his face, but she didn't have to see the weary lines to know they were there. "You must be tired after fighting all that traffic in Branson and then the drive home."

She leaned back against the door frame, and he rested a forearm above her head. It brought them very close. Close enough that she felt his breath on her face—it smelled of the spearmint gum the kids had passed out on the drive home.

"Yeah, I am." His chin made a raspy sound as he ran a hand over it. "But we had a great time, Meg. The kids will remember this time for as long as they live. And I don't think I said thanks properly."

He referred to the fact that she'd insistently paid for everything, telling him it was holiday money she'd already set aside for the year and she planned to spend every cent. In truth, she would've spent far more to vacation in Europe, she'd told him.

"It was my pleasure, Kelsey."

"Well, no need for you to get up early tomorrow. The kids will probably sleep late."

"That's an idea," she mumbled over a yawn.

"Good night, Meg." He closed the gap of mere inches between them, placing his mouth on hers with a swift firmness. Meg knew immediately this was no mere gesture of friendship or a kiss of thanks; his lips communicated all the lively interest a woman could hope for from a brand-new husband. Meg sighed, feeling her body respond, and let all of her love flow into the kiss.

The rustle of one of the kids turning over came to their ears. Kelsey drew away first. He stood a moment in silence, then whispered, "Sleep well."

She climbed the old twisting staircase alone, suddenly wide-eyed, flipping on the light switch to the bare bulb hanging from the sleeping porch ceiling and wondering how long it might be before Kelsey decided they'd had enough adjustment time. That it might be time for them to become truly married.

The next morning Meg woke slowly as the sun's first rays streamed through the oaks and maples to make beams on the fold-up bed where she lay curled. A breeze whispered, sending a refreshing coolness through the open room, and the birds chirped and sang from branches that nearly touched her screen walls. The back kitchen door creaked as someone went out...and she smelled coffee. Her eyes drifted closed and she sighed deeply.

An irritating scratching against a screen persisted until she opened her eyes again. Coffee? She sat up, blinking away her desire to go back to sleep.

Something, a small rustling just beyond the tail of her eye, made her turn her head. A small figure sat in the juncture of a tree staring into the sleeping room. A two-legged jeans-clad bare-footed figure. Phillip.

"Phillip!" Leaping from bed, Meg felt her hair stand straight out as she rushed to close the distance. She came up against the screen like a splayed toad, her first instinct to get him out of the tree and off the precarious limb equal to that of a fireman getting a victim off the top of a twenty-foot building. "Phillip, what're you doing there?"

"I was waiting for you to wake up." He blinked calmly, matter-of-factly. "You're the mom now. You promised to cook breakfast."

"So I did. How did you get up there?" Twelve feet off the ground, sitting on a limb no thicker than her arm? Her heart jumped to her throat. What if he should fall? Scrabbling at the screen's metal lifts, she found they wouldn't budge.

"Climbed."

"Well, obviously, but what do you think you're doing?" Where was everybody? Where was Kelsey? Listening for one breath-held moment, she decided the other children hadn't been disturbed. Yet surely Kelsey was up; he'd made coffee. Or Bennie?

She gave up on the stubborn screen. The old paint held it fast in its tracks. She could only stare at him through the screen and try to keep her cool.

"Phillip." She licked dry lips and took a calming breath. "Phillip, can you get down?"

"Sure."

"Safely?"

"I can get to a lower limb, then I'll have to drop—"

"No! No, don't do that. Wait. Just...just climb down to the lower limb and wait there till I can get a ladder."

"Okay."

Grabbing jeans and a T-shirt, she yanked her clothes on in record time. Not wanting to disturb the others, she practically slithered her way down the stairs, past the sleeping girls and into the kitchen. A yawning Bennie exited the boys' bedroom as she plunked herself down on the kitchen table bench to pull on her sneakers.

"Mornin', Meg."

"Bennie, do you know where Kelsey keeps his ladder?"

"Reckon it's in the garage, Meg. What do you need it for this early in the morning?"

"To get Phillip down from a tree."

"What's he doin' in a tree already?"

"I haven't figured that out yet myself, Bennie." Frustration at the need to explain made her want to snip, but she didn't think that would help matters. "Maybe you should run down to the barn and find Kelsey."

"Dad doesn't like to come back to the house when he's already started on his chores," Phillip said, opening the kitchen screened door and waltzing in as calmly as though just in from a Sunday stroll.

Meg let her eyes close in gratitude, hoping her heart would soon cease its snare-drum thud, then opened them to stare at the unconcerned nine-year-old. "Phillip, you scared me half out of my wits. Do you always climb trees? How did you get down? You didn't hurt yourself, did you?"

"Uh-uh. I slid down the trunk. Wasn't hard."

"Mmm... Well, why don't you get your shoes on now."

"Okay," the boy said, blinking owl-like before he turned toward the living room where he'd left his sneakers.

Meg turned slowly and made an effort to bring her nerves back into a reasonable state. Calm might be nice, she mused. London mornings or wake-ups at her mother's house were never like this.

Perhaps she should start the morning all over again.

"Morning, Bennie. I'm going to have a cup of this coffee that Kelsey made. Do you want one now or do you want to wait for breakfast?"

"I'll take one now," he said, rubbing his rumpled head. "Don't wake up so good without it."

"Me, neither," she admitted with a sigh as she poured the dark brew into two mugs. She didn't think her hand trembled too much. "And I've grown too dependent on city ways as well, I guess. Learning to get up with the dawn will take some getting use to."

Not to mention finding a child staring at her the very first thing when she awoke in the morning. Even sharing with Heather hadn't been difficult.

And so far she'd had only a taste of responding to the daily needs of six other people on a regular basis. It had definitely been fun on vacation, but now the real world was at her door.

The first order of the day was breakfast, she supposed.

And after three days of watching the kids eat everything in sight that was edible, she recognized her days of merely nibbling a breakfast of toast or a bagel were over.

While Bennie sat down at the kitchen picnic table she rummaged through a lower cupboard until she found a skillet, then glanced into the refrigerator to see what it contained, only to find it rather bare. A half-dozen eggs wouldn't feed everyone, and a half-gallon of milk wouldn't go far, either.

"Don't know how well stocked I am here," she said, realizing for the first time that grocery shopping would take immediate priority on her morning list of things to do. "But I think we can at least manage some pancakes for right now."

"I love pancakes," Bennie answered. "Those'll do just fine."

"Aha! Sausages!" She held the freezer door wide as she dug into a back corner. "Now I hope the microwave is in good working order."

"Yeah, it works just fine. Leastways to heat frozen dinners," Bennie said, swallowing a last gulp before setting his cup on the counter. "Think I'll go on out an' see what Kels is up to. Y'know that bull might just make champion this year at the fair, if he ain't too fractious."

"All right. You men plan on heading in for breakfast in about thirty minutes, okay?" He nodded and left as Meg found a mixing bowl and an electric hand beater and started to work.

She turned from the sink to find Phillip sitting at the table, blinking at her with Kelsey's keen gaze, his cheek in his hand, his elbow braced on the table as he watched every move she made. She hadn't heard him come in at all.

"Oh, well hello, Phillip. You've finished dressing, I see. Are you hungry?"

"Uh-huh."

"Good." She turned back to the sausages, sliding them back into the microwave for further thawing. "I'm making pancakes and sausages. How many can you eat?"

"'Bout fifty."

"Mmm... Guess I should stir up more batter. And find a bigger skillet."

"Why don't you use that griddle?"

"Oh, that's just the thing. Do you know where it is?"

"Yeah. It's in that buncha things you got at the wedding. It plugs in."

Surprised, she turned to look at him. Phillip, usually so quiet that she'd begun to worry about him, actually had quite a personality. He hadn't said two words to her till this morning. "We received a griddle? How do you know?"

"Andy told me that's what Aunt Kathy and Uncle Jack gave us. It's the biggest the store had, he said."

"Imagine that," she said with a laugh.

"Want me to get it? There's three big boxes of presents in the living room."

"Mom must have brought them while we were gone," she murmured, her heart warmed by her mother's thoughtfulness. She hadn't expected it, had planned to stop in for them when she made her rounds this morning. "Well, we'll have to find something nice to do as a return favor, won't we? Phillip, do you suppose you can tell which one it is?"

"Yes, it's got a big white bow on it and it's long an' flat."

It wasn't the first time Meg had noticed how observant Phillip was. She had a real suspicion he took in far more of what went on around him than most nine-year-olds. More than Kelsey would guess, she'd bet.

"Could you get it without waking Thad?"

"Sure," he said as he scooted from the bench. "He sleeps through anything. Even storms an' lightning an' stuff."

Meg listened as Phillip slipped into the living room. All she detected was a faint rattle and shuffle before the boy returned with a big, wrapped package. Sure enough, it had a huge white bow that looked like her sister-in-law's handiwork.

"Let's open it, okay?"

Phillip nodded and tugged at the ribbon until he'd removed it, then tore the wrapping off. The box indeed showed a picture of a top brand electric griddle. He pulled it out and inspected it with a thorough eye. "See, it's got lots of settings," he pointed out.

"Yes, it's a dandy. Now where should we put it?" Meg wondered aloud, shooting a glance around the small kitchen. It had so little counter space, and what there was already held more than its share of odds and ends of cooking chaos.

"Why don'tcha put it on the end of the table over here. We can plug it right there." He pointed to a low wall plug.

Lissa wandered in, smothering a yawn, and a minute later, Thad. He plopped down beside his brother while Lissa pulled a can of orange concentrate from the freezer and reached for a plastic container. "Thad, don't sit there. Set the table," she ordered without looking his way.

"Not my turn," Thad said, refusing to move.

"Thad, you come after Aimee," Lissa pointed out. "She set the table last week."

"Don't think so," he insisted. "It's her turn."

"Thad," Lissa gritted out with all the normal irritation of an older sister when a younger sibling refused to cooperate.

Meg, having washed and dried the new appliance, set the griddle on the table end and plugged it in. She couldn't decide if she should merely let the children argue it out or intervene. Anyway, she didn't know their usual schedule. Besides, she was loath to move into a heavy stepmother roll so soon.

"I did it last week." Aimee entered the argument from the doorway just as Kelsey and Bennie approached across the backyard. Meg sighed with relief. She'd let Kelsey settle the matter. She had plenty of time to ease into things.

"Well, Phillip—" Thad started again.

"He helped me clear up," Lissa declared. "He has to empty trash this week."

"Well why can't Heather start doin' her share? You never make her do anything. And now that we have Meg, I'm not going to do any more kitchen work, and no more laundry, either.

Girls're supposed to do that stuff. That's why Dad got married to Meg, isn't it?''

"Thad!" Lissa's shock came through.

"You little brat," Aimee stated, her narrowed eyes threatening.

"Well, isn't it?"

Meg stilled, her back to the room. Part of her wanted to laugh outright at the child's old-fashioned views. Gracious, he had a lot to learn. She wanted to point out that his attitude wouldn't win him any brownie points with the girls in his future, but she thought him too young to grasp her meaning. But then again, she felt an unreasonable jab hit her just below her heart. Is that what he thought, that his dad had married her to become the housekeeper? Where could he have come up with that on his own?

No, he wouldn't have. Obviously he'd overheard someone say it, and she knew that viewpoint had been bandied about when she and Kelsey first decided to marry. She'd rightly ignored it. And then she recalled hers and Kelsey's discussion over their division of duties on the day they'd picnicked down by the river. Yet Kelsey's conversation held nothing of this "a women's work" overtone when he'd asked her to take charge of the house.

From behind her, Kelsey made a sharp command. "Thad, go to your room. I'll talk to you later."

Meg whirled, her back rigidly against the sink. Kelsey's face looked pinched with fury. He didn't look at her, but Thad did. He threw her a fulsome gaze of his own wrath before he stormed from the room, clearly blaming her for his sudden fall from grace.

From the griddle, pancakes sent a burning odor into the air.

Chapter Twelve

❧

"**I** can't believe my own brother! Thad's just a little brat," Aimee repeated later that morning as Meg drove into Sedalia for groceries. Aimee and Heather had chosen to accompany her while Lissa volunteered to stay at home to start the laundry. The temperamental old washer that stood on the back porch had to be understood, Lissa said, though the newer dryer gave no trouble.

"When you've been so nice to us..." Aimee rumbled on.

"Don't worry about it, Aimee." Meg didn't want more made of the incident than it was. "Everyone behaves like a brat once in a while. Even grown-ups."

Truth was, Meg didn't like housework much herself—she just liked everything to be clean and orderly. But someone had to take on the responsibility for keeping things together, whether in a business, the corporate world or a household. And now the well-being of this household had fallen to her. Odd. She hadn't felt a threat to her feminist side when she and Kelsey had discussed her taking it over. It made perfect sense to her; she didn't know anything about Kelsey's business of *farming*, but she knew how to organize and prioritize a *business*. A household couldn't be that different.

Besides, she'd already been considering the need to keep

Mary Claire on to help with the housework a few mornings each week, especially since Meg wanted to continue working part-time with Clive. Now she decided Mary Claire was an absolute must.

Aimee wasn't quite ready to let it go. "And *we're* the ones who begged you to *marry* Dad! I mean..."

"Let's let your dad take care of Thad, okay?" Meg had expected adjustments might be a little strained for all of them, but she hadn't thought they'd start so soon. However, now that the excitement of the wedding was over, Thad seemed ready to let his real feelings be known. Her puzzlement came in not knowing why Thad resented her. She sure hoped when their daily routine returned to normal, Kelsey would tell her. Perhaps then she could set about repairing whatever it was.

"We've got oodles of our own things to do this week before the fair starts," she said, changing the subject. "How do you think your lamb will do?"

"Don't know. Dad wanted us girls to have something in the 4-H this year, but I'm not really interested in sheep. I like horses, though, and I love the Appaloosa..." Thankfully, Aimee started talking about what to expect during the run of the fair.

Meg sighed, and listened with one ear while her thoughts wandered. She *was* curious to know how Kelsey handled his talk with Thad, what he would say. After breakfast he and Bennie'd taken the boys out to tackle barn chores, and they were still there when she left.

She wanted to make a quick stop at Justine's to check whatever may have come in through her e-mail or fax or new phone message center, but after glancing at her watch, decided it would have to wait. A slight grimace caught up to her, a heretofore unadmitted feeling of impatience. Old habits died hard, she supposed; this need to be in touch with her working world was still very important to her. Anyway, she'd told everyone she'd be out of touch for the entire week. No need to hit the panic button.

Grocery shopping proved to be a bigger challenge than she'd even imagined; she hadn't taken the time to make a list, so she and the girls bought everything that took their fancy as well as staples. They easily filled two shopping carts to overflowing.

Meg didn't mind. Stocking up would give her plenty to choose from to make meals for the next week, and real menu planning could wait until she'd caught on to all the family's food preferences.

By the time they'd returned home, put away everything Meg could find room for in the limited storage space, helped Lissa finish six loads of wash with four loads postponed to the next day—not even including towels and sheets—made a few phone calls, made lunch and supper and accomplished the cleanup, Meg had a glimmer of what she'd let herself in for. Never mind the limitations of the tiny house; laundry and meals for seven, twenty-one times a week, would be the major challenge.

Yes—if she was to keep working even part-time, Mary Claire definitely had to become a permanent household help.

Bennie stayed through supper and almost objected when Kelsey handed him a check to pay for his time.

"Feels sorta like I oughta pay you, Kels. Enjoyed it so much."

"We appreciate your coming to help us out, Ben," Kelsey assured him.

"Well, if you folks need me again, just give a holler," Bennie said as he climbed into his late-model red pickup truck. "I'd rather work out here where I can feel the earth an' sky close anytime of day you ask me, than in town."

Meg waved as he sped toward the county road.

"Do you think he'll ever really return to farming?" she asked Kelsey as they watched gravel dust plume.

"Don't know," Kelsey said with a shake of his head. He slung an arm across her shoulders companionably as they headed toward the back door. "Miss Maybelle would like to think he might, but I don't think Bennie could really settle into it. She hated to sell the old place, but she finally faced the fact that none of her children really wanted it, and it became too much of a burden for her to keep it."

"She seems happy enough in town, now," Meg murmured, turning back to the house. The shifting problems of the generations was a topic she'd given a lot of thought to these past few months. Not for the first time a gladness stole over her for being geographically closer to her own mother.

"Maybe so, but I've offered her good money for that last piece next to my south property line and she keeps turning me down. She's just not ready to give it up."

After the evening tasks were done, Meg and Kelsey gave in to the kids' nagging and settled down in the living room to unwrap the wedding gifts that overflowed the three cardboard boxes. Meg sat in one corner of the couch where Heather immediately claimed the seat next to her. Thad and Aimee busied themselves shoving the boxes into the center of the room, Lissa sat on a footstool near her dad, and Phillip perched on the opposite sofa armrest. Kelsey snagged a foot around his computer chair and pulled it into the circle.

"Why don't you kids help," Meg suggested, glancing at Thad. He hadn't spoken to her since his surly outburst that morning. "I think most of them are for all of us, anyway."

"Yippee," Aimee responded.

"All right!" Lissa agreed.

They made a game of it. Kelsey held up each package singly, and by matching the wrappings to the personalities they knew, they had three guesses of who might be the giver. Then they had a try at what the package contained. After the package was opened, each of them taking a turn at tearing off the wrappings, he described in detail what it was and how it could be used. Hilarity piled up as Kelsey became more eloquent with each gift.

The *very* long white tablecloth. "Notice, my good friends, the tiny roll-stitched hem, the washable quality of the cotton. For Thanksgivings and Christmases, to make our humble picnic table into one of glorious feasting...and a pretty good finger wipe, too."

"Not quite," Meg protested, waving one of the twelve matching napkins so everyone could see.

"Spoilsport," Kelsey muttered, eyebrows raised, a grin tugging the corner of his mouth.

A salad bowl set—one large one and six small ones. "Obviously, the big one is for the head of the house. But since I'm an old-fashioned meat-and-potatoes kinda guy, I'll let the big-gest salad eater use it. Which would be-e-e... Thad!''

"Nuh-uh." Thad let his feelings be known in no uncertain terms, his dark eyes lively. "Not me."

A set of inexpensive blue glassware. "Mmm, the giver ob-viously has never experienced the delight of drinking from our own exquisite, very exclusive jelly glasses."

"Eight glasses, all alike," Lissa said, enraptured, lifting one to shine in the lamplight. "They're so pretty. Now the table will look more matched."

"What happens when we break a couple?" Thad asked.

"No, you don't!" Lissa gave her brothers a fierce gaze. "These are for when we all sit down together, not for only when you want a drink of water or fruit juice or something. And don't any of you dare take 'em outside, either. I found three glasses out and around the other day that *somebody* forgot to bring back in the house."

"Wasn't me," Thad jumped to deny.

"Me, neither," claimed Aimee.

"Don't look at me," Phillip put in.

"Um, guess I'm guilty at least once, honey," Kelsey admitted with a sheepish expression. "Sorry. I'll try to remember next time, okay?"

"You'd better, or I'll sic Meg on you," Lissa teased with a straight face.

"Oh-oh. That might be, um," Kelsey murmured, and leaned closer to Meg's ear, "kinda interesting."

Meg felt her heart thud an off-beat rhythm. Could being in love honestly give a woman an enlarged heart or something? How transparent was she?

Heather had long since left the sofa for the more interesting floor space near the gifts, but Phillip, close by, gazed at her intently. And Thad, after a brief disgruntled glance, pointedly went after another gift.

"*Interesting* is what you'll find it if you mess up the kitchen rules," she flung back at Kelsey in diversionary style. Kelsey gave her a lopsided grin and set the box of glasses out of the way behind his chair.

"Okay, men and women. Now hear this. The new keeper of our couth has spoken. No taking the good glasses outside and no wiping our hands on the tablecloth."

"What's that word, Daddy?" Heather asked.

"I'll explain later," Lissa told her.

Kelsey continued on with several more packages.

"I should've become an auctioneer," he stated about halfway through the proceedings as he raised a very large square box. "Mmm... This one's real heavy. Real heavy. Okay, ladies and germs, er, gentlemen," he said, then stopped to give a stern-eyed stare when Meg groaned at the old joke. "Don't mess up my material, Mrs. Jamison."

"Er, I won't except when you need to find fresh jokes, Mr. Jamison."

"But this audience hasn't heard all my old ones yet."

"Yes we have, Dad," Aimee said. "And you *seriously* need to find some new jokes."

"I like Dad's jokes," Thad insisted.

"But we've heard 'em a million times," Aimee protested.

"Why is *germs* a joke, Daddy?" Heather asked, counting how many packages remained unopened.

"Never mind, Heather," Lissa said. "I'll explain it later."

"Okay, okay." Kelsey called their attention back to their purpose. "Now, guess number one. What d'you suppose we'll find in this fancy box with the big white bow?"

"A big food mixer," Phillip stated bluntly. "Top of the line with all attachments from Aunt Audrey."

"How could you know that?" Lissa turned her green eyes directly on her youngest brother. He returned the stare passively.

"I just know."

"You were snooping! Phillip, that's not nice." Lissa turned to Kelsey. "Dad, you've got to do something. He—"

"I wasn't snooping. Andy told me."

"Lissa, honey, it's true," Meg defended the child. "He knew about the griddle from my sister-in-law, too, and this package has the same wrappings and the same kind of bow. Andy probably did tell Phillip what were in the packages."

Phillip gave her an unreadable gaze which made Meg wonder

if he'd never had anyone to take his side in anything before. He said so little, choosing silence more often than not while in a crowd.

"Well, the prize goes to Flip," Kelsey said, peeking under a torn corner of the wrapping. "It's pristine white with aluminum bowls."

"Goody. Can we make a cake tomorrow?" Aimee asked.

"Me, too?" chimed Heather.

"Chocolate," Aimee added.

There were two dozen things on her priority list to do tomorrow, Meg thought. But in an instant, they were no longer the most important. "I'll see what I can manage. Anybody got a birthday coming up?" she asked innocently, knowing full well Kelsey's was two months away.

"No, not till Heather's in a couple of weeks," Lissa said. Faces fell along with the disappointed groans.

"Well, then we'll just have to have an unbirthday cake, I guess."

"Remember that pineapple cake you made once a long time ago?" Kelsey asked beneath the happy response to her suggestion.

Remember? As if Meg would ever forget. At fifteen, she'd hoped for a perfect cake to take to one of their church teen picnics. She'd wanted to impress him and Dee Dee and all their friends with the powers of her culinary art. After all, she couldn't look petite and dainty-cute like Dee Dee.

It had turned out awful.

"Better toss it in the garbage," Dee Dee had advised, giving it a cursory look. The cake sagged in the middle and looked overbaked around the edges.

"But I promised a cake," Meg replied in a forlorn tone as she stared at the dismal results of her best efforts. She stood poised with a spatula in one hand over the bowl of powdered sugar icing when Kelsey knocked at the back door, there to take the two girls.

Dee Dee let him in. "We'll be just a minute, Kels. Meg just has to junk that cake and clean up the mess before we can go. Aunt Audrey'll have a tizzy if we don't."

"Junk it? What for?" He hung his chin on Meg's shoulder and gazed at the cake sitting on the counter directly in front of her. "It doesn't look so bad."

"I don't think it got done in the middle," Meg explained, flustered by his closeness. "Mom said our oven is giving out...."

"Well, why don't you put some sauce on it or something. Call it a pudding cake. No one will know the dif."

Hope made her lift her eyes to his. Their green depths held a sweetness she'd always afterward associated with his gentle fondness. "What kind of sauce?"

"We don't have time for a sauce, Kelsey," Dee Dee protested from where she waited by the back door, looking slender and pretty in her red shorts outfit. "We'll be late if we do that."

Meg envied her cousin's brown curls, too, saucily hovering just above her dark brows. Her own light brown tresses hung straight down, giving her no distinct difference from a dozen other girls her own age.

"Oh, not that late. C'mon," Kelsey insisted, returning his gaze to the cake. "Let's try it."

They decided on pineapple because Meg had no lemons and there was sure to be a chocolate cake among the other offerings.

They spent twenty minutes making the sauce, Kelsey reading directions from a cookbook while Meg stirred. Dee Dee finally hurried the proceedings by loading the dishwasher as fast as they finished with a pot or utensil, rushing them out the door the very second they'd finished.

At the picnic, Kelsey declared the pineapple pudding cake the best of the desserts. He'd eaten two helpings. But not until after he'd played lawn darts with Dee Dee as his partner and personally shown her how to improve her baseball swing. Meg wasn't the only girl with an envious sigh that day, she recalled. And afterward, he'd sat on the front porch steps with Dee Dee until all the stars had appeared.

"Yes, I remember." She recalled his kindness to a teenage girl who desperately wanted his admiration. She'd never noted quite that look from Kelsey again over the years that followed, but something in his gaze reminded her of it now.

"How about a pineapple cake tomorrow?"

Before she could agree, Lissa interrupted her thoughts with an insistent, "Give it to Meg, Aimee."

"Keep your shorts on, will ya? I'm only looking at it."

"Well, it's not ours. I don't think you should open it."

"All right, already." Aimee handed Meg a package shaped like a shirt box. "This one has just your name on it, Meg. But there's no card, so I don't know who it's from."

Meg tugged at the lavender satin ribbon and unfolded the matching paper. Lifting the lid, a black silky sheen caught the light. Automatically she slid a hand beneath the fabric. Lace and satin. Spaghetti straps. The small card inside read simply, "Elizabeth."

Her co-worker from London. Clive had said something during the reception about sticking a few packages on the gift table from the gang back in England.

"What is it?" Heather asked, scooting closer to peer into the box. "Can I see?"

Meg, her cheeks heating, snapped the lid back on with a swift shove. Obviously this gift had not been intended for mass ogling. "Uh, it's not—"

"Aw, that's not a wedding present," Thad complained in disgust. "That's just somethin' for Meg."

"I'm not so sure it was intended *exactly* that way," Kelsey murmured very low. Something in his comment caused Meg's color to flame higher. She bit her lip, wanting to look at her husband but not quite daring to—not in front of the children, anyway.

"Oh," Heather responded to Thad's remark. "Well, what is it?"

Aimee giggled and Lissa dropped her gaze, embarrassed. Thad shrugged and Phillip, as usual, said nothing.

"Oh, it's just one of those things to stick in a chest someplace," Meg struggled to answer. "It's not really, um, practical."

"Never mind, Heather," Lissa said. "I'll explain..." Lissa let her promise die on her lips and changed directions. "There're two more here. Why don't you open the last ones, Dad?"

"That's a good idea," Kelsey answered, barely smothering his laughter. He rose then, and gathered up the gift cards, shuffling through them as though to remind himself of each giver. "Then after that we can divide up the thank-you notes. Everyone can write at least two."

"Why do we haveta do that? That's not my job," Thad began before he caught Kelsey's uncompromising stare.

"Let me write the one to Sydney Burroughs," Aimee said with a mischievous set to her mouth. She held out her hand. "I want to tell her a proper—"

"Perhaps I'll do that one," Kelsey hastily stated. The only impractical gift they'd received, a china tea set, was from Linda Burroughs and Sydney.

"I don't know how to write yet," Heather complained. "I can only do my name."

"I'll share mine with you," Meg suggested, watching Kelsey pick and choose among the cards, shoving a bunch into his shirt pocket before handing her the rest. "You can put your name on the thank-yous I write."

Later that night when the house grew quiet, she pushed her pillows to form a backrest behind her against the rough wall, thinking of all that must be done the next day. She and Kelsey had talked only briefly about the fair preparations they needed to take care of, and he and the middle-three kids planned to leave the house in a couple of days.

She pulled out her handful of cards. She had almost two dozen. Surely Kelsey had at least a dozen, and between them, the children almost as many. Her heart warmed as she looked at the familiar names on the gift cards. Warmed not only by the generosity of their family and friends, but by the kindness of so many of her church family, people who had known her all or most of her life. Their love and support had been steadfast for as long as she could remember.

Then she noticed the absence of one card she expected to find. The lavender one from Elizabeth, her London associate. Kelsey wouldn't have given that one to any of the children to answer. So he must have included it among his own. But...what could he possibly intend by it when the gift had been so very personal?

Chapter Thirteen

A few days later the fair opened. After every full day's work, Kelsey spent the last few countdown evenings helping the boys and Aimee prepare their animals for judging. They had one dilemma to solve: the boy's had to show their bull at the same time Aimee had to show her lamb.

"Sorry, kids," Kelsey said as he sat down at the supper table the evening before the opening day. "With so much going on lately, I just realized it." Kelsey shook his head over which one he'd attend. "Guess we'll have to toss a coin for which of you I'll be with. Maybe we can get Mr. Miller to stand in with the other, if his schedule allows it. I'll call him."

"That's all right, Dad," Aimee volunteered, plopping paper napkins down on each plate. "You go with the boys, since Fred has a real chance of winning this year. I can handle Betsy Ross on my own."

Kelsey gazed at his second-born daughter, feeling torn. It wasn't fair to her that he wanted to see the bull judging more than he wanted to follow the sheep judging, but he was honest enough to admit he did. Yet he wanted to cheer Aimee on, too, and show his pride in her, every bit as much as he did the boys. He just liked cattle better. How could he make it up to her if he chose the boys' event over hers?

"I'll sit in the stands to cheer you on, Aimee, if that'll help," Meg offered, as she set a huge meat loaf in the table's center. "But I'm not very good with animals, I'm afraid. I wouldn't know how to help you with Betsy Ross."

Kelsey watched Meg set a bowl of steamed broccoli next to the meat loaf, his gratitude for her offer rising with the steam. She seemed to know by instinct when to step into the gap. Especially when it concerned the older girls. He often thought he failed to either understand Lissa and Aimee or to know how to help them as he should.

Thad stared at the meat loaf and made a face that noted his disgust. Before he could open his mouth to complain, Kelsey lowered his chin and glanced at his oldest son from under his brows. Meat loaf wasn't his favorite meal either, but he was going to eat it and be happy. He'd have no more of the disrespect that Thad had displayed during their first breakfast at home. It bothered him not a little to still not know why Thad felt the way he did. After a moment Thad dropped his gaze to his plate, his chin thrust out in muted rebellion.

"Can I say the blessing?" Heather asked.

"It's Phillip's turn," Thad stated, his mulish attitude still evident.

"No it's not," Phillip answered. "It's yours."

"Uh-uh," Thad insisted. "I'm not saying it."

"Well, it wouldn't hurt either of you, if you ask me," Aimee put in her two cents. "Lissa and I've been saying—"

"That's enough, kids," Kelsey said firmly. "I'll ask God's blessing and say thanks."

Meg stilled. Kelsey hadn't offered to lead prayer since she'd been back home; she hadn't realized it until now. Probably because the children had vied for the privilege at mealtimes. And he seemed to listen only perfunctorily at bedtime.

In the old days, he'd prayed freely whenever the need or request arose, she recalled. Had he become distant to the Lord's voice? Or had life's busy demands crowded out his daily walk?

Sweetness of her own daily devotions rose and she thought about the many times she, Kelsey and Dee Dee had shared gratitude for the Lord's goodness around this very table. Doing so had been as easy as sharing the meal. Without thinking about it, she lay a hand over his. "Let me," she murmured in gentleness. "I feel like giving thanks this time."

At Kelsey's nod, she bowed her head. "Father, we thank you for today and this food, and ask your wisdom to find answers for every challenge we face. And, Father, thank you for giving me *each* member of this family as *my very own*. Amen."

When she raised her gaze, Meg encountered Thad's stubborn one. His slowly changed to one of confusion before he quickly stared at his plate. For a moment the others remained silent. Then Kelsey squeezed her hand before he let her withdraw it, his brief gaze warm and understanding.

"Well, pass the dumb meat loaf," Thad said, as though going to an execution. "Guess I'll get it over with."

Meg ducked her head to hide her laugh. Beside her, Kelsey sidetracked a grin by shoveling a bite of bread into his mouth.

"I can help you, Aimee," Lissa said, passing a bowl of sliced tomatoes. "And I can take care of Bets if anything happens."

"Yeah—" Aimee's face lit with delight "—that'll be super. See, Dad, the girls in this family can take care of each other. We don't need any of you men."

"Well, I didn't aim at widening the gender gap," Meg said with a outward laugh, glancing pointedly at the boys as she took her seat next to Kelsey again. She'd been up refilling the bowl of corn.

"You didn't," Kelsey said with a no-argument-there tone. "But you have solved our problem. Thanks, sweetheart. And you, too, Lissa."

Sweetheart. The word, spilling easily from his lips, filled Meg all the way to the top with delight. It meant the direction of his thoughts was changing. She wasn't just a friend anymore. And she wasn't even going to think of how long it might take before he meant the endearment. She could buzz on it all week, she mused.

If she had time. Her "to-do" list seemed to be growing like yeast dough on a warm day. She and Kelsey hadn't stopped or even slowed down to share a private moment since the night they'd returned from Branson. Each night she'd climbed the stairs to the upstairs sleeping porch alone. Each night she'd listened to the quieting of the household, the crickets, the snuffling of the dogs, the sigh of a breeze, while falling asleep as though isolated in an ivory tower. Alone, but hopeful. Lonely, yet counting down those nights like calendar points to when she and Kelsey might become one in truth as well as name.

As planned, Kelsey and the kids pulled out early the next morning, hauling the trailer with Fred behind. The lamb and Aimee shared the truck bed, cushioned and penned in by hay bales and old quilts. The truck bed also held folding chairs, coolers and more trappings than Meg would have thought possible. She didn't hope to see much of Kelsey or the boys until the fair ended, though she planned on running Aimee back and forth each day. The "men" were camping in the fair camping area specifically designated for exhibitors.

Of course, she would take in the sights with Lissa and Heather and run whatever errands were required.

After they left that morning, and between times during that hectic week of the fair, Meg and Lissa concentrated on organizing the house, room by room, tiny closet by tiny closet. But the dimensions were totally inadequate for seven people, even with the most careful use of the space. Especially with five of those people growing steadily larger every day.

That didn't surprise Meg at all; she'd known what she was getting into. At least that's what she kept telling herself. Still, she'd hoped to find some measure of overlooked or otherwise mismanaged space she could utilize for the new school clothing and supplies the children needed, as well as some space for herself. There didn't seem to be any.

Kelsey's clothes were neatly stacked in one single-tier chest. Mostly jeans, T-shirts and flannels. Mostly dark colors. Meg sorted through, discarding the garments past redemption and counting the rest. His tiny closet revealed only a few more things. He needed an update on his wardrobe as badly as the children. It looked as though he hadn't purchased anything new for years, until he'd bought his wedding suit. She noted his sizes for her expanding list—the one under the "Department Store" heading. Brick red, light blue. Green, any shade, and a few selected grays. Kelsey would look terrific in all of those shades.

They came upon a number of Dee Dee's things, left behind by accident or ignored, Meg suspected, simply because it was the easiest thing to do. She and Lissa silently packed away the keepables into the top of Kelsey's closet together, stacking the other things to give away into a box that afterward went right into the van, ready to be carted to town. When they came across a set of old diaries, Meg handed them to Lissa, saying very little. Both of them felt a wrenching.

Lissa spent a few moments gently smoothing her hand over the imitation leather, then murmured, "I think I'll put these away until I'm older, and Aimee and I can read them then." She glanced at Meg, a hint of tears surfacing. "Mom loved us all a lot, but sometimes..."

"Sometimes?"

"At the last she sometimes didn't talk to us much. For days and days, and then weeks and months. It made Dad unhappy, and he spent more and more time working with the cattle or down at the barn at night. We kids didn't know what was wrong. I'm not sure Daddy did, either. She didn't tell anybody she was sick, and then just before she died, she spoke of you...."

"Oh, Lissa. I wish I'd known."

"I don't think there was anything you could've done for her, Aunt Meg," Lissa said, letting her old form of address slip out. "She could've written or called you if she really wanted. She didn't want anybody, I think. But she did write in her diaries a lot. Only, now, I...I think I'll wait until I'm older to read them. D'you suppose that's all right?"

Meg reached out and gathered Lissa in a gentle hug, her own tears pooling with the understanding that this oldest child of Kelsey's had quietly carried so much emotional burden. "Oh, sweetie, I think it's very all right. God's word tells us there is a season for grieving and a season for living. I think Dee Dee would want you to put away the sadness of her passing now and concentrate on all the living ahead. You have some wonderful growing-up years just ahead of you—it's time for you to enjoy being the teenager you are."

Lissa's hug tightened before letting go. "Thanks, Meg."

Without more comment, they moved on to tackle the closet in the boys' room, but after the hours of rearranging, discovered that straightening and sorting helped only minimally. There was simply too much to be stored in the tiny space.

All the closets were totally impossible. It made Meg sigh and grit her teeth in frustration. She wanted everything in order by the time school started, and she couldn't find room in the kitchen for even half the new small appliances and kitchen linen they'd received as wedding gifts from the church family. How could she keep any order at all or maintain any kind of schedule in such cramped quarters?

How would they manage with only one bathroom when school started?

One morning, when Meg actually made it in to her corner loft space at Justine's, she interviewed Mary Claire. Thankfully, the young woman agreed to come out to the farm twice a week permanently; she'd kept the routine Meg had set up for Audrey a month earlier.

"Justine, I can't thank you enough for finding Mary Claire for us," Meg told her friend as she gathered her things to leave. Lissa and Heather huddled around one of the computers, playing games with Justine's son.

"No prob, Meg," Justine said, lowering the top of her best, biggest copier. "Glad she's working out for you. Her sister helps me out now and then. I'd be lost without her. And for Steve Carter, here," she said, gesturing to the dark-haired mid-forties man waiting by the counter, and then made introductions.

"Hi," Meg said politely.

"Steve came to town a few years back about the time you left," Justine explained. "He's the builder of those new houses out south of town."

"That builder?" Meg drew an excited breath. She had briefly seen those houses one day when she'd been out and around with Kathy before the wedding. They were well done, nicely designed.

She glanced at the girls; they paid her no attention. Taking a step closer, she moderated her voice. "Tell me, Steve, if I wanted to add a room or two..."

Twenty minutes later Meg left Justine's with her head whirling with more than a few facts and figures. Her excitement level was high. Kelsey had casually talked of adding a room to their small house; now she could hardly wait to bring the subject up. Building on. But they really needed more than a couple of rooms. Too bad they couldn't simply pick up one of those beautiful brand-new houses and transplant it to the farm like they did tomato plants or begonias.

"Is Mary Claire gonna come see us again?" Heather asked as Meg opened the van door.

"Uh-huh. Next week. Won't that be nice?" Bliss was more like it. "Another pair of hands to help with the chores." Meg scooted into the driver's seat and started the engine. "If she can simply do most of the laundry and handle the kitchen twice a week, we might have room to breathe."

Twice a week might even expand into three after she got her part-time consulting thing going, Meg mused. But one thing at a time.

"Yeah, Meg, it'll be terrific," Lissa said. "But what's Dad going to say?"

"What do you mean, Lissa?" Meg pulled onto Broadway, heading for the fairgrounds.

"Well, he didn't like the last two women he got to help out. One spent most of the time on the phone, and Dad couldn't get in one day when he tried to call us from town, and, well—"

"Ouch. I spend a lot of time on the phone, too. It's the nature of my job."

"That's different. You live there now. Besides, you're not just a gossip, and you're working when you do talk."

"Thanks, honey. Remind me to hire you as my defense lawyer if I ever need one. I've been thinking we should have another phone line, anyway—now I think it rises to the top of the list. Now about Mary Claire. Didn't she do a good job for us last month when I was in London?"

"I guess. At least she came when she said she would and Aimee liked her. She didn't get upset when the boys spilled fruit punch all over the kitchen floor, but she made them help clean it up.''

''A woman of strength,'' Meg said with a smile. ''But why don't you think your dad will like her?''

''Well, she's kinda bossy.''

''Ahh, bossy, huh? Was it over something she needed to be bossy about? I'll have to remember to—oh, oh—'' she eased her foot on the gas pedal and looked at her watch. ''I completely forgot to pick up my fax messages from Justine's. I should have a message about the closing date on Serenity. But that'll have to wait, I guess. We promised to be there for Aimee's lamb showing at one, remember? Too bad we can't be in two places at once.''

After Meg dropped Lissa off to join Aimee, Meg parked the car. She and Heather threaded their way through the crowd to the sheep pavilion at almost a run, squeezing onto a third-row seat as the first introduction came over the loud speaker. They waited and watched and cheered when Betsy Ross placed third.

''Shoulda taken second, at least,'' Aimee complained later, when Meg and Heather caught up with the girls back at the pens. ''But that's okay. I know the kid who got champion, and he worked hard with his sheep.''

''There's always next year,'' Meg suggested.

''Yeah, but I don't want another lamb. I like Betsy Ross okay, but I want to go out for sports in school now that I'm in middle school, and I won't have time.''

''I had no idea,'' Meg answered as she searched Aimee's face.

''I already told Dad about it. But see, I'll have to have extra rides and things. He said it depended on you.''

''Well, we can discuss it after we get the school schedules.'' Meg made a mental note of adding Aimee's desires to the list. ''Lissa wants to try out for the choir, too. I'm sure we can work something out.''

''Can we have some ice cream now?'' Heather asked.

''Sure, honey. Right after we find out how the boys made out with Fred.'' Meg turned to Lissa and Aimee. ''We'll bring you girls some ice cream later, okay?''

"You go ahead, Meg," Lissa answered. "We'll wait our turn."

Outside the cattle judging arena, Fred stood warily having his picture taken, with Thad and Philip at attention, pride and shiny-eyed excitement on their faces, on either side of him with firm hands. Kelsey waited, talking with a couple of men Meg didn't know and their neighbor, Bill Miller.

He turned as the girls approached, giving them a wide grin and a thumbs-up, then continued his discussion.

"They did it," Meg murmured in wonder, keeping her voice even so as not to startle the animals. She felt a burst of pride.

"They really did."

She hung back with Heather and waited. The photographer lined up another shot. When it was over, the boys led Fred toward their father.

"Way to go, boys," Meg told them, wanting to hug them, but holding her impulse in check. They weren't quite ready to accept her affection like the girls did, especially in public. But their faces nearly split with happy grins at her congratulations. "All your hard work paid off."

Kelsey introduced her to the two men who nodded their greetings.

"Looks like we have our winner, Mrs. Jamison," Bill Miller said, looking pleased. Meg smiled and made polite conversation, but mostly listened to the farm talk and the men's opinion of the various animals. Shortly thereafter, the two other men left.

The rest of them turned to head toward the animal pens, Kelsey walking ahead with Fred and the boys.

"This will put the Jamison farm into the spotlight this year," Bill Miller remarked. He was only about ten years older than Kelsey, yet spoke as though he knew all there was to know of the cattle business. "Kelsey's been trying to gain a reputation for breeding black Angus. It surprised me when they decided on raising that Hereford."

"I'm thrilled for the boys," she replied. "They've worked hard and babied Fred along like mother hens, according to Kelsey."

"Yep, that's what it takes, besides having a fine animal to

begin with. My son never did half as well as those boys in spite of having more to choose from. We've favored the Herefords from time to time, but we've cut back some now. But for a small operation, Kelsey does well.''

"Yes, I guess he does." She glanced in pride at her husband and boys. "Too bad he hasn't been able to expand."

"The timing hasn't been right. Prices too high." He shook his head and clicked his teeth. "I'd sure like to push my boundaries. I'd even offer for Kelsey's place if I thought he'd sell it to me at a reasonable price. I've been after Miss Maybelle to go ahead and sell me that field I've been renting from her for the last few years, but she won't hear of it. Don't know why she wants to keep it. I'm going to try again soon's the weather cools.''

So he was after Miss Maybelle's piece of ground, too. And Kelsey's? But Kelsey would never sell out, that was a certainty.

Bill Miller went on his way, and Meg and the girls parted company with Kelsey and the boys outside the animal pens. Kelsey promised to meet the whole family later for supper.

That evening felt a little anticlimactic. The boys and Kelsey accepted many congratulations during their meal at one of the big church vendors, leaving no time for the family to talk or celebrate among themselves. Meg had hoped to broach the idea of adding on to their house with Kelsey, but it didn't take her long to realize the subject would have to wait.

The drive home with the girls felt lonely, too. Already Meg felt incomplete when tucking in only half her family at bedtime. Ah, well. The fair would last only a few more days. Then the return to school would be upon them, throwing them all into a new routine.

Long after she'd gone to bed, Meg lay half-asleep listening to the night sounds, welcoming the cooling air that reached her through the screens, thinking of where she could stretch the house, refusing to allow loneliness to take its toll. Until she heard a car.

It sounded like Kelsey's truck.

She threw back the light sheet as the truck door snapped closed. She heard the faint padding of the dogs, a low bark, a hushed command. Hand on the lamp switch, she paused. What if it wasn't her husband? Footsteps crunched on the drive, then ceased. She held her breath, wondering if she should hurry downstairs. Yet nothing seemed out of place, and she heard no sound from the girls, below.

"Meg," a masculine voice called up to her. "Are you awake?"

She stumbled toward the screen windows opposite her bed, relief flooding her at recognizing Kelsey's voice.

"Kelsey. What are you doing home? Is anything wrong?"

"No." He stood as a shadow beneath the spreading maple, mysterious and yearning, his face raised to see her through the dark. "Sorry. Didn't mean to scare you."

"Where are the boys?"

"Bennie came by and offered to camp out with them. He seemed really pleased about Fred and wanted to stay. I left them swapping tall tales with one of the other old-timers, and the boys had company of their own age, too."

"Sounds like they're having a great time."

"Yeah. I s'pose they'll remember this fair for the rest of their lives."

"Then what brought you home?"

A long pause ensued. Only the wind whispered to fill the quiet, fluttering her cotton nightgown and cooling her bare shoulders. It felt refreshing through her hair after the day's heat.

"I wanted," he huskily murmured, "hoped..."

Meg's breath caught up high in her chest, and she couldn't let it out. She licked her dry lips. "Kels? Would you like to come up?"

"Yes. Yes, I—" He turned and disappeared from view.

Before Meg could reach the stairway, she heard the kitchen door squeak open and closed. She waited, barely breathing. A muffled thud reached her before she heard a stair creak. He came through the door and stopped, his boots dangling from his hand. The breeze ruffled his hair, and she caught the clean odor of soap and tangy aftershave.

"Ah, Meg..." His husky voice reached out and wrapped around her leaping heart. "I came home for you."

Chapter Fourteen

As soon as she had breakfast cleared away the next morning, Meg headed into town with only Heather. They'd received a card in the mail from the school Heather would attend, inviting them to an early orientation. Thad and Phillip were students there, and she was sure Heather had been there before, but she felt it would help Heather to gain some independence to visit the classroom.

Heather wasn't too sure about that. Her feet lagged. Meg held the small hand firmly. "Why can't Lissa come?"

"Lissa's a big girl and is going to attend the school for the big kids, remember?" And to forestall the next protest, "And Aimee will be in middle school, just like we talked about."

"But I don't like Mrs. Danes. Thad says she has a mean look and her nose is so long it nearly touches her chin. He says—"

"Now you know Thad said that just to scare you. Lissa told me that Mrs. Danes is an excellent teacher and has a special play corner filled with a big papier-mâché giraffe. It's taller than your daddy. I'm eager to see that, aren't you?"

"I don't like giraffes."

"Have your ever seen one?"

Heather shook her head.

"Then how do you know you don't like them? Didn't your

dad ever take you to the zoo? He didn't? Well, we'll have to remedy that, won't we. I'll put that as number one on our 'to-do' list for this fall, okay?''

By that time they'd reached the kindergarten room. Heather's feet dragged slower and slower. She crunched Meg's hand and stepped on her feet in an effort to disappear into Meg's skirt. Until she heard her name called by a little girl named Ashley she knew from Sunday Bible class.

To Meg's relief, it didn't take much coaxing after that.

Meg talked a few moments with Mrs. Danes, then stepped down the hall to the office with the intention of introducing herself. The quicker she became involved with the children's school, the easier it would be to deal with their school career, she thought. Something on which Kelsey had asked her help.

Yet she came away from talking with the school principal a little troubled. Thad had almost failed math the previous year and needed tutoring if he expected to keep up with the current year. Kelsey hadn't mentioned it.

They pulled away from school with Heather talking about where she and Ashley planned to sit when school started. Meg relaxed behind the wheel. She wished every problem were so easily solved. And finding a tutor from the three names given her at the school office should result in a solution for Thad's need, but it was one more thing to put on her list, one more schedule to keep up with.

"I wanted to stay and play with Ashley," Heather told her. "But Ashley had to leave, too. Can we have lunch now?"

"Lunch already? It's only eleven o'clock."

"But I'm hungry," Heather wailed.

"Well, let's see what's open. What sounds good?"

The streets were crowded, and as Meg glanced at her watch, she decided to run by her mother's house first and maybe get a bite there, before checking in at her office. The doctor had suggested to her and Jack that some older patients slipped easily into depression when living alone, and Meg planned to stop by to see how Audrey was getting along now that she was on her own again. Later, she could put an hour or two in at her computer. She'd also made an appointment to see Steve Carter and to look at house plans.

She still hadn't discussed her ideas with Kelsey, but fair week wasn't exactly good timing on her part to expect him to focus on the house. She'd made one attempt as he dressed in the early hours to return to the fairgrounds. His thoughts already turned to the day ahead, he took in only the understanding that she wanted to make changes in the house.

Bending to kiss her goodbye, he nuzzled her neck. "Mmm...you smell good. What's that stuff you wear?"

A light breeze rustled the trees outside, sending cool fingers to flutter against her cheek and ruffle his hair. Brushing it from his eyes, Meg could barely see his features in the gray light. "It's nothing special. Just something I buy across the counter."

"It's just right." He touched her lips once more, tracing her mouth with a finger. "I hate to go," he murmured, then with a sigh, said, "Whatever you want to do with the house is fine with me, sweetheart. Whatever works."

Meg sighed now, driving through town. Her nerves still tingled with the memory of what they'd shared, of knowing that all her girlish expectations—her dreams—had become reality. Their loving had been most sweet and tender. Yet in her own honesty, she had to admit Kelsey hadn't once said he loved her.

But that would come. Surely, it would. She could only hope their intimacy had taken them forward.

And last night had unexpectedly been easily arranged. Spontaneous and joyous, as though they'd fallen into a special time-out from demanding children and crazy schedules.

But given their circumstances, their togetherness wouldn't always be so easy until they shared a proper room. If one could call Kelsey's sneaking back to the house, tiptoeing barefooted past sleeping children to climb that creaky staircase, then leaving again at dawn, easy. Picturing it made her chuckle. They sounded more like teenagers than two grown-ups, properly married. Married folk shouldn't have to sneak around to gain a little privacy. And come winter, they wouldn't have even the old sleeping porch.

Meg shook her head as she had to stop once again for bulging fair traffic. She tried to ignore the delay and think of a solution to their dilemma. They *had* to have a room of their own or their marriage might remain just as clogged as these streets, she mused.

By the time they reached her mother's house, Heather was campaigning even harder to eat.

"Hi, Mom," Meg said, kissing her mother's cheek when Audrey opened the door. "Can we bum lunch from you today? The lunch trade today is great for the eateries, but a tough competitor when you're not quite five."

"Oh, my, yes, but," Audrey said, looking down at the old summer duster she wore, "you've caught me before I've even dressed. I wasn't expecting anyone today. But sure, Meg. Come on in. I don't have much in the house besides peanut butter, though."

"Peanut butter! Mmm. Haven't had a p and j sandwich in ages," Meg said, glancing at her mother's unkempt hair. Perhaps it was a good thing they'd stopped in to see her early. "How about it, Heather? You want to eat with Aunt Audrey?"

"Uh-huh. Is Sara coming?"

"No, honey, I'm sorry to say," Audrey answered. "She lives too far to come very often."

"Oh." Heather's face fell.

"Well, how about a tea party?"

"What's that?"

"You've never had a tea party?" Audrey glanced at Meg in surprise. "Well, I suppose a tea party is rather an old-fashioned concept. But it's still fun. We'll have to do something about it. Your mother and Meg used to have tea parties when they were little, and...you know what?" A dawning light entered her eyes. "I miss having tea parties."

To Meg's complete amazement, her mother entered into the game with happy anticipation. Excusing herself, she hurried to get dressed. When she came back downstairs, she'd found an old rag doll of Meg's to sit with Heather. She even pulled out the miniature china tea set Meg had given her for Christmas one year. The three of them chatted and munched, and Heather told about the big giraffe in her new schoolroom. Meg was more relaxed with her mother than she'd felt in weeks, until finally she glanced at her watch.

"We really have to go, Mom. I have an appointment, then I have to make a stop at Justine's."

"Do we haveta?" Heather complained. "I get tired at Justine's."

"Why don't you leave Heather with me," Audrey suggested. "She and I can find things to do until your business is completed. I think we might even find a picture of a giraffe in an animal book I have upstairs."

"You're kidding." Meg could hardly credit her own hearing. Having fourteen-year-old Lissa as a guest was one thing, but offering to watch Heather? This was the woman who had complained about her taking up with Kelsey and his children only months ago? Who fussed at the way her antiques might be roughly treated? "You're not?"

"Well, honestly, Meg," Audrey said, affronted. "I'll have you know I can still entertain a child."

"I know you can, Mom." She studied her mother's face. Audrey did seem less tired these days and happier. Maybe she'd misjudged her mother's emotional well-being earlier, because now she seemed perfectly fine. "I recall lots of time when we had great fun. It's only that...I wasn't sure you really wanted to."

"Why not? I don't have anything else to do today until Paul calls for me."

"Oh, Paul is taking you out, is he?"

"Now, Meg, don't read anything into it," Audrey insisted while a blush crept up her cheeks. "We're only friends."

"Uh-huh. Better watch out, Mom," Meg teased. "What will your *other* friends say about your spending so much time in Paul's company?"

Audrey made an exasperated sound and turned pointedly to the little girl. "Let's put it to Heather. Would you like to stay and play with me? I could teach you how to read the piano notes."

"Can I learn that song Sara knows?"

"Sure, why not?"

"Okay. I'll pick you up about four, Heather," Meg said as Audrey and Heather headed toward the living room, hand in hand. But she doubted either of them heard her.

Rain poured down as she left her mother's house, further slowing and clogging traffic. Idly, she wondered how Kelsey and the boys got along in the downpour or if they even paid it any mind. Had they packed rain gear? Then once again, she laughed at how ridiculous she sounded to herself; Kelsey had been parenting for years while she'd brought only a few weeks to the job.

She spent longer with the builder than she'd planned.

Happily, she now had a better understanding of the process of building a house and current costs. But the more she thought of merely adding on a room or two to Kelsey's little house, the more she realized she wanted a new abode altogether. Something large and fresh with lots of expansive windows and enough space to accommodate their growing family. And why not?

That small cottage on the farm had been right for Kelsey and Dee Dee when they were just starting out together, and she knew they'd worked very hard to pay for it. For that matter, Meg wasn't sure if it was free and clear yet; Kelsey hadn't mentioned what he might still owe on the farm. But he had spoken of having nothing more than what she saw…what was obvious. And if that was all she and Kelsey were ever to have or could ever afford, as long as they shared it, Meg could make the best of the tight space and be content.

Then she laughed out loud. Mere contentment? How foolish of her. She'd be deliriously happy! She'd still have the man she adored and five lovely children. And one to come, if God blessed her and Kelsey with a child of their love as she hoped.

But she had enough money socked away from investments that, if she sold it all, she could build twice the size house they needed, two or three times over. But she wouldn't have to. If she kept her best stocks and then continued to draw from her part-time consulting, she could pay for a house in only a few years. The kids needed more growing room—they could use a study or den—and a huge, modern kitchen wouldn't go amiss.

Why not build an all-new, easy-to-keep, easy-to-live-in house to make life run smoother for all of them? Why shouldn't she?

She and Kelsey should have a frank discussion about money soon, Meg supposed; he'd never asked her about her financial assets. He'd made no objection and asked only a question or two when she'd mentioned keeping an office of her own. But honestly, they'd been apart more than they'd been together. When things slowed down, when school kicked in its routine and the children had regular bedtimes, then they'd have those couple times, those late nights when they could talk and share their thoughts and dreams, and that bowl of popcorn Kelsey had mentioned.

Meanwhile, he'd said she could do anything about the house she wanted to do. And she *wanted* a new house. She'd loved Dee Dee wholeheartedly, but she wanted a home that was her own.

She found a parking spot behind Justine's building and hurried in while dreaming big dreams of the perfect house. Where could they put it? What would make a good home site? Every bit of Kelsey's acreage was in use. How much work and how long would it take to run utilities in a new direction?

"Hi-ya, Meg," Justine greeted, flipping her chestnut-colored hair behind her shoulder. "I was beginning to think you wouldn't make it in today. You have a few faxes left over from yesterday and a couple that came in this morning. Oh, and your business mail has started coming through. It's there in your box."

"Thanks, Justine." Meg accepted the folder with her fax messages and reached for the handful of business letters and a few cards. When word had spread about her marriage, congratulations from old colleagues had trickled in steadily. "It's been rushed."

"Yeah, isn't it just. School starting soon. Fair week. And traffic," Justine said, wrinkling her nose in disgust. "Can't blame those people who take off for the lake to avoid it all."

Meg looked up from shuffling through her messages and chuckled. "You ought to see traffic in one of the *big* cities, Justine. It's sometimes ten times as bad, and without a state fair to clog streets. Well, I've got to hit the computer and respond to these.''

Meg had four e-mails from Clive, two from clients who lamented her loss as their adviser, and several from Elizabeth wanting advice on how to handle something. She still needed to answer half of them. Her faxes were full of queries for investment advice, or high-powered, big-concept investments that someone wanted to sell her. She answered them in order, plowing through most but putting a couple on hold.

Among other things, Clive wanted an answer to their invitation to attend the five-day opening of Serenity during the first week of November. He urged her to come.

Should she? The idea intrigued her; the Serenity exchange had been the only resort investment she'd done in recent years and perhaps her last, if she stuck to her resolve to keep her business interests to a few clients. She'd like to celebrate the success with Clive and the Neels. But she no longer had only herself to consider, she couldn't simply rearrange a few days with an office staff, pack her bags and go. Impossible.

Rising, she stretched her back and went downstairs by the back staircase to grab a cola from Justine's fridge, behind a partition near the rear wall. Tossing the money for it into the cup, she leaned against the counter and popped the top, thinking about how much of her own, the children's and Kelsey's schedule had to be rearranged if she were to accept the invitation.

Yet it shouldn't be any more difficult than when she'd gone to New York, she decided. She had Mary Claire coming into the house twice a week now, and the kids would be in school. Five days weren't that long. Besides, she didn't have to make a commitment yet.

The front door opened, setting off the subdued *ding* that announced a customer when Justine was away from the front counter.

''Hello, Justine. I always declare not to budge out of my house during fair week,'' she heard a familiar voice complain. Sandy Yoder. ''But somehow, something always manages to demand a little extra attention, and I get caught up in all this traffic. This would be the year for Mrs. Lathrop to take her vacation in August when I volunteered to fill in at the church office. She's always taken it in July, before, y'know. I do think it's time we found an assistant secretary for the poor dear— someone younger. The work has become just too much for one woman, to my thinking, and now Pastor wants this extra insert in the bulletin. If the church copier hadn't broken down, I could've avoided the worst of it, don't y'know."

"I'm happy to be of service, Sandy," Justine finally broke in. "How many copies should I run?"

The front bell dinged again, and Meg heard Justine say, "I'll be with you in a minute."

"Four hundred, Pastor said," Sandy answered. "I declare, I don't know why he thinks we'll need that many when we only have about two hundred members coming during the last of August."

The bell indicated more customers had entered, so Meg ambled around the kitchen partition toward the front counter. "Can I help, Justine?"

Justine threw her a glance of gratitude mixed with a grin, and Meg turned to the older woman on the other side of the counter. "Hello, Sandy. Why don't I run those for you while Justine attends someone else."

"Well, if you're sure. Do you know how? I mean, those new copiers are really different than the old things we have at church, y'know."

"I think I can manage. Why don't you step around here and tell me how the week's been going while you've been filling in as church secretary?"

"Oh, well, all right I suppose. But really, Pastor Reynolds is so much busier than old Beaker was, y'know. He's even been holding regular counseling sessions and such, which is all well and good, but he insists on making those appointments himself, and then when people call, I simply don't know what to tell them. Miss Maybelle came in yesterday and wanted to speak with him about a new time for the seniors activities, and he wasn't there or at home. Came in fifteen minutes late. And poor Miss Maybelle had to wait."

"I'm so happy to know Miss Maybelle remains active," Meg commented.

"Oh, my, yes. But y'know, she's still driving, and I'm not sure if she should at her age. She complained she had to drive all the way around town to avoid traffic. Too bad Bennie or one of her other children won't move back to Sedalia to be close by like you did. But at least she sold that farm out near you folks a few years back or she might be trying to live there herself."

"Yes, Miss Maybelle loved living in the country," Meg answered while her mind jumped like a cricket in three directions at once. She'd faced her own mother's ill health with those same thoughts of needing to live closer as Audrey grew older. And she recalled Miss Maybelle's wistful expression when first mentioning she still owned twenty acres next to Kelsey. That acreage had no improvements on it. It held only a couple of rocky outcrops, roughly a six-acre stand of mixed hardwood trees, and the rest in open pasture. But there was a lovely rolling rise only a quarter of a mile from Kelsey's drive, with easy access from the road, that would make a perfect setting for a house.

And Bennie had grown tired of his city job. He'd even mentioned wanting to help Kelsey out again with the animals. Would he by any chance be looking to make a change? Could she convince Bennie to consider taking a part-time job with Kelsey right away? Kelsey wanted to expand his beef herd, and if they had a small house to offer rent-free in the bargain, perhaps if not Bennie, then someone else would be interested in hiring on.

"I remember she and Grandma Hicks used to quilt together and can fruit when I was little," she chatted aimlessly with Sandy, stacking the printed sheets neatly together. "They were great friends. Did she get back home all right?"

"Oh, yes, I'm sure she did. Said she had nothing better to do this afternoon than to nap."

Meg finished the copying task and cheerfully helped Sandy carry them out to her car. When she returned to the office, she waved at Justine, beaming with good cheer, and took her cola up to her office space. A moment later she punched in the phone number she'd looked up in the town directory.

"Hi, Miss Maybelle, this is Meg Jamison. Did I wake you? No? Well, I'm just wondering if you might give me an hour this afternoon...."

Chapter Fifteen

❧

In spite of the late hour, Meg slowed the car to a bare roll as she approached the twenty acres adjoining Kelsey's south property line. Hers, now. Miss Maybelle had sold it to her this afternoon; it hadn't taken near the persuasion she'd thought it might. Miss Maybelle found it a lovely idea for Meg to own the land, especially since none of her own children wanted it. To make sure, Meg waited while Miss Maybelle phoned her two daughters and received approval for the sale. She hadn't bothered to phone Bennie at all.

"The more I've pushed with Bennie to go one way, the more he was determined to go his own," she confided, her face puckering with old worries. "If you and Kelsey want to offer him a place with you and he takes it, I'll be pleasantly surprised. Although I must say, he's been showing more common sense of late and more interest in his roots than he used to. But don't count on anything. And for heaven's sakes, don't tell him you suggested the idea to me first. It might send him in the opposite direction. You remember it was Justine who suggested to him to help you folks out when you and Kelsey got married."

"Yes, I do remember. All right," Meg said, patting the older woman's hand. "When the time is right, we'll approach the plan with care. It'll be toward the end of the year, anyway. By Christ-

mas, if we're in luck. By the same token, Miss Maybelle, I don't
want anyone to know of my plans just yet, either. Kelsey really
wants that pasture, but I aim to claim about three acres on that
front rise.''

"It'll be our little conspiracy, Meg, dear.''

Afterward, Meg had wasted no time in starting the paperwork
with the young lawyer Justine recommended.

She glanced at the back seat where Heather had fallen asleep
holding on to a bag of groceries. Dinner would be late, but she
had all the makings of a quick stir-fry dish that she knew the
girls would like.

She let her gaze swing back to the horizon line where it
dipped slightly before reaching a final gentle hill. That was the
spot. She braked the car, turned off the motor and stared. Finally
she eased her door open and quietly exited, vowing to find out
how far she could see from the top.

Meg climbed the rise, her white canvas sneakers sinking into
the soft ground, still wet from the earlier rain. Her skirt hem
was becoming damp from the tall grasses, too, but she didn't
care. She drew a deep breath and let it out slowly as she turned
in a circle, observing the lay of the land. From here she saw
more of Kelsey's barn than she did of the house; a dip in the
ground and the line of trees allowed her to see only a corner of
the rooftop. The garages and sheds weren't visible at all. Beyond
another hill in the opposite direction were the Millers, the people
who had bought Miss Maybelle's original place, their buildings
appearing as large blobs against the sky. Across the wire-fenced
road lay rolling pasture and cattle.

Tears unexpectedly shimmered against her lashes. It was a
lovely piece of ground, and Meg felt an attachment she hadn't
counted on feeling. How could she love and want mere land so
suddenly? But the feeling was there, strong and sure. Grandma
and Grandpa Hicks had often spoken lovingly of their four hundred acres, closer to town, and had tended it with care. This
feeling of belonging must have come from them, must have
been how they felt, Meg mused, and how Kelsey felt. An unusual regret that her family no longer owned the old Hicks property swept over her.

Yet keeping it after her grandparents died had been imprac- tical for her parents, she knew. The place had not been mod- ernized beyond the fifties. Times had changed and left the old place hopelessly behind, and her mother had never felt the con- nectedness her grandparents felt nor wanted the isolation or work of it. Neither was her father interested in farming; he'd been perfectly content with his law practice in town. Ah, they all succumbed to time's march, Meg supposed.

She started back to the car, excitement still bubbling along her veins. She could hardly wait to tell Kelsey of her purchase. He'd mentioned wanting to buy the adjoining piece from Miss Maybelle more than once, and so had Mr. Miller, only Miss Maybelle hadn't been ready to sell before now. Now it was hers and Kelsey's. A pride of ownership was an awesome thing, making her want to crow like Peter Pan.

Almost reaching the vehicle, she saw Heather pop up in the open window, crying. "Me-e-eg."

"Here I am, honey. Don't cry."

"Where were you?"

"I had to stop a moment. I like the look of that hill," she said to redirect the child's thoughts. She reached for and hugged her close. "Do you? Isn't it pretty?"

"Uh-huh." Heather gazed at where Meg pointed, then back at her in puzzlement.

"Never mind, honey," Meg told her with a chuckle. "Let's go home and cook dinner."

Meg had no time to mention her day's activities to Kelsey. When he called her from the fairgrounds, he spilled over with the news of two offers for Fred and the decision of the boys not to put the bull up for auction but to take the offer from the breeder. Thad especially liked the idea of starting with a new calf next year provided by the breeder at a very fair price while Phillip simply didn't want Fred to end up as somebody's steak, Kelsey told her. But Betsy Ross had been sold at auction and Aimee, while happy with the sale, felt a bit of parting blues. He'd given Aimee permission to spend the night with her friends, so Meg needn't worry about picking her up.

He ended by telling her Bennie had agreed to run by that

evening to see to the routine cattle check, and they'd wrap up the fair next day. She could expect him, Aimee and the boys home sometime the next afternoon.

Meg sighed, folded four loads of clothes and put them away, ran the vacuum, changed her bed sheets, and set aside clothing that needed mending or to be taken to the cleaners the next day. Tomorrow she had to take Heather for her physical checkup and order a cake for Saturday's birthday dinner. Heather would be five, just under the wire for kindergarten.

Her last task for the evening before climbing the stairs to bed was to finish cleaning her one stir-fry pot. Tiredly she stooped to place it atop two other pots in the lower cupboard next to the stove. It balanced precariously, and she took a moment to reposition it.

She was halfway up the stairs when a sudden rattle and crash made her jump nearly out of her skin. Lissa let out a loud squeal, and a second later Heather began to cry.

Meg spun and leaped down the stairs and into the kitchen, snapping on the overhead light before coming to a sudden halt. A swift glance at the back door assured her it was still locked. Nothing moved beyond the windows but the breeze. Except for her own heavy breathing, she heard nothing.

Lissa appeared at her side wearing her blue sleep T-shirt they'd bought in Branson, green eyes wide and questioning. She held a baseball bat against her shoulder in ready-to-swing position.

"It's all right, girls," Meg soothed, her hand on Lissa's trembling arm. Together they stared at the pile of pots and pans that had caused the cupboard door to burst open as they spilled onto the floor. The old latches seldom held firm. She mentally ordered her heart to stop leaping like a bullfrog. Heather still sobbed.

"Hold on a moment," she murmured to Lissa. Turning, she fetched Heather from the bedroom, scooping the little girl up and taking her into the kitchen. "Look, honey. It's nothing to be scared of. It's only the pot cupboard telling us it ate too much for dinner. It burped."

Lissa rolled her eyes at Meg and started to giggle.

Heather giggled, too, in the midst of rolling tears and receding sobs. "At least it's not a critter," Lissa muttered, letting her guard down. "Once a racoon got into the house and we chased it for an hour before we got it out. And last year we had a hard time with a squirrel in the attic. Remember, Heather?"

"Uh-huh. That really scared me."

"What happened?" Meg asked.

"Daddy had to do a plug-up job. He kept going back up to the roof until he found out where the squirrel kept getting in and finally plugged it. Boy, did he grumble."

"Well, old houses need lots of repair, don't they?" She thought the girls' nerves sufficiently settled, so she said, "Let's just let those pots and pans sleep where they landed for the night, okay?" She waited for Heather's nod.

They started back through the hall, snapping on lights as they turned off the kitchen's, but at the bedroom door, Heather's arms tightened around her neck. Her little body stiffened.

"Meg, will you sleep with me?" her voice quivered.

Meg eyed the narrow bunk. She glanced at Lissa, who would eat worms before admitting that she was anything close to scared, too. It must be too much excitement, too much on their minds, Meg thought. Neither of them had shown any fright before.

"I tell you what," Meg said, deciding to indulge them this one time. She shifted Heather against her hip. "Get your bunny that you sleep with, and you and Lissa and I will all go up to sleep in the big bed." Though only a double, it would afford more space than one of the narrow bunks. "How's that? We'll have a three-girl slumber party. After all, this is the last night we'll be alone before the guys and Aimee get home."

"Okay," Heather sniffed with a nod.

"I'll get bunny and the pillows," Lissa said. Meg noticed she didn't offer a single objection to sharing the upstairs bed.

"I'll tell you a story about Grandma Hicks and Grandma Audrey," Meg said a few moments later, settling in and pulling the sheet up to their chins. Heather relaxed a little but tucked her head firmly against Meg's shoulder. On the other side of Heather, Lissa sighed deeply.

Meg began in a modulated low tone. "One time Grandma Hicks was making jelly. Cherry jam, to be precise, and..."

Meg signed the contract with Steve Carter the next morning. She offered a sizable bonus if he could complete the house by Christmas; he agreed it could be done. Visions of spending the holidays in a big, new dwelling decorated with all the bright things that made Christmas beautiful and filled with music and good food, and finally, surrounded by loving family and friends with smiling faces—all of it danced in her head like the proverbial sugar plums.

A dream, to be sure.

Lord, I know Christmas isn't about things and tinsel and glitter. Or even feasting and songs. Christmas is about celebrating You. If we were to have nothing more than the stable You had, we'd still have You in it and feel blessed. But, Lord, we do need more space and I have the means....

And she'd always honored Him with her tithes and offerings. According to Grandma Hicks's teachings, that was an important part of worship; Meg also felt comfortable in recalling her father's agreement with that Old Testament directive. Two years ago, she'd quietly and without fanfare given the money to purchase a new piano for the youth department and contributed nearly half what was needed for a much larger sanctuary organ. Even now, her mother didn't know of her giving practices, although she sometimes felt Miss Maybelle did.

She decided to wait to tell Kelsey of the land purchase until after the rush of school starting and Heather's birthday party and a heavy round of clothes shopping. Surely things would settle down by then. She'd been thinking about how he'd been reluctant to accept her purchase of the van and it seemed wise to wait and tell him when she could do it quietly, without a crowd around.

Oh, he'd be wildly happy about her plans, about gaining that piece of ground—she just knew it. Didn't she? He hadn't been very keen about her other surprises. Finally, she admitted to herself she really couldn't guess just how he'd react to the news.

But she still thought it best to wait until things slowed down before telling him.

Just before three the next day, her mother appeared unexpectedly.

"Mom!" More than a little surprised to see her, Meg swung the screen wide, Heather crowding her side, to invite Audrey into the house. "What—I mean, is anything wrong?"

"Hi, Grandma Audrey."

Audrey glanced in distaste at the ragged old shorts Meg had on for cleaning the back porch and laundry area. "Wrong? Does something have to be wrong for me to visit my daughter? Hello, Heather, dear."

"No, of course not. But you've never come out to the farm before." When had Heather begun calling her mother Grandma? Meg wondered. Even more surprising was the way her mother seemed so easy with the new name.

"Well, I was bored with the town crowd...." She gazed around at the small living room with a critical eye; mercifully it was neat and clean for the moment. "And when Justine said you had a couple of faxes that looked important, I decided to take a country drive."

"That's sweet of you, Mom," Meg said, taking the two sheets of paper and laying them on Kelsey's desk to ensure they wouldn't be lost. "Want some iced tea?"

"Yes, that sounds lovely."

"Come see my bed, Grandma," Heather begged. "Meg bought me a new spread. It's part of my birthday. Meg's gonna make a party in three days. Are you coming?"

Outside, the crunch of a vehicle on the gravel drive, followed by children's voices, told Meg the fairgoers were home at last. After that the afternoon and evening degenerated into a mass of short tempers and the cyclonic force of seven people trying to do their own thing. What was worse, Audrey accepted Heather's invitation to stay for the evening meal and witnessed most of it.

Kelsey dove into catch-up work immediately. After a brief greeting, with a quick peck on her cheek and a mumbled hello for Audrey, he disappeared outside, reappeared when called for supper, ate quickly, almost silently, then left the house again.

The boys and Aimee had a harder time returning to routine. Camping gear and dirty clothes promptly reduced all Meg's and Lissa's efforts at bringing order in the house to near shambles once again. Lissa was defiantly cranky over trying to enforce a sense of responsibility in the boys to pick up or pack away as they pulled things out. They ignored her. Aimee wasn't much better, but promised to take care of her camping gear first thing the next morning.

"Lighten up, Lissa," Aimee said on her way from the bedroom through the kitchen to the back porch laundry center. "I'm getting my stuff sorted, and I said I'd put in the first load, didn't I?"

Thad, rummaging through a bag of chips only an hour after supper, popped up, saying, "She's only being good about the laundry 'cause she wants that green outfit clean to wear for *Neddie* when he comes around."

"Thad, you hush your mouth," Aimee started, swinging around with a threatening frown.

"Who's Neddie?" Meg asked mildly, entering the kitchen. She'd left her mother reading to Heather in the living room.

"Never mind," Aimee muttered, and disappeared behind the back door.

Lissa called from the bedroom, "Aimee, don't start any laundry now. We won't have any hot water for showers."

Meg heard the washing machine click and the intake of water.

"He's a new kid from town. The same one that Lissa thinks is cute." Thad raised his voice a mocking notch with each sentence. "We met him at the fair when Dad got talking with his dad. Aimee *likes* him!"

"Aimee," Lissa shouted her protest, overlaying Thad's voice.

"I think we should change the subject," Meg ordered Thad in a gentle tone, deciding to take one thing at a time. Heather yanked on Meg's jeans, asking for a bedtime snack. The only child not clamoring for attention was Phillip, Meg mused. She glanced around. Where was Phillip?

"I think I'll go now, Meg," Audrey said from the doorway. "Before it gets completely dark."

Thad gave Meg a rebellious look and continued. "But she *does*."

"Thad!" Aimee reappeared with her chin pushed out and her hands in fists.

"Nedeee! Nedeee!" He defiantly crunched his way through three big chips along with his chant.

"Meg, did you hear me?" came from Audrey. Meg glanced up to catch the I-told-you-so look her mother took no pains to hide.

Lissa appeared in the kitchen door, her hands on her hips, while anger sparkled in her eyes. "Shut off the machine, Aimee. I was about to get in the shower."

"Yeah, Mom, okay," Meg said, raising her voice to be heard.

Before she could see her mother out the front door, the back screen swung open—just in time for Kelsey to snatch Aimee around the waist as she started for Thad in full battle stance.

"Well, I can see things are back to normal." Kelsey set Aimee back on her feet but held her in place with a hand on her shoulder.

"Okay, kids. Listen up. Phillip, you, too." He paused, and Meg watched in amazement as Phillip crawled out from under the table. Vaguely she heard her mother's car start and leave.

Oh, great! Now Audrey's worst suspicions would be confirmed in her own eyes. Just as Meg had been winning points with her, too, and she'd started to think better of the Jamison clan. She would probably never come back.

Kelsey proceeded to snap out straightforward commands, which included a pointed look for Thad and Aimee, his tone indicating he would brook no argument or more delay. To Meg's relief, within the next half hour most of the obvious clutter became neatly stacked, put away or carted to the laundry baskets. It didn't take much coaxing after that to get the kids through a lineup of showers and into bed—but by that time Kelsey had fallen asleep on the living room floor.

Meg slid down the wall and folded her legs beneath her. Only a stream of light from the kitchen shone into the darkened room.

She gazed at him for long moments, feeling again that sense of delight that God had made it possible for her to love this man with a free heart. She loved the shape of his mouth. Leaning over, she tentatively traced his lips with her forefinger.

"That tickles," he said without opening his eyes. "And I'm sleeping."

"Mm... So you are. Notice anything?"

"Like what?"

"Like blessed quiet."

"You mean all the kids are down for the count?"

"Yep. Five accounted for and it's barely nine-thirty."

He blinked his eyes open, gazing at her from under droopy lashes. "Meg, you're a miracle worker."

"Nope, miracles aren't my department. You're the one who played top sergeant and they all marched in time. I think they were all just too tired to fuss any longer."

He lay a long moment, fighting to keep awake. "I guess it's my turn in the shower."

"That's the bad news, Kels. There's no hot water left."

He groaned and rolled into a sitting position. "That's hardly a surprise. I suspected as much. But at least it's not wintertime— that's been known to be a real test of courage." He rubbed his eyes with the heel of his hand. "Someday I've gotta put in a bigger heating tank. This one's gonna blow anytime now. I'm going to market some cattle soon, then we'll see."

"Well, don't worry about it tonight," she said, offering him a hand up. "And the bathroom's all yours."

Kelsey sleepily gathered clean underthings and stumbled his way into the bathroom. He closed the door gently so as not to wake anyone. Then stared. The tub was filled to three-quarters full with fresh water, but it wasn't cold. Steam rose—not much, but enough. An empty cooking pot sat on the commode lid. He realized Meg had heated water on the stove to give him a warm bath.

Thirty minutes later he climbed the stairs and slipped into bed beside her, leaning to whisper in her ear, "Macho jargon aside, Meg, that warm bath was just the thing to ease a tired body. It was real thoughtful of you to see to it."

He punched his pillow and stretched out, his hands behind his head. "When ol' Solomon said having a wife is a good thing—" he yawned "—I guess he knew what he was talking about."

She chuckled. "He should. He had lots of them."

"Rest easy, Meg, *I'm* not planning to take on any more."

"Well, I should hope not," she teased, leaning her head back and, like him, tucking her hands behind her head. "But think of all the fun Solomon must have had sorting out the household routines and children. Can you imagine lining them up for evening baths?"

"Uh-uh, no thank you." His mutter was slurred. "I've enough trouble with just five children."

"It might not always be so, Kels. What if we had more bathrooms, hmm? Wouldn't that be better? Kelsey?"

But his deep breathing indicated he'd returned to sleep.

Chapter Sixteen

Meg ordered a clown cake for Heather's birthday, found streamers and balloons for Lissa and Aimee to string above the picnic table and bought washable paint and brushes for an idea she'd been tossing around in her mind. Then between scrolling her e-mail on her computer at Justine's and shuffling through half a dozen faxes, she took a deep breath of determination and called her mother.

"You want me to what?"

"Paint faces. C'mon, Mom. It'll be fun and the kids will love it. Besides, Heather's never had a birthday party, and I think Jack and Kathy and their youngsters will come."

A long pause ensued. After the total chaos the other night, Meg was sure her mother wanted to refuse attending the party altogether; her mother had no patience for clutter and the normal disharmony that sometimes erupted among tired people. And she'd witnessed the kids at their worst. Yet Meg held out hope for the growing fondness Audrey felt for the children. At least for Heather and Lissa, which was a start.

"Do you think you can manage everyone in that small house?" Audrey finally answered.

Meg didn't think she could manage at all, if it rained. But

Heather was going to have her birthday party just the same. "We'll cook out on the grill and sit under the trees."

"Oh." The distinct lack of enthusiasm had Meg gritting her teeth, but before she could think of how to coax her mother any further, Audrey spoke again. With a deep sigh, she said, "I've never done anything like that before."

Meg gave a silent *Yes!* and moistened her dry lips.

"It shouldn't be hard, Mom. Not for you. Remember all those special invitations and things you used to do? And surely you've seen that sort of thing at craft fairs and the like."

"You mean the little rainbows and hearts on little cheeks?" Audrey's voice began to lift. "I suppose I could do that. You said it's a clown cake?"

"Mmm-hmm."

"All right. It might be rather fun, at that. And why don't I find some clown hats, too?"

"Terrific, Mom. You're a peach."

"Yes, I am," Audrey said staunchly. "And please try to put a little discipline into the children. I'm bringing a guest."

"You are?" Meg put a grin in her voice. "Okay. Tell Paul to drive his old truck this time."

Dinner was a hit: corn dogs on sticks, French fries and corn on the cob, for the children, and steak kebab and a huge, healthy green salad for the grown-ups. Jack and Kathy, Sara and Andy, brought caramel corn, and Paul hauled out a huge watermelon from his truck bed, chilled in a tub of ice. He suggested a seed-spitting contest. All the children but Lissa howled with delight, and Paul, Jack and Kelsey ended up joining the fun.

And so was the face painting a hit. Audrey patiently brushed hearts and flowers, Indian stripes, rainbows and teddy bears as each child chose what they wanted. Even Lissa sat still to have musical notes dotted on her cheeks and temple.

"Grandma, can you do this again sometime?" Sara asked. "For my birthday?"

"Sure I can. You just let me know when to be there," Audrey answered, her face soft and pleased. Meg's heart swelled. Her mother looked more herself all the time, and happier.

After cake and presents, the children—except for Lissa who

felt too old to indulge in such rambunctious play—ran in tag teams and ended by throwing seeds and cups of water at each other. After that, Jack and Kathy packed their two into their car and left. When the first squabble broke out, Kelsey squashed it with the announcement that it was bedtime. Over protests of his being *seriously* and *majorly* unfair, he stuck to his decision even with Lissa. They needed to go to bed at a decent hour, he told them, in readiness to start school.

One by one, they dawdled toward the house, Heather running back one more time to hug Grandma Audrey. "That's enough, now, pumpkin," Meg told her. "You'll squeeze all the breath from her."

"Goodnight, sweetie," Audrey responded for the third time, her voice soft. "You can tell me about school next time we see you."

Slinging an arm around Meg, Kelsey strolled with her down the drive toward Paul's old truck, pausing as Paul opened the passenger door for Audrey.

"Audrey..." At the hesitation in his voice, she turned. "Um...thanks. Thanks for coming. You gave Heather's party something special."

"I was glad to do it, Kelsey." Audrey's voice was crisper than when she spoke with Heather, and he wondered if she was now trying to deny her generous contribution to the party or that she didn't want to recognize his gratitude. "I'm glad it was such a big hit with the children. But it was Meg's idea."

"Yeah...well, thanks again." He let it go. He had other things to concern him, besides trying to figure out his mother-in-law. "See you folks."

Meg said her goodbyes, and they walked toward the house.

"The party did turn out nice, didn't it?" Meg asked.

"Yes, it did. But whatever happened to the unspoiling Heather idea?" he teased as they went up the three back steps to the house. "It seems to me she gets most of the attention around here."

"Oh, do you feel neglected, Kels?" she said, her hand on the porch back door, her voice full of laughter. Inside, the normal bedtime routine sounded more subdued than usual. Was there hope it might go smoothly?

"Not me, but I'm wondering if we haven't set a pattern, here." He leaned against the washer, his feet spread, loath to enter the house just yet. "All the kids will want birthday parties now."

"Oh, I think we can manage." Meg leaned against the freezer opposite. A light from over the kitchen sink shone through the back door window, giving a little illumination to the porch enclosure. But he couldn't see her eyes, and for some reason, he wanted to. Yet he didn't want to signal the kids they were there by turning on the overhead porch light, either.

"Sometimes a little spoiling helps them think about doing the same for others," she continued. "But thank goodness their birthdays are scattered around the year. Are you sure you're not feeling a little neglected?"

"Naw, that's not it."

"When was the last birthday party you had?"

"I can't remember." He actually did recall the last one—the only real one he ever had—quite well. Meg and Dee Dee had thrown him a surprise party the year before he and Dee Dee got married. All the youth group from church had attended. Now that he thought about it, he'd bet dollars to donuts that Meg had been behind that party. Dee Dee had never gone to so much trouble after they'd married.

Meg had always been the more generous of the two girls, he suddenly realized. His appreciation for her sweetness rose, and an overwhelming yearning to partake of it settled around him like the night.

"Well, your birthday is only a month—"

Without warning he scooped her against him and lowered his mouth. A little surprised, she swiftly tucked her arms behind his shoulders, her fingers splaying through his hair, and returned his kiss. Her mouth, like her heart, gave generously; he took it all, all she offered, giving everything he could in return.

They broke apart only to draw breath. From inside, they heard Aimee call something and Lissa's murmured answer. The bathroom door slammed. Kelsey tightened his embrace, drawing her closer, kissing her for long moments as though he'd never before known its like and might never experience it again.

"Let's...let's..."

"Turn in early," she completed.

"Um...as soon as the kids..." He couldn't seem to stop kissing her.

"Uh-huh."

It seemed forever, but they made the most remarkable use of the back porch utility room while waiting for the house to grow quiet.

In the wee hours of the morning, Phillip woke with a sore throat and fever. Meg gave him a pain tablet, and Kelsey sat with him until he went back to sleep. She insisted Kelsey return to his old room for the remainder of the night to be closer if Phillip needed him, and instead of climbing the stairs to her sleeping porch, she curled up on the living room couch. With all its lumps. She didn't get more than a doze, and she suspected Kelsey didn't, either.

Phillip missed the first three days of school; it turned out to be strep throat. Kelsey slept near him at night, and Meg entertained him throughout the day. By the third day, Meg welcomed Mary Claire's presence with fervent thanks and begged her to stay all day. They compromised on an extra hour.

Meg spent the time running between the doctor and pharmacy, popping into the land office to make sure the transfer of papers had gone smoothly, dashing into Justine's to answer her dwindling mail and check stock markets and other pertinent markets. She responded to Clive's complaint that Elizabeth just didn't have her insights, and she picked up Aimee from her first track practice.

No one complained about Mary Claire's stew that night. No one had enough energy to quarrel. Aimee leaned desultorily on her elbow and Thad nibbled a potato cube from his fork. Heather said her throat hurt. Meg gazed helplessly across the table at Kelsey. He appeared a little glassy-eyed, himself.

"All right, that's it," Meg pronounced. "We're *all* checking in with the doctor tomorrow."

"No way," Thad started, clanking his spoon down. "He'll want a throat culture and I always gag."

"I'm better. I don't haveta go, do I?" Phillip responded.

"Mom's right," Lissa said, frowning slightly. "We should have the doctor look at all of us. I was talking to the school nurse this morning, and she said strep is very contagious."

"That doesn't mean anything—" Aimee began.

"Well, I don't plan on missing a lot of school again this year, Aimee."

Kelsey tugged at his ear and glanced at Meg. "No one's asking you to, Lissa. Not unless you need to for yourself. Last year was...not that good, I admit."

"But this year, you have me," Meg hastily added. She wondered if she was the only one who had caught Lissa's reference. Had it been a mere slip of the tongue or had Lissa really meant to call her Mom? Regardless, she felt warmed by the acceptance and rewarded by the appreciation she saw in her husband's eyes. "I'll be here to take care of the home front."

Sumac along the roads had just begun to turn its fiery shade three weeks later when Kelsey came through the kitchen door as though chased by one of his bulls; he reached for his truck keys from the hook by the back door.

Meg looked up with interest from where she was stacking the last of the breakfast dishes. "What's wrong?"

"Something's going on up the road."

"Which direction?" Was it what she hoped for?

"It's Miss Maybelle's ground that adjoins my south line."

"Well, what's happening?"

"Don't know yet." He ducked into his old bedroom for his wallet, tucking it into his back pocket as he reappeared. "But I intend to find out. There's some big machinery coming in."

"Wait, I'll go with you." She threw the dish towel on the counter.

He turned, jiggling the keys in impatience. "Aren't you planning to go into town this morning?"

"Um, maybe later."

Kelsey started the truck, driving faster than he should on the gravel drive, then gunned up the tarmac road. The fencing lay rolled aside, affording a wide entry at the place that gave the easiest access from the road. But the activity centered on top of the rise at least three hundred feet away. Several men stood about, two of them checking stake lines while another sat waiting inside a bulldozer cab. A smaller machine was parked out of the way, but nearby.

Kelsey pulled over to park on the road shoulder, swinging his door open almost before he shut off the motor. Meg slid out of her seat, stretching her legs to keep up with Kelsey's long strides. But she couldn't help the smile that played across her face; she hadn't imagined she'd experience such excitement over building a house. She'd started to worry that the paperwork and other delays would slow the builder, but now they were actually beginning construction.

"Kelsey, there's something I need to tell you."

A tall, graying man wearing denims and a dark T-shirt was checking a wide, unfurled paper. He turned at their approach. "Mornin', folks."

"Morning." Kelsey didn't seem ready to give more than a terse acknowledgment. His gaze skittered to each point of intrusion, each red-flagged stake. "I'm Kelsey Jamison. I own the property next door. Can I ask what's going on here?"

"Kelsey, I know about this," Meg said, beginning to get the feeling she'd made a royal mistake by not sidetracking Kelsey at the house long enough for an explanation. Kelsey glanced at her but didn't reply; he didn't look happy. Her smile faded.

"Why, it's just what you see, Mr. Jamison," the other man said. He offered his hand. "I'm William Doroughty. We're contracted to put in a foundation here."

Kelsey shook hands, then remarked, "I wasn't aware anyone but Mrs. Maybelle Harden owned this ground, and I know for a fact she didn't plan to build here."

Doroughty unrolled his paper again, checking the county numbers. "This's the right parcel, all right. I don't know a Mrs. Harden, but you can check with Steve Carter if you have any questions. He's the builder."

Kelsey pursed his mouth, then nodded. "Thanks, Mr.

Doroughty. I will." He glanced briefly around once more before heading toward the truck at a rapid clip. Meg usually had no trouble matching her steps with his, but she found herself almost running to keep up.

Meg waited until they were out of earshot of the building crew and almost to the truck. "Kelsey, I have something to tell you."

"All right, but can it wait?" He yanked his door open and slid one leg in. "I want to get on the phone and find out who's behind—"

"I can tell you what you want to know."

He'd switched the motor on, but let it idle as he looked up at her. "You know what's going on? Well, why didn't you say so?"

"I'd planned to, Kels. Soon. I—I should have before now." He stared at her, his gaze slowly taking on the color of dark moss as it hit him that she meant something more than that she had something insignificant to tell him.

It dawned on Meg she'd never in her life seen Kelsey angry. Not really angry. Nothing in their shared youth or brief months together had occurred to indicate he had much of a temper. But there was both deep anger and temper etching his features now, however controlled.

Without another word, he U-turned the truck and drove the short distance to their own driveway. He parked, but made no move to get out. He pushed himself back against the seat, then gazed at her sideways, his eyes shaded by his straw cowboy hat. He studied her for a long moment.

"All right," he said in a tight voice. "Why don't you tell me now. What's going on with Miss Maybelle's ground? Do you know why she didn't sell it to me?"

"Yes." She nervously smoothed her hair behind her ear. "She sold it to me. I'm having a house built there for us. A big one...."

She'd hoped the news might ease those lines around his mouth and lighten the look in his eyes, but it didn't. He merely waited for her to give him more information, looking like thunder.

It shouldn't be so hard. Or so nerve-racking. She'd given presentations to some of the wealthiest businessmen in the world and presented hundreds of packages of detailed information covering every aspect of a proposal she wanted to sell, including the negatives as well as positives. Now she could only sit in misery while her stomach knotted at the disappointment she saw in her husband's gaze. To her dismay, she recognized distrust, as well. She licked lips gone dry and tried to repair some of the damage.

"I'm sorry—really sorry, Kelsey." She bit her lip. "I should have told you right away. There's just been so much happening with first one thing and then another. The fair and the kids being sick. School."

"How long?"

She didn't pretend not to know what he meant. "Miss Maybelle and I agreed on the sale during fair week. You were tied up with the boys and Aimee and Fred, and I thought—well, never mind what I thought. I put a rush on the job with Steve Carter. He's a reputable builder, Kels. I've seen his work. He say's he can have us in by Christmas."

He gazed down at his hands, splayed against the wheel. "Why?"

"Why!" She thought the reasons obvious. "Because we *need* it, Kels. We're so crammed..." He wouldn't look at her.

"No, that's not—" Kelsey clamped down on his words, looking as though he wanted to pound something. He gripped the wheel until his knuckles turned white, then suddenly thrust his door open and got out, heading toward the barn.

Meg shoved at her own door, then ran to catch him. She laid a hand on his arm. "Then what, Kels?"

He didn't slow down. She held his pace.

"All right, so I didn't tell you right away. Let me tell you now. You said you wanted the land. You can't be upset over that...."

He whirled to face her, halting his rapid pace so suddenly that Meg stumbled into him. Automatically his fingers curved around her arm to steady her. His eyes blazed like the sun.

"Yes! Yes, I wanted the land! I wanted to expand and grow,

to have enough to offer something to my kids when they're grown if they should want it. I've waited on half promises for years and worked at putting a little extra aside besides paying down my mortgage. I thought Miss Maybelle knew how badly I wanted that land. What did you pay, Meg? You must have offered a premium.''

"No, I didn't. Only the going rate, Kels. Not a penny more.''

He considered that a moment. "How much did you have to borrow?''

"I didn't borrow anything. Not a cent.''

"What do you mean? Surely Audrey didn't give it to you—she wouldn't.''

"Why wouldn't she?'' Meg asked, momentarily wondering why his thoughts had taken a rabbit run. "Mother is a very generous person.''

"Not toward me, she isn't. At least be honest about that, Meg. She doesn't like me much. In fact, she hates the very idea that you married me in the first place. She felt the same when Dee Dee and I got married.''

"That's not true, Kelsey. Well...um, not anymore, anyway. But you're right,'' she said, thinking to bring their focus back to the main issue. They'd have to tackle the emotions of family feelings at another time. "Mom didn't give me the money for the land.''

"Then where did you get it? From Clive?''

"That's a low blow, Kelsey. There's no need to insult me.''

Silent a moment, he glanced away. Meg turned her head and blinked back tears, the hurt shafting through her so sharply she wondered if she might bleed. How could he say...imply... Although she wouldn't hesitate a hiccup to borrow money from Clive in a business deal; Kelsey must know that. But that wasn't what he'd meant.

"Yeah...'' Instant remorse softened his tone. He tugged at his ear, then stared at the ground. "That was unfair. I know you better than that, Meg. I just—I let my temper do the talking, I guess.''

He ambled over to sit on the picnic bench under the linden trees. After a moment Meg followed. They sat not touching, a good foot of hardwood bench between them. It felt more like a chasm to Meg.

From a distance a rumbling whine of a heavy machine began. The first shovelful of dirt being dug for their foundation, she mused. He made no acknowledgment that he'd heard it.

"All right, Meg." He removed his hat, swiping at his forehead, then laid it on the table behind them. "Let's start again. Where did the money come from? For all of it, land and house."

"I paid for the land outright."

"*You* did?" Open curiosity and surprise laced his question, displacing his anger for the moment.

They should've discussed this topic when they first agreed to marry. She hadn't wanted to, glad when he hadn't asked her any questions. She'd been afraid of his reaction. But had she been totally honest by being silent about her finances?

"Kelsey," she started in a tentative tone. "I've made some money over the past few years. Quite a lot, actually, and I didn't see a reason to borrow for the land, but—" she took a deep breath "—now that I've cut my workload, my income will be only a little more than a third of what it was last year, and I didn't want to liquidate any more investments right now, so...I've borrowed sixty percent for the house."

"Only sixty percent?" he said in a doubtful, teasing tone. Then when he realized she was serious, gasped. He narrowed his eyes in dawning suspicion. "That means you laid out forty percent cash?"

She nodded.

"Plus the price of the land?"

Again, she nodded, biting her lip. She didn't know whether to feel ridiculously insulted or a bit triumphant at the astonishment he displayed; she'd long been aware that most of her family and friends wouldn't or couldn't really see her as someone who'd run with the big guys. She might be a big girl in size, but most of them still viewed her as a simple hometown girl with nice, well-kept small town manners, including attitude and intelligence. Why, only a generation ago a woman might inherit money or marry it, but never earn it on her own. They thought of secretaries or teachers. Real estate agents or insurance brokers. Even female bankers, a sprinkling of lawyers and doctors would do, these days. But make it big on her own? That would stretch imaginations.

Disappointing to think it, but Kelsey was no different. It hadn't even occurred to him to imagine she'd made it into the big leagues.

"Just how much cash are we talking about?" His complexion had taken on a funny hue, not quite colorless but not really his usual healthy glow, either. Perhaps he was imagining, now.

Still nibbling her lip, she named the figure.

"And that didn't touch your investments, so to speak. Should I ask how much—what you have invested? What you made last year? How much you're worth?" His questions came in rapid fire.

This was the hardest to answer bluntly, but she figured it couldn't do any more damage to give it to him straight.

"On paper, I have over a million—nearly one and three-quarters. I haven't factored in my commission from the sale of Serenity yet. But lately I've let things slide, rather, and passed things on, so my portfolio looks a little stagnant..."

All at once he shoved his head between his wide-spread knees and sucked in air as though starved for it. Then blew it out slowly. He repeated the process several times.

"Are you still angry with me?"

"Angry? What makes you think that, Meg? Just because I want to charge like a bull and butt my head against something hard—anything—to make me feel better? Because I feel like the victim of a charity case? Like a sucker for being so easily led? You wait weeks to tell me you've spent an enormous amount of money, money that I don't have, you buy a new house as though it's a new toy you can't do without, don't discuss it with me and finally tell me only when I found out, and you wonder that I'm madder than a charging bull?"

"Kels, you did say that I was in charge of the household, remember?"

"Yes, I remember. Which only makes me more of a fool. I

knew what I had wasn't much to offer you. But I thought you accepted what I had. Accepted me!''

He got up and stalked off toward the barn. She didn't think he wanted her company. Silently her tears rolled to drip off her chin.

Chapter Seventeen

Kelsey threw tools, wire, and materials into the back of his truck and sped off over the rough ground along the inside of his north fence line—as far away as he could get from his south property line and the tearing up of the ground there. Rocky and hilly, this section of his land was far from the sights and sounds of civilization. Whenever he went there he enjoyed complete silence from any man-made noise. Only the rare airplane reminded him of the twentieth century; otherwise, he might think himself living a hundred years ago.

The place really suited his mood today. Sometimes he wished he could return to those simpler days, slower times. Like now. He could get into a period when a man was undisputedly the king of his castle and the boss of his own family. Then perhaps he would have a wife who spent her time pleasing her husband first and making a haven from the outside world with what he provided, instead of running on the moneyed fast track...even being in the forefront.

His mind still couldn't grab hold of the amounts she'd told him. That kind of income was for other people, men and women who somehow lived on a different planet, occupied a different kind of skin. Not him. Nor his *wife!*

Why on God's green earth had she married *him?*

Father, I need to understand... Please, please help my mud-dled thinking.

He stepped from his truck and snapped the door closed. He had a few cattle back here and hadn't checked them of late. He knew the fence was weak—he'd postponed fixing it last month because it would take him more than a day to get it done, and after so much time apart during the fair, he hadn't wanted to spend such long days so far from the house. He'd savored Meg's presence in his life; her companionship stirred a growing new excitement. He enjoyed spending a lunch hour with only the two of them alone in the house, though it rarely happened. Since the day he'd asked Meg to marry him, he'd looked forward to the special pleasure of having her to himself for a whole day.

It had seemed forever before all the youngsters had gotten over the strep throat and were back in school full-time. Then Mary Claire had become a semipermanent fixture. He wasn't sure how he felt about Mary Claire yet. He liked her well enough on a pure friendship basis, but the very reason for need-ing a household employee was an irritation. He hadn't liked it before, either, when it was a highlighted necessity. An outsider in the house always changed the balance of things.

He startled a cottontail, a young one that shot away into the brush. A covey of quail nested back in there last year, he re-membered. A year back he hadn't had time to even consider hunting. Hunting wasn't a passion of his, anyway, so it was no loss. He was happy enough spending his time raising a product that he could then sell, trading his dollars for whatever else the family needed. And he'd done well enough, he supposed.

But he did like this isolated part of his land. He always felt at peace here, felt less encumbered with the daily demands that sometimes drained a man of energy and enthusiasm. This was where he'd come the day Dee Dee told him of her illness. Where he'd sat for long hours knowing she'd deliberately kept him ignorant until she could no longer hide it. Until she had only a little time left.

He'd cried his tears here that day and one other. The day of her funeral. He recalled one other emotion from that day. He'd cried out Meg's name, wanting beyond reason, beyond understanding, the one other adult person in his life to whom he'd ever felt a deep connection, to be there to share his toughest hour.

He'd cried out to the Lord, too. After a time he'd felt solaced. He felt drawn back to his children and able to pick up his life, and theirs. It wasn't a bad thing to have been so busy, so needed. Yet only now did he realize how much he'd longed for Meg to come home.

Lord, I know you were with me then. I'm sorry I've...turned away from your presence. Forgive me...

Pulling up a wobbly fence post where a section sagged almost to the ground, and testing several more, he stood back and assessed the amount of work to be done. More than he'd thought, actually. Enough to warrant renting some equipment and maybe hiring someone to help get it done. Only heaven knew why he hadn't had straying cattle before now. He needed to bush hog some of this back area, too. He shouldn't be neglecting his back pasture.

He pulled a small roll of wire from his truck bed, pulled on a pair of heavy gloves and set to work. A patch job wasn't the best solution, but better than nothing until he could do the whole thing right. He may not have lost any cattle over that downed section yet, but there was no need to push his luck. He'd done that already with Meg.

A heavy sweat rolled down his face and back, soaking his shirt. He paused to find his kerchief and wipe his forehead. He didn't mind the heavy exertion; sometimes it was good to work a body to exhaustion. Near his feet he spotted a basketball-sized stone, and he bent to harvest it from the ground. Every time he was back in this section he dug a few rocks from the pasture and stacked them onto a rock wall along his property line. After fifteen years his efforts showed; maybe he ought to forget about putting in more wire.

No. The wire was most practical and efficient. Besides, one man working alone would never be enough.

He guessed he didn't really want to live back in the old days, after all, when every blessed thing had had to be done by hand. He loved talking with the old fellows, though. It always gave him a sense of destiny, a connection with the land. Old man Miller, his neighbor's grandfather, could tell some fascinating tales. He'd farmed here in Missouri right through the Great Depression with his father, and he could tell some hair-raising stories of his father and grandfather, all farmers, before that. Of times when a man and woman had to put in back-breaking days and long kneel-worthy prayers to keep from starving.

He pondered on that awhile. Naw! He didn't really want to have lived back then. Most of today's life was no longer such a struggle. He was glad—*majorly* glad—he lived in the present time.

Seriously!

He thought of the day he and Meg had split their sides over the way Lissa and Aimee had proposed for him. In spite of himself, a smile caught him. He liked his kids, they'd been concerned about him. Their boldness was still mind boggling. Meg's response...

He still didn't understand Meg's reaction, but he recalled his own. He liked Meg, too, enormously. Always had. She was a sweet girl and so pretty. They'd been best buddies.

Dee Dee told him once, years ago, that Meg had a huge crush on him. He hadn't thought much about it then. In some ways she'd been more of a teenage playmate than Dee Dee. She matched him in tennis, swam as well, helped him anchor the church baseball team—chums. He wondered...

But now it was more, so much more. She was a woman. His leap from liking to thinking of her as a wife made him feel as though it had been—oh, ordained or something. Preplanned. Like she'd been waiting in the wings. She drew him into a companionship unlike any he'd experienced before, and their nights as husband and wife had turned out...revealing. He'd found a deep, sweet fulfillment.

Aw, why had Meg married him? For pity? For the children's sake? Or for the need to have children? Were all women secretive?

Bending to grasp a heavy jagged stone, he hefted it the few yards to the rock wall, scraping his arm in the process. He frowned at the line of blood beads popping up along his skin.

Secretive? Where had that thought come from?

Dee Dee. For the first time, he faced a reality he hadn't wanted to see before. Dee Dee had kept more than her illness from him. She'd kept her own thoughts to herself about a lot of things; about her feelings of dislike toward his father, for one, until some of her actions spoke for her. She hadn't treated him with a lot of kindness. She'd hidden her disdain for their livelihood until he overheard her true feelings as she'd discussed her lack of ready money with someone at church.

He recalled other things, mostly little things, but now he realized Dee Dee's behavior, her attitude, sat poorly with him. Over the years she'd grown more silent, even sometimes totally withdrawn. He'd never stopped loving her, and he was sure she'd continued to love him, but that widening gap indicated a lack of trust between them. Sometimes he'd felt so alone in their marriage. Why hadn't he seen it?

Were all women thus? His mother sometimes kept secrets from his father, too. He recalled she hid money or new clothing or even friendships. She once carried on a flirtation with another man behind his father's back. Kelsey was sure it had never been anything more serious than a mild recognition between a man and a woman, but the division it caused was the same. His father had turned a blind eye, and his mother had died before they ever had a chance to talk things out.

Perhaps, like his father, he'd been afraid to discover why Dee Dee did those things, felt as she did. But would knowing she wasn't perfect have dimmed his love? *Was that it, Lord? Am I a coward, unable to face that maybe I failed Dee Dee some way?*

Perhaps he hadn't been a perfect husband, but he'd loved Dee Dee. That she was human enough to sometimes disappoint him didn't diminish what they had together. He loved Meg, yet he was ready to admit she could be perfectly human, too. He'd felt disappointed that she hadn't told him up front about her finances or about her contracting for the new house or even about buying the twenty acres he'd wanted to add to his own place. Yet he couldn't honestly say he loved her less.

The astonishment came then. *He loved Meg!* He stopped what

he was doing and stood perfectly still, throwing back his head
to stare at the sky.

Do you hear that, Lord! I love her!

He did, and the soaring feeling had nothing to do with that
limpid, pallid emotion of simply good friendship. He felt happy
around her, she understood a piece of him nobody else ever had.
And his disappointment melted into the bright blue above him.

He'd been unjust. Vastly unfair. Unfair to expect Meg to be
the same girl he'd known, not the woman she'd become. He'd
wanted her to understand his every need, to come into his and
his children's lives with all that that entailed and with all those
limitations, without wanting, taking anything of her own back.
Hadn't he expected her to be changed at all?

He'd mulled over her reasons for marrying him once or twice,
but not very deeply. He'd been a coward, not wanting to see
that she might be marrying him because of some sense of mis-
placed loyalty toward her cousin. Or pity toward his motherless
children.

Perhaps both those reasons were true. Would she ever tell
him if they were? Did she harbor other secrets? She'd been very
blunt about her monetary worth; she could buy him out twice
over. But this thing with the emotions—had what Dee Dee
said—could it be true? Would Meg tell him if he asked?

All that money. He couldn't get it from his mind, or adjust
to it.

He'd asked her to move into a sleeping porch with second-
hand furniture where she didn't even have a closet. Her clothes
hung from one of those metal rack things on wheels. He'd worried about spending all her savings on the van and the honeymoon weekend in Branson. It was laughable.

Would he have asked her to marry him if he'd known?
Uh-uh... No way, he'd have squashed that notion quicker than
squashing a potato bug, kids begging or not.

And what did that say about him? That he was full of wrong-
headed male pride? Just about rock-bottom pure right, he
guessed. But he couldn't help it and didn't want to, just at the
moment.

Yet for all that, he knelt on the rocky ground. For the first time in more than a year, his heart felt ready to hear his Heavenly Teacher.

Oh, Lord! I am a fool. But I've fallen in love with Meg, and I'm willing to listen....

He didn't come in for lunch. Meg waited forty minutes, then wrapped his sandwich, tuna salad on rye, one of his favorites, in a sandwich bag and shoved it into the fridge.

She hadn't exactly planned on being at home for lunch today, she fumed later as she drove into town. Heather had gone home with her friend Ashley for the afternoon, and she needed to take advantage of the time to catch up on some office work. She'd delayed her own plans to try to smooth out Kelsey's hurt, angry feelings, and he had ignored her lunch bell. She had a day's work waiting for her that she would now have to squeeze into a few hours, and there were three errands to run as well. Dinner would be late. And she didn't care!

She turned onto the south highway and shoved the gas pedal down. The van roared toward seventy-five.

He *had* told her she was in charge of the household. Several times. He hadn't wanted to take time to listen about her ideas or thoughts. *Now* he complained she'd spent too much money without telling him first. What did he expect, that she'd ask him for every nickel and dime as though she were Aimee or Lissa?

Well, two could play the anger game.

Only, she felt so miserable over their quarrel she wanted to run home and throw herself on her bed to cry. And beg his forgiveness. Which she'd planned to do, if he'd only come in to lunch.

But she hadn't been the only one in the wrong, and she felt as though the rules of the game had been changed behind her back. How was she to build a strong bond between them if Kelsey played on an uneven playing field? She was likely to step off a sudden drop at any time.

If only she didn't love him so completely that a smile from him could draw her like a hummingbird to nectar. It made her heart go to mush. Maybe her brain, too, she mused with an offbeat humor. And thought how even that observation would make him chuckle if she could share it.

Was that part of the problem? Had she been so eager to gain Kelsey's love that she was overdoing everything? Trying too hard to be everything he or the children needed? For years she'd taken charge of her own world and made many decisions that directed many another's finances. But this was a different situation, and she had to gain an understanding of the balance. And she had to stop trying too hard. Time, she mused, to attend her own business a little closer.

Going straight to the office, she spent unusual care in answering every inquiry, e-mail and fax. She made several long distant calls, catching Clive as he was leaving his office for the day. At least with Clive and the investment world, she knew her ground. People appreciated her there.

"Hello, luv. How's the country mouse?"

"Starting to let my mind catch up with my heart."

"What does that mean?"

"Oh, nothing. I'm only trying to sort through some, um, rather interesting things that have cropped up. Um, sorry. Excuse the pun, please."

"Finding a few weeds in the garden are we? Well, let me know if you find anything I should know about, hmm?"

"I'll do that. Now tell me what you know about a rather small firm..." She continued to keep her tone professional, asking all the pertinent questions that would give her enough information to make a decision about whether to buy or otherwise advise her clients to invest in the company. Just before she was ready to hang up, she said, "Please tell the Neelses they can count on me being there for Serenity's grand opening week. I wouldn't miss it."

"Fine, I'll do that. They'll be pleased to hear it. Bringing anybody with you?"

She hesitated a moment. "Yes, certainly. There will be two of us."

"Very well. That's only weeks away. I'll look forward to seeing you."

They hung up, and Justine called up to her. "Meg, I took a

message for you while you were talking. Thad says he missed his bus. Can you make a swing by to pick him up?''

Meg squeezed her eyes tightly closed. Why couldn't the child have been where he should have been at the right time? She didn't have time for an unexpected errand. She really didn't, if she was going to get the prospectus to her clients by morning. She'd already postponed it once, and she didn't want to do that again. But… ''I'll take care of it. Thanks, Justine.''

She let the van motor idle as she waited for Thad to come out of school. He tossed her a sheepish glance, but got in and buckled his seat belt without thanks or apology.

''Did Phillip get on the bus?''

''I dunno. 'Spose he did.''

''How did you come to miss it?''

''Teacher said I had to do a paper over.''

Meg waited a moment for further explanation, but wasn't surprised when none was forthcoming. Thad just didn't talk to her like the girls did. Even Phillip talked to her more than Thad, although it was usually when they were alone. Phillip just didn't like to compete with the others.

''All right,'' she said, deciding not to tackle the issue of why he had to do the paper over. But she thought it was time for Kelsey to have a conference with the boy's teacher. ''We have to pick up Heather, too. Then I have to run back to the office for an hour or two.''

Thad's face twisted in distaste. ''Why do I have to? I don't like hanging around there. Can't you take me home first?''

''No, I can't. If I take time to run you out to the farm and then turn around to come back into town, I'll waste an hour.''

''But I don't have anything to do there.''

''Well, I do. You may do your homework. There's an extra desk near mine where you can work.'' She glanced at him from the corner of her eye. His sulky face stared straight ahead. She sighed in frustration. She shouldn't take her irritation with Kelsey out on Thad.

''How're you doing with the math tutor?'' she said in a softer tone.

Thad shrugged his answer with one shoulder.

"Don't you like him?"

"I don't like math. What's the big deal about it, anyway? I'll never use half of it in real life. Adding and subtracting and multiplying and dividing—I can do all that with a calculator, anyway."

"Yes, that's true, but what if you lose the calculator? Or it breaks?"

He shrugged the other shoulder. "I don't care. I hate math."

Meg picked up Heather from her friend's house and headed back downtown. It was nearly five, and Justine was getting ready to close the shop.

"Justine, I need to hang on for a couple of hours yet, is that all right with you?"

"Sure, Meg. Just check the locks when you leave, okay?"

Meg guided the children toward the wooden stairs that led to her office in the open loft, then paused as an idea struck her. She turned to catch Justine before she left.

"Justine, can I boot up that machine you let the kids use for games? I promise I'll shut everything down when we go. And I'm going to take one of your education programs, so please add it into my bill tomorrow, all right?"

Meg made a call home to let Lissa know she, Thad and Heather would be late. Phillip and Aimee, Lissa reported, were safely at home.

Meg didn't ask for Kelsey or even ask where he was.

She got a package of potato chips and a soda for each child from the vending machine and set Heather to coloring. Then she cracked the cellophane on the math tutorial, popped the software in and showed Thad how to run it. It was designed for the user to follow along at whatever pace was comfortable and it was a level she knew Thad could easily achieve.

"This is awesome," she heard him mutter a few minutes later. She left him alone with it, telling him to call her if he really needed her assistance. He grunted, his gaze glued to the screen.

Holding back a smile, Meg returned to her own desk. Periodically she heard him whistle to himself or mutter. After about thirty minutes when Heather became bored, Meg suggested Thad find some way to entertain her.

"But I'm up to my third phase. This is easy, Meg. Can't Heather do something else?"

"We'll take it home with us, I promise. But you have to earn back your time on the computer by helping to look after Heather now. I'm almost finished with my work for today, and after that we can go home."

Meg completed her report and put it into a special, overnight delivery envelope, ready for the earliest pickup the next morning, before strolling over to see how the kids were faring.

Heather sat on Thad's lap. She giggled at the animated game Thad was guiding her through while he grew more impatient.

"No, Heather. Like this."

Heather immediately did the opposite.

"That's not it! Why don't you *listen.* You're just messing it up."

"We can go now, kids." She looked at her watch. "If we're lucky you can eat supper before it's your turn in the shower, Thad."

The drive home was rather quiet until Heather asked what was for dinner.

"I'm not really sure, Heather. Something quick, though."

When Meg thought about the evening she still had ahead of her, she felt all her energy drain away. She was still out of temper with Kelsey and didn't yet know how to resolve it. Was he still furious with her?

Oh, Father, she began. But it was the only thing her heart could say.

Chapter Eighteen

A smoky cloud drifted near the kitchen ceiling when Meg pushed through the back door just behind Heather and Thad. On the table were flatware and glasses. The old chipped plates sat on the counter near the stove. Where was the new ironstone she'd purchased last month?

She sniffed. Fried potatoes, onions and sausage. Her tummy growled. Bless her, Lissa must have started dinner. Although Meg'd been trying to introduce a more healthy, less fatty diet into the family eating habits, sometimes comfort food was exactly the thing.

But it wasn't Lissa who turned from the stove, a dish towel tied snugly around his waist to protect his clean denims. Kelsey, freshly showered and shaved and wielding a spatula like a baton, acknowledged her homecoming with a sober, uncertain glance. Barely peeking at her, he tried to assess her mood, she guessed. Which she wasn't at all sure about herself. She let her gaze flicker, wariness making her shy while she made a stab at guessing his.

"Um...dinner smells good," she offered. Neutral ground, she hoped. "It looks like you're about ready."

"Yeah. Thad called."

"He did? From the office? I guess I didn't hear him."

"No. You were tied up with an overdue something or other."

"An analysis of a new stock offering. Really looks promising...." She let her voice drop. Kelsey cared little for this kind of market. The figures would bore him. Turning, she hung her keys on the hook by the back door.

"Thad, don't leave those books on the table. We're about to eat," Kelsey thundered.

"Sorree!" The boy grabbed the books, glancing up guiltily, then scooted out of the kitchen on speedy legs.

"And tell your brother to turn off the TV and wash his hands." He lifted his voice to be heard in the next room. "Aimee, you wash yours, too."

"Daddy, I don't like sausage," Heather whined.

"I'm sorry you don't, Heather." Kelsey's grumpy tone allowed no room for argument tonight. "But that's what's for supper. If you don't like it you don't have to eat it."

Heather's mouth turned down. Her lip trembled. Tears loomed.

Kelsey sighed and set his spatula down, going to his haunches. "Sorry, honey. Maybe you'll like supper better tomorrow."

"Yeah," Aimee said, coming in. "Meg's a better cook. Dad, I think something's burning."

"Uh-oh."

He jumped up and grabbed for the old iron skillet, barely getting the hot pad around the handle before he lifted it. Meg reached around him to shut the burner off. He stepped back against her, and she automatically flattened her hands against his back to let him know she was there. Holding the sizzling skillet aloft, he twisted to look at her over his shoulder, his mouth grimacing in comical surrender. His eyes went all soft then, with sudden humor, that look that never failed to cause Meg to fall in love all over again.

"I wish just once I could manage to cook a meal—just one—without burning *something*. How in the world do you manage, Meg?"

"It's called motivation and focus, Kels," she answered, her own mouth quirking into a tentative grin. "And timing. Two of those characteristics you display in admirable quantities when it pertains to your work. As for timing... Perhaps we both need a little help in that area."

She wasn't referring only to preparing a meal, and she was certain he knew that as well.

"So..." He shifted his gaze to see how near the children were, then leaned closer, lowering his voice. "I think I need to focus on talking more with my wife, if she's still speaking to me. I wouldn't blame her too much if she's put out with me, but I hope..." His gaze dropped to her mouth. "Or just...focus, maybe. At least my motivation's in the right place."

Meg's emotions rapidly went from humor to meltdown at the gleam in his gaze. A knowing...a new element shone there. What had happened, where had his anger of the morning gone? Yet they still had issues to settle between them even without the anger. Especially without the anger.

"You could never accuse me of being the quiet type, now could you?" she said with humor. "Talk to me and I talk back."

"Yes, thank goodness," he responded fervently. "That's what I'm counting on. Straight on, Meg."

"Are we gonna eat or what?" Aimee said.

"We're doing a little of both, I guess," Kelsey said, turning back to the stove. "Call the others."

"Both?" Aimee asked, tipping her head in puzzlement. Yet she pursed her mouth and raised her brows as if she knew something was happening between them that she wasn't getting. "Eat and what?"

"That's right," Kelsey answered, checking the table to make sure he had everything he needed.

"Oh, is that all," Aimee said, pretending to lose interest.

"And tonight the men are cleaning the kitchen."

"Aw, Dad." This time Phillip was the first to complain. Meg turned away to hide her laugh. On the very rare occasions she recalled her own father offering to help in the kitchen, Jack had responded in like manner. And though she knew Kelsey could do a very creditable job of cleaning the kitchen these days, she was just as sure he didn't have the patience for it. And probably never would.

"Dad, I appreciate that you try hard, and I sure don't object to the boys doing their share of kitchen work, but would you mind letting us girls do the cooking from now on?" Lissa said a few minutes later as she pushed over-crisped potatoes around her plate. "You just don't have a knack for it."

"That ain't saying anything new," Thad muttered.

"Don't say ain't, Thad," Lissa corrected her brother.

With an immediate sputtering reaction from Thad, Kelsey deliberately set his fork down and held up his hand. "That's it. I'm not putting up with another fight at mealtime. I'd like a little peace and quiet, and we're making a few new rules in this house. First of all, Lissa, you're no longer responsible for correcting your brothers and sisters. You neither, Aimee. That's my job and Meg's."

Aimee let her mouth drop in shocked denial, while Lissa's eyes grew large. "But I only said he shouldn't use *ain't.*"

"I know, and you weren't wrong in that. But from now on, I *or Meg* will do the correcting. You don't have to worry about it."

"Ha! See? See Lissa? You're not boss," Thad said in glee. "You either, Aimee. Dad just said so."

"Thad," Kelsey warned.

"Oh, all right. But—"

"No 'buts.' Do you understand me?"

"I guess." Then with one last glance at Kelsey's stern demeanor, he muttered, "Yes, sir."

"Good. Now that we have that one settled, listen up. I want no more fuss, no complaints, not one tiny argument during mealtime about anything, especially the food. From now on if you have something negative to say to the cook—" he glanced around at each of them "—about the food or each other, you may put it in writing."

He waited a moment to allow the groans and grimaces to subside.

"Compliments, however, may be made verbally and often." He lightened his tone, allowing his playful side to show. "Now you see what would happen if we didn't have Meg, don't you? You'd go back to eating my cooking. Is that what you want?"

At their vigorous denials, Kelsey nodded and raised his glass of milk as a toast. "So I'm going to start off our new attitude. Meg, thank you for those wonderful applesauce pancakes at breakfast. And the tuna sandwich I found later when I came in. It hit the spot for a tired, hungry man."

Meg felt her cheeks flush. She'd been so angry when she threw that sandwich into the refrigerator, she hadn't cared about Kelsey's well-being. At that point, she hadn't cared if he'd starved, so focused was she on her own hurt and frustration. Now she was glad she'd followed her instinct and Grandma Hicks's training of saving food instead of throwing it away.

"Yeah, Meg," Aimee jumped in. "I liked breakfast, too."

"Everything Meg cooks tastes good to me," Lissa said. "I'm learning a lot of new stuff from Great Grandma Hicks's old recipes, too."

"I like hot dogs," Heather said, not wanting to be left out.

"I liked last night's supper," Phillip supplied. "Chicken and noodles."

Thad stared at his burned potatoes a moment, then muttered, "Yeah, the chicken and noodles were okay."

"I'm glad, because that's an easy one," Meg murmured, near tears. She didn't care if Kelsey had prompted their appreciative expressions, she felt a warm fuzzy in hearing the words. "We can make that in the Crock-Pot in the morning and it's ready that night."

It had been a day of emotional contrasts, and she felt Kelsey had made a big effort to make a way back between them from their morning quarrel. But she wondered if it was only his sense of fair play or if he honestly wanted an equal footing for them both. Only time would tell, but much of the leftover morning hurt drained away. After all, he was making an effort.

Later, while Kelsey and the boys tackled the kitchen cleanup, Meg examined Kelsey's computer. She'd known from early on it was a very basic operation. Now she wondered about the amount of memory and power they might need to run the math tutorial she'd bought.

"Looking for something in particular, Meg?" Kelsey asked as he entered the living room.

"Oh, just checking things out." She swung the computer stool around to face him. "We need to upgrade your system as soon as possible, I think. Thad really needs to stay with this program I got from Justine. At least he seems to like it well enough."

"Wait a minute, back up. What program? What are you talking about?"

"I bought a math tutorial. Thad's not that happy with what's-his-name, the young man tutoring him, and he seems to like using the computer. Maybe this will do the trick. But his teacher says he's really in trouble, Kelsey."

Kelsey frowned. "I don't get it. If he's that much behind, why haven't we heard about it before now?"

"She said you were sent a note at the end of last year. Didn't you get it?"

His frown deepened. "I don't recall one, but I did know he wasn't too swift in math. It's really that bad?"

"According to the teacher he's been falling behind for a long time. Probably since his mother died, really. Why didn't you make an appointment for a conference, Kelsey? She said she's called twice."

"Now wait a minute. I didn't talk to her, and if she called when we weren't here, there would've been something on the answering machine." He stopped and thought a moment, then pivoted and went to the door. "Thad, come in here, please."

"Yeah?" Thad appeared at the door. "What?"

"Come in here, Thad."

The boy came farther into the room, his gaze growing suspicious.

"Meg tells me your teacher has called twice for a conference. I don't remember getting her calls on the answering machine. Do you know anything about that?"

The boy threw her an accusing look. "Uh, well...well, uh...not really, Dad."

"Thad? Don't look at Meg, she has nothing to do with this. Own up. Did you know that your teacher wanted to talk to me?"

Thad's gaze filled with guilty misery. His head slumped forward, his chin touching his chest. "Yeah. I, um, erased it. I thought, you know, you were too busy to—"

"That won't wash, son. Busy or not, if you're in a pickle at school or anywhere else, I want to know about it."

Thad's head came up. "Well, it's just too hard. I try, Dad, I really do. It's not my fault I don't have enough time to finish anything."

"Son, if you knew the material, you wouldn't have any difficulty in finishing an assignment in the allotted time. Now, that's not the problem, is it?"

"I 'spose not."

"Thad," Meg interrupted. This was the child most like Dee Dee. She'd watched him for the last few minutes with a growing certainty: Dee Dee hadn't known how to ask for help when she needed it, either. Instead of asking for help, she sometimes became defensive or secretive and withdrawn. Like his mother, Thad had, effactually, run away by ignoring the problem. "Thad, can I ask you a question?"

He looked up at her, giving her his usual shrug when he didn't know how to answer. His brown eyes shone raw vulnerability before he dropped his lashes, and her heart went out to him.

Meg gentled her tone. "Was it your mom who usually helped you with homework?"

"Yeah."

"But you've tackled it on your own for the past two years, haven't you?"

"Well, yeah."

"With no one else's help?"

"Nope."

"Your mother was a good coach, wasn't she?" Meg waited for the boy's nod. "And when she was gone," she said very softly, "you thought no one else could help you, is that it? No one else would ever understand you? Or be patient with you?"

The boy said nothing.

"And math is supposed to be an absolute. How could any of it be right when your mom died? She was your mom..."

Thad and Kelsey both stared at her with an arrested gaze. Thad's eyes began to fill with tears. He stood frozen, silent, the

unexpected truth peeling away his protective layers to wretch-
edness.

Meg felt her own eyes sting and her chest hurt. Thad still
grieved for Dee Dee, probably more than any of them realized.
No wonder he'd resented her. He thought his father guilty of
replacing Dee Dee as though he'd lightly put aside one living
wife for another, irrational as it sounded, as though it was a
wrong done on purpose.

She lifted her gaze. Kelsey's mouth stretched harshly against
his teeth as his arm snaked out to draw Thad tightly against
him. A sob broke from the boy. Above his head Kelsey's eyes
related heart-shattering sorrow and guilt.

His gaze skittered from hers, and he swung to hide his face.
He couldn't look at her, draw comfort from her.

Quietly Meg rose and walked around them, leaving the room.
Leaving father and son alone to share their grief.

She wasn't sure if her own heart could mend over this one.

She'd give a vital organ to seal away the hurt and fill the
void, if that would do it. But perhaps it never would. How could
she ever hope Kelsey could love her as he'd loved Dee Dee?

Meg slowed to wave at the building crew as she did every
morning now, if someone was there. Every afternoon on her
way home, she stopped to look at the home site. She never got
out of the van, merely stared at it from her window.

The concrete foundation had lain embedded in the ground like
a giant, ragged tooth for a week, curing, waiting for the carpen-
ters. A huge truck sat by the fence line, its open back end revealing stacks of lumber and sheets of plywood. They would
complete the initial flooring by tonight, Steve Carter had assured
her, and by the end of the week the shell would be up. With a
full crew, the roof would take them no more than two days, and
the traditional dark red bricks were ordered, ready to deliver any
day.

She put the van into gear and headed into town.

It was time they told the children about the new house, she
supposed. They couldn't keep them from knowing much longer.
Someone, somehow, would tell them. She'd hoped she and Kel-

sey could present it together, but his lack of enthusiasm hadn't encouraged that.

Until now, she'd brushed aside the one or two curious questions and remarks Lissa and Aimee had made after they'd discovered the gaping foundation hole. Thad speculated a house there would be occupied by someone from the city, either St. Louis or Kansas City, who wanted a country place, since twenty acres weren't enough to really farm. Phillip absorbed a great deal in his usual silent fashion, but made no comment. Heather wondered if the new house being built so close by would have a little girl she could play with.

Meg didn't know if Kelsey had fended off any questions. Kelsey hadn't mentioned the house since that day a week ago. In fact, he hadn't talked about much of anything at all and pretty much kept to himself lately.

Sighing, Meg parked the van in her slot at Justine's. She sat a moment without moving. Looking at her nails, she gave a disgusted hiss. They looked in need of a good manicure in spite of her best efforts. She smoothed her hair back at the temple. A decent haircut would do her a world of good, too. It had grown so long that today she'd French braided it after shampooing, something she usually reserved only as a last resort. Well, now she was down to the last resort. There'd been no time of late for many "personal" days, as she thought of them.

She stared unseeingly at the "to-do" list for the day; she didn't really mind being so busy—and she could squeeze those personal indulgence things into her day on occasion. What really bothered her was the nowhere direction of her relationship with Kelsey. Why couldn't they seem to get beyond their disagreement? Or Thad's resentment of her? Or the past?

There had been so much promise in that earlier exchange between them that night after their fight, and then it seemed to all drain away with Thad's tears. It felt as though Dee Dee had died only a month ago, and Thad's and Kelsey's grief was fresh and new.

Although she should be grateful for Thad's breakthrough— and she truly was thankful, for Thad had slowly begun to respond to her offer of help—it seemed to put Kelsey in a deep well of guilt. He'd taken to sleeping on his old cot in the downstairs bedroom.

She was willing to give him room and time and space to mull things through, to take whatever steps he needed to in order to come to terms once more with his feelings, but she missed him. Dreadfully. What hurt the worst, what scared her the most, was the thought that maybe *he* didn't miss *her*. That maybe he didn't need her.

Oh, he needed someone. There never had been a doubt about that. But did he want her? She swiped at a tear running off her chin and stared into space.

Oh, Father…here I am again. It's me, Meg. I'm sorry to bother you with the same old lament, but I just don't know what to do. Please, please help me to have a little wisdom with Kelsey. I've been so foolish. I hurt his pride over the house, supplanted his place as leader of the family, spent too much money. Now he feels guilty over failing his son when Thad needed him, and I'm the one who pointed it out. He's probably a world of sorry that he married me. Lord, what should I do? Give me a direction….

Into her memory popped her grandmother's voice with an admonition she'd heard often as a child. "Whatever your hand finds to do, do it." Meg rather thought it came from scripture somewhere. She determined to get Grandmother Hicks's Bible out tonight to look up some of her favorite verses again. Perhaps she'd find that one among them.

A car beeped loudly next to her. Startled, she lifted her gaze only to groan aloud. With all the things she had to do, this was bound to add to them.

Her mother smiled brightly at her from the passenger's seat of Sandy Yoder's car, and the two women waved eagerly. Obviously they wanted to talk to her. Was this another "Whatever you find at hand?"

On pretense of reaching for her purse, Meg swiftly wiped her tears before she turned to get out of the van. She put on a smile and returned their greetings. Then her smile became genuine, imagining the Lord chuckling along with her. She had asked, hadn't she? And she'd been praying so hard she hadn't even heard another car park beside her.

All right, Lord, whatever Mom and Mrs. Yoder need, I'll try to help. And whatever my next step with Kelsey is to be, I'll trust you to have it all in hand.

Chapter Nineteen

"What can I do for you, ladies?" Meg asked, slipping her keys into her purse. This part of town wasn't among her mother's normal routes, so she was pretty sure Audrey wanted something in particular.

"We want to talk to you about an idea we had, Meg," her mother said.

"Why didn't you call? I could've run by the house."

"This is business. We thought we should visit you in your place of business," Sandy answered. "I checked with Justine to see when you'd be in today, and here we are. Could you spare us a few minutes?"

"All right. Come along upstairs."

Meg led the way into the store, greeted Justine and collected faxes and her mail, then the three of them climbed to the loft. The sun shone through the ten-foot, arched front windows, bathing her desk with natural light. Meg had had a multicolored hand-woven rug laid beneath her desk. Room-sized, it gave her space definition and softened the stark wood beams and red brick walls. Every scrape of her chair wasn't screeched through the entire shop any longer, either. Her mother took a few moments to gaze around.

"Why, this is rather inviting. It's modern and old at the same time," Audrey said in surprise. "I'd imagined it to be dark and dank."

"Justine had a lot of work done on the building last year to open it up," Meg replied as she set her purse and mail down on her desk. "I came along at just the right time to take advantage of it."

The edge of an envelope with a logo she recognized edged between the stack. Her airline tickets, first to Florida, then to the small island where Serenity was located.

She still didn't know if Kelsey would go with her, although she'd mentioned the event. They hadn't discussed it, and she was under the impression he didn't want to, although the first week in November should work out for him. She hated to go without him, but she must. She'd given her word.

This last week made her wonder if he'd even miss her.

Thankfully, Mary Claire had agreed to put in extra time with the laundry while she was gone, and she'd stored a couple of casseroles in the freezer. But there wasn't a lot more she could do to prepare the family for her absence, short of bringing in a full-time housekeeper to help out. Kelsey would hate that. He'd rather be thrown back to how he'd managed before she'd reentered his life.

Maybe that wouldn't be such a bad thing. For five days.

Mentally Meg shook her head. This wouldn't do; a pity party wouldn't accomplish a thing. Besides, she'd asked for all of it when she married Kelsey, hadn't she? The valleys as well as the mountaintops. She'd just have to work harder at climbing the mountain.

"Now what can I do for you?" she said to the two women, putting on her best smile, gathering a couple of straight chairs into a semicircle. She sat in her computer chair. "May I get you some coffee? Soda?"

"No thank you, Meg," her mother said, her face intent. "We have business to discuss. Now Meg..." Audrey scooted to sit on the edge of her seat, her eyes alight and her mouth edging on animation. Meg hadn't seen her mother this excited since she'd found an old piece of first-edition sheet music. "We were talking at bridge the other day about insurance and savings and things.''

"What things?'' Meg prompted, looking from one to the other.

"Investments,'' Sandy supplied as though telling a grand secret. "The stock market.''

"And since you've done quite well with them, we thought you'd be the very one to give us some advice,'' Audrey said with triumph.

Meg couldn't have felt more surprised if her mother had told her she wanted to throw out all her antiques and refurnish her house in crates. She'd never been interested in banking or finances when her father lived.

"Mom. Sandy. May I ask what brought on all this sudden interest?''

"Oh, nothing earth-shattering, Meg dear,'' Sandy said. "Miss Maybelle came by the other day while we were at bridge—she doesn't play, y'know, but she likes to visit and stay for dessert.''

"And she mentioned she'd just come into some money,'' Audrey added. "She was very pleased, really, and said she wanted to invest it.''

"Did Miss Maybelle say where the money had come from?'' Meg asked, picking up a pencil, concentrating on making circles on a yellow legal pad.

"Not really.'' Her mother pursed her mouth in thought. "Something about selling a piece of land. I didn't know she had anything left except that twenty acres out by you, Meg.''

"Ah...well.'' Meg laid the pencil down and folded her hands in her lap. "Now tell me, ladies, what you have in mind. The stock markets can be very risky. A gamble. Are you sure that's what you want?''

"Oh, not in a big way, dear,'' Sandy replied, reaching forward to pat her hand. "None of us has that kind of money. And we certainly don't want to gamble! Oh, not at all! We're speaking of investments. But they do say, don't they, that you should never invest anything you can't afford to lose. And that's why we want your advice, don't y'know. For an investment club.''

"I see. How many people want to be included?''

"Oh, we've counted about ten of us who said they wanted in," Audrey said. "Babs and the others. And Miss Maybelle, naturally. Paul, now. He doesn't need any more investments, but he said he'd go along for the fun of it."

"When do you want to do this? And how soon?"

"Oh, we'd like to meet every week. Make it real. We were hoping you would teach us how to read the papers and understand what it all means."

Meg bit her lip. The suggestion was a good one; too many times she'd seen older people, especially women, avoid the responsibility of handling their own money. At Audrey's request, she and Jack had set up investments for her after their father died, but heretofore, Audrey had shown no real interest in it. Now she could learn about the world of finance in a friendly group that wouldn't overwhelm or insult her.

And that spawned another thought. It was her own fault that Kelsey had been caught flat-footed over the fact of her having made so much money. She hadn't given him, or even her mother, a clue all these years as to how successful she'd been. She wondered now if she'd been afraid of revealing her success, perhaps in some way fearing it would set her apart from the people she loved most, causing them to see her differently. Different from "good old" Meg. Perhaps she ought to change that.

"All right," she said, suddenly excited by the notion of advising these old friends. It would be fun to share her knowledge, and very rewarding to give something back to people who had loved her since she was a child. "But only if we don't jump into actually investing any money for a while. Say about three to six months? And then we'll start very small."

She wrote on a pad and tore it off, handing the paper to her mother. "These are the titles of a couple of books to study. You can read them, discuss them among yourselves, and we'll begin when you're ready after that. Okay?"

Audrey rose. "Thank you, Meg. Oh, by the way. I suggested to Lissa that she come into town on Saturday. I promised her I'd help her practice for the choir solo she's auditioning for, and then Babs's granddaughter Courtney is coming down to visit. The two girls have formed quite a friendship it seems."

"Yes, I know." Lissa had confided that she wanted to invite Courtney out to the farm to spend the night, but with no room to share, had refrained. Another reason to hurry the house along, Meg mused. After the new house is completed, the kids could invite a friend out whenever they pleased. The huge office and den she'd planned would make it a hundred percent easier too, and not only for the kids. She could work at home; she and Kelsey would each have their own workspace. And she'd planned a computer center for the children, as well. "You've been a peach to help Lissa out with her music. You always treat her as a grown-up, too, with respect for her opinion. She likes that."

"Well, the child is your father's grandniece, after all, as well as my own grandchild by marriage now. She needs me." Audrey's whole face softened and her voice became animated as she continued. "I'm the only one she and the others have, really, to represent the older generation."

Meg was struck by how much blossoming Audrey had actually done over the past few months. There was pride and eagerness when her mother spoke of the children. For all of them, Sara, Andy and Kelsey's five.

Her heart lifted. In God's own time, she thought—the promise Kelsey had made. *Thank you, Lord. Thank you.*

"You're very lucky to have so much family," Sandy remarked a little enviously as she gathered her purse and stood. "I wish my daughter visited me as often as your children."

Audrey's face lit with delight. "Yes, and little Heather? She's begun to call me Grandma, you know, and she asked me to come to her school when they have Open House. I just wish I could take her with me to St. Louis next week to visit with Andy and Sara. I promised to show her a real giraffe at the zoo."

Well, here was one person who would be enthusiastic about the new house, Meg decided as she walked them to the top of the stairs.

"Mom, why don't you come out to dinner tonight? There's something I want to show you."

* * *

Kelsey drove out to his south section, pausing to look his stand of walnut trees over, then carefully followed the dirt track around the lower pond. The water level was a little low; they needed rain.

He braked the truck, put it in neutral and got out to open a wire gate. He kept a small herd of black Angus beef cattle in this wedge-shaped pasture, the ones he was shipping to market. The cattle trucks would be here in the morning.

The animals bunched on the near rise away from his boundary line, spooked by the noisy activity going on in the next field. He didn't blame them. Hammering from half a dozen sources hit the air, reminding him that a house would soon occupy the heretofore peaceful ground. As if he needed reminding.

He could no longer avoid it. And in spite of himself, he was drawn to the fence to watch. He leaned a forearm on a post and simply observed for long moments. A black truck with a Carter Construction logo printed on its door arrived; a man got out, consulted with one of the crew, then let his truck tail down, revealing a large cardboard box and a huge drink dispenser. The hammering let up. After a moment the truck driver began to hand out boxes from a well-known chicken restaurant and cups filled from the dispenser.

Kelsey glanced at the sun. Close to noon. Yet he'd never known a construction boss to feed his crew on his own before. Workers usually brought lunch from home or took a break to run by a fast-food window. Well, he guessed he might just as well find out if curiosity really killed the cat. Or himself.

He put his booted foot against the bottom wire, stretched the middle one high, and bent to step through. The wire twanged as he let it go and headed toward the truck.

Several of the men nodded a greeting; one looked slightly familiar, yet Kelsey couldn't quite put a name to the face.

"Hi, there," the young man said, coming forward. The dark eyes held a friendly glint. "You're Mr. Jamison, right?"

"Yeah, I'm Jamison. Just thought I'd see how you're getting along here."

"Great! Just great. I'm Carl Hays, from church?" At Kelsey's enlightened nod, he continued. "The subflooring should be in by the time we knock off tonight. You sure got some quality lumber here. Mr. Carter don't accept the poor stuff.''

"Ah..." Kelsey made a noncommittal answer, glancing at the stacks of lumber hanging from the back of the huge vehicle parked against the far fence line. Meg's boundary line, now.

"Your crew is good-sized. Isn't it larger than most?''

"Yep, it sure is. And we're the best he's got, too,'' young Carl said with pride. "That's because Mr. Carter wants the shell up quick, and this is a big'un. Says he wants it ready for the roofers in a week.''

A big'un. Kelsey tugged at his ear and wondered just how big. He hadn't asked Meg anything about the size or style of the house she'd chosen. He wanted to know, but he guessed he'd look pretty stupid to ask those basic questions of the building crew. He'd find out soon enough, he told himself.

"That's fast,'' he remarked, not knowing anything else to answer. The builder's promise to have the dwelling completed by holiday time seemed well on its way to being honored.

"You want some chicken?'' Carl asked. "It's mighty nice of Mrs. Jamison to have it sent out. The rumor is she's gonna send a hot lunch out on Fridays to whoever's here until the house is done. Makes it something to look forward to.''

"Well, my wife has her own way of doing things,'' he replied, surprised, but then not, to learn of Meg's generosity. She'd always been generous and caring. Hadn't he counted on that when he'd asked her to marry him?

He touched his finger to his hat, nodded more greetings and left the way he'd come. He checked his cattle. Satisfied, he drove slowly back to the house.

Mary Claire was there scrubbing the kitchen floor, her plump body wielding a wet mop with lethal vigor. "It you weren't going to get a brand-new kitchen soon, Kelsey Jamison, I'd tell you just what I think of this sorry thing you call a floor. It's so worn down it won't come clean any longer. These here countertops need torn out, too, and new ones put in. A person can only do so much to make it look nice.''

Now how in the world did Mary Claire know about the new house? She hadn't heard it from the kids. But his youngsters might very well find out about it from Mary Claire if he didn't watch out. He and Meg ought to tell them.

"Communication," he muttered under his breath, citing something he'd read in a parenting magazine. Sure as the sun rose, he and Meg needed more communication between the two of them.

He thumbed through the old recipe box he kept his phone numbers in, searching for the number of the cattle hauler. Double-checking always made him feel better. "'Good communication is the successful results...'" Or was it a business mag? "No, that's not it. 'Good communication leads to better understanding between colleagues and therefore, achieves better results.'"

He'd already fumbled badly in that field with Thad.

He hadn't been too swift with his wife.

Where in the world was that blasted number? Meg'd suggested he wasn't utilizing his computer like he should, but when did he have time to put addresses into a machine when he couldn't even find one hour in the day to—

Mary Claire burst into song at the top of her lungs.

"Mary Claire!"

"'Lord above how we adore thee—'"

"Mary Claire!" The singing ceased. He let out his breath. If it wasn't one of his kids it was someone else.

He should've stayed out of the house this morning.

Should've remembered it was Mary Claire's morning to clean. How could a man be expected to get anything done with all that interference?

Finally finding the card he'd been searching for, he dialed the number and left a confirming message on the answering machine when no one responded. He'd have felt better if he could've talked to the trucker direct, but at least he'd left a reminder that he was expected first thing in the morning.

Communication.

He supposed they were going to have to talk about things. He and Meg. Settle things. He felt miserable about the uneasy way he and Meg had been just *existing*. He wouldn't call it living together. Certainly not as man and wife.

There had been far too much going off in different directions.

He'd sure missed her, too. He hadn't had enough time with her by a long shot. It dawned on him that she never bored him and, though he'd always liked having her around, now he really felt deprived if he didn't see much of her during the day. If that were Meg singing in the other room, it wouldn't bother him at all—even when she sang off-key.

She'd been right to want the bigger house. They did need it, desperately.

She hadn't been wrong in taking the initiative over it, either. Left in his hands he'd probably have mulled and stalled until next year, or the year after. He should tell her that, and he would. Soon. When he felt less...threatened, he guessed.

Late that afternoon Kelsey headed back toward the house after spending the afternoon working in his back field. The house was quiet, the van absent, but something in the oven smelled delicious. Meg must have prepared an oven dinner before taking Heather with her to pick Thad up from his tutoring session.

He glanced at the wall clock. That meant he had about ten minutes to hit the shower early. If he dawdled even long enough for a cold lemonade, he'd miss his opportunity and have to wait until after the kids went to bed.

He'd just pulled a clean, dark green shirt over his head when the school bus dropped Lissa and Aimee at the end of their drive. Ever since Meg had told him she loved the way the shirt matched his eyes, it had become his favorite. He wore it often.

Phillip came in thirty minutes later, with Meg driving in very soon after that. Thad lumbered into the house as though he carried a weighty boulder, while Heather spilled from the car at a run, the dogs barking behind her.

"Look, Daddy. I got two smiley faces on my paper."

"That's great, honey." Heather ran to show her papers to Lissa and Aimee, and he glanced at Thad. "What's your problem?"

"Nothin'." The boy made a beeline right through the kitchen toward his bedroom.

Kelsey raised a brow and glanced at Meg.

"Oh, Kels," Meg said, her eyes lighting up as she took note

of his freshly washed hair and clean shirt. "I'm glad you've showered early. Mom's coming to dinner."

"Ah... That's nice. What's with Thad?"

"Um." She paused and turned from where she was washing her hands at the kitchen sink to peek past him until Thad was out of sight. She lowered her voice. "He's got a new tutor. A girl, this time."

He leaned against the counter, crossed his ankles and continued to gaze at her in puzzlement. "What's wrong with that?"

"Only sixteen?" She dried her hands, her eyes sparkling with humor. "Pretty?"

"Ahh," he answered, catching her meaning. "Thad's discovered *girls!*"

"You got it. Now help me set the table. I want to have everything ready when Mom arrives, and I want the kids to start right in on their homework. I think it's time—"

"To show them the house," he finished for her, taking the white-on-white patterned plates she handed him.

"Yes."

"Yeah, I've been thinking the same. Mary Claire said something today about our getting a new kitchen." He set the plates and turned to get the blue glasses. Meg always wanted the table to look nice, but especially so whenever her mother was around. "I'd like to know how Mary Claire knows anything about it, but I thought right then I didn't want the kids to hear it someplace else besides this house."

"Exactly. And it's time Mom—"

"Or she'll be terribly hurt by being the last to hear."

"Uh-huh. Besides, the kids will need to pick out carpet and paint colors for their rooms."

"Me, too?" he asked.

She halted near the table, flatware in hand, and tipped her head to look at him. She studied him, trying to gauge his mood. He liked the way she did that sometimes, the way she tried to burrow into the center of his being. Like she really wanted to know how he thought. Or wanted to become a part of him. Like becoming one. One of mind and heart?

They weren't there yet, but he thought it was time he made

an effort to do his part. The least he could do was appear interested in the new house. It was important to her. To them all.

He was more than a little interested, actually. He was a lot interested. He just felt too shamefaced to admit how poorly he'd behaved.

Finally she softly murmured, "Yes, you too. If you want to. If you feel—"

"That the house belongs to us...all of us."

"Uh-huh. But I don't want you to resent it."

"No. I won't do that, Meg. I don't now. There're some things—"

"You-hoo. I'm here," Audrey called from the front door.

"Some things?" Meg prompted, ignoring the interruption.

"It isn't the house, Meg. Really. And I don't resent your wanting something nicer."

"Not nicer, Kels. Enough space." She turned back to the table, her shoulders curled inward as though she buffered herself against a strong wind. Had he said the wrong thing again?

"Is anyone going to let me in?" came her mother's plea. Then, "Oh, thank you, Phillip dear. I was beginning to think everyone had become deaf. Or that I'd become invisible."

Chapter Twenty

"Are you serious?" Lissa asked, her eyes as large as teacups.

"Perfectly, *seriously* serious," Meg replied, setting her iced tea glass down. She watched the children's changing expressions with happy anticipation, and Kelsey's from the corner of her eye. She prayed Kelsey no longer felt so uncomfortable with the project. Admitting to the need wasn't exactly the same as shouting hurrah. What she counted on was that he'd gain some perspective once he saw how much improved their daily routines would be. "The new house going up next door is ours. It will be ready by Christmas, hopefully, and we'll have a lot more space, more bathrooms...."

Everyone stared at Meg, their mouths open. Audrey carefully laid her fork on her plate, her face almost comical with mixed consternation, perplexity and disbelief. Almost in unison, they all turned to stare at Kelsey.

"Don't look at me. This is Meg's show." But he smiled while saying it. Meg flashed him a look of conspiracy, hoping to tease him back into a sense of fun. They were presenting this surprise together after all.

"Well, Meg," her mother sputtered, patting her mouth with her napkin. "I don't understand why you didn't tell us before now. You let me sit in your office this morning and prattle on and on about Miss Maybelle having sold some land, when it was you who bought it.''

"Yeah," Aimee said. "How come we didn't know this already?''

"Why, um, well, I...we're telling you now," Meg began, glancing down the table at Kelsey. Fat lot of help he was, Meg thought. He merely shrugged. He leaned back in his chair and played with his silverware.

What could she say? The truth? That she and Kelsey had quarreled over her buying the land and the house itself? That she hadn't told anyone because the whole thing had caused a rift between them and they hadn't yet completely resolved it? That Kelsey still wasn't altogether thrilled with it?

"What Meg means is, she, ah, wanted to surprise you," Kelsey finally said, his glance telling her nothing more than he wanted to help her off what had become an uncomfortable hook. "And now that the structure is underway, it's time to let all of you in on it."

"You mean we're moving?" Thad said, frowning in puzzlement.

"Well, duh, Thad," Aimee said. "But you can stay here in this house if you want to. I won't care."

A flush crept up the boy's cheeks, and he gave his sister a heated look. "I only meant—"

"It's all right, Thad," Meg said. "You've never lived in any other house but this one, and the thought of moving can be a little startling. But we'll all have time to grow used to the idea."

She daren't glance at Kelsey now. Her mother would notice it. So would Lissa and Aimee.

"Will the new house have an upstairs?" Phillip asked.

"As a matter of fact, it will," Meg answered brightly, glad the focus had veered a bit. "Why do you ask?"

"Because I like upstair houses. Will it have an attic?"

"Yes."

"Where will I sleep?" Heather asked.

Kelsey wanted to ask that same question. Like his children, he was self-centered enough to wonder about his own place in this new household—which probably made him a little childish, too, he suspected. But he did wonder.

"That's one of the things we have to discuss, sweetie. It's time for Lissa and Aimee to move into a bedroom all their own. They're growing up and need more space. A big girl's room."

Heather's eyes began to overflow. "But—"

"But you have a choice from two."

"Two what?"

"There'll be a small room close to Lissa's and Aimee's on the upstairs floor or another room downstairs, close to the master bedroom. You can choose which one you want."

Kelsey watched Meg from under lowered lids. She had plans for each of the children. And five bedrooms? Had he grasped that right? Did that mean he was relegated to the small room next to the master if Heather wasn't using it? Or would he be invited into the main bedroom, the one usually intended for the master of the house?

He knew without a doubt he didn't want to spend any more time in a lonely bed without his wife. Without *Meg!* Was he going to have to wait three or four months to find out if she planned to include him in the master suite?

He didn't think so.

"Can my room be in the attic?" Phillip asked, sidetracking Heather. And Kelsey.

"Why would you want the attic, Flip?" he asked.

"I like being up high. If I could be up high I could see a long, long ways."

"Hmm…" Meg sipped the last of her tea. "I suppose that solves the riddle of why we keep finding you in trees. Well, I don't think the attic will be accessible for a bedroom, Phillip, but, I tell you what. There's some pretty tall trees close to the new house. Why don't you collect some of the scrap wood over the next few months and build a tree house?"

"That's a cool idea," Aimee said.

"Yeah!" Thad no longer felt any doubt, it seemed, that moving would be a good thing. "A tree house."

A scowl settled on Phillip's face. "Mom said it to me. It's gonna be my tree house."

The protest from Phillip was unusual. He seldom balked at anything the other children arranged, nor did he often object to being the one squeezed in the middle. Meg shifted her gaze toward Kelsey with delight. The child was learning to stand up for himself at last.

Kelsey glanced back at her, a smile hovering. They understood one thing together very well, he thought. His children. And if he had to use his biggest asset to continue to court her into love, then he wasn't above using it—her delight with his children. "Well, *Mom* did say it to Phillip. But I think we can make it big enough to accommodate the bunch of you."

At the opposite end of the table, pleasure heated Meg's cheeks. Phillip had called her Mom, and Kelsey had noticed it while she hadn't. And he'd made a point of acknowledging it in front of her mother. Yet his gaze held far more warmth than merely the fact that she had gained her place and fit into the family so well. There was a husbandly gleam in his green eyes that made her want to clear the kitchen of everyone except the two of them. She caught her breath, a tremor of desire running along her nerves until it settled deep in the pit of her stomach.

"I'm only surprised you haven't built one already." Meg broke the spell by averting her eyes, rising from the table with her plate and glass and heading to the sink. If she didn't move she was likely to embarrass the lot of them.

"Never had time, I guess," Kelsey murmured, covertly watching Meg's retreat over his shoulder. Her hands trembled slightly, and she wouldn't quite meet his gaze. She'd guessed what was on his mind, no doubt.

Maybe she hadn't married him only for the children's sake. Maybe she wanted him as much as he wanted her. Could she possibly love him, as well?

"Well, why would you?" Audrey defended him.

Meg turned abruptly, nearly dropping in shock the gallon of milk she carried for refills. Her mother gave her a lightning glance, lifted her chin, then continued as though she'd never held an adverse opinion of Kelsey Jamison in her life.

"It seems to me you've had your hands full just keeping body and soul together with five children to raise. Farm work, even in today's modern times, is hard enough on anyone, much less without a woman in the home. You've done extremely well in the fair, too, which shows proof of your skills."

"Thank you, Audrey," Kelsey returned on a quiet note.

"What's the house going to look like?" Thad asked, bringing them all back to where they started.

"Oh. I have a sketch and house plans we can all look at later. But right now I think we should go and look at it. See what progress has been made today." Meg glanced around at the plates. Untouched green vegetables and rice remained on two. "As soon as supper is over."

"Well, I'm finished," Lissa said, spooning the last of her rice into her mouth. She scooted off the end of the bench with her plate and glass in hand, eager to clear the table.

"Wait a minute, young lady," Kelsey began. "We haven't—"

"Me, too," Aimee said, already standing, one foot on either side of the bench. Thad and Heather both stuffed their mouths with green beans and chewed as hard as chipmunks.

"It looks as though we're going before the dishes get done tonight," Meg said, laughing. "Okay, the last one into the van is a rotten egg."

Outside, the clouds looked streaked with apricot and purple in the setting sun. Near the horizon the sky had a dense opaque appearance and the air had cooled by ten degrees; a storm front moving in, Meg supposed.

They walked and crawled around the home site until dark.

Her mother gave up first, saying she needed to be home to receive a telephone call. When they returned home, the two older girls pored over the house plans and hunted up the yardstick to measure rooms, then matched their findings with what the plans said. Phillip seemed happy with the idea that the window of his room would face east, the view being the woods.

Kelsey asked her nothing. After kicking off his boots at the back door, he went straight to the blinking answering machine and listened to its messages. Meg heard the murmur of his voice as he returned a call. She let the children run through their excitement without interruption, cleaning the kitchen alone, but insisted they go to bed on time.

Later Meg wandered into the living room with a bowl of popcorn. Kelsey scribbled something on a yellow pad. The front door and window were opened wide to let the fresh air cool the stuffy room, but she knew before morning she'd need a blanket on her bed. The nights, at least, declared the time of year.

"Want a munch?" she asked.

"Sure." He sniffed without looking up. "I never turn down popcorn."

"What's up?"

"Oh," he said and let his breath out. "One of the cattle trucks I expected tomorrow had a breakdown. My hauler gave me two choices. Find somebody else to do it or wait for him to get it repaired."

"Mmm... How long does he think it will be?"

"A week, probably."

"So what are you going to do?"

He threw down his pencil. "Well, I can get trucks from a fellow on the other side of Sedalia. Never used him before. But he has only one driver, so it looks like I'm it for the second truck. Do you mind?"

"No, why should I?"

He grabbed a handful of popcorn. "Well, besides the trucking change, I'd like to take my cattle to a different market this time, too. I've been coddling and hand feeding this particular herd along without additives. You know, growing them the natural way. Miller seems to think I'll get a better deal for my specialty from a plant near Chicago. Called the man he's dealt with and he's quoting a good price. But I'll be gone overnight, most likely."

"Oh. Don't worry about us. We'll get along just fine."

"I suppose."

"Then what's the matter?"

Outside the breeze had picked up. A wheezy sway of tree branches bent them lower to the ground. The door creaked in the wind.

"Nothing. Nothing at all." He stood and reached for her

hand, pulling her up against him. He held her there, his arm
snug around her waist, leaning his forehead against hers. "I'm
tired of sleeping alone, that's all."

"You can climb those stairs anytime, Kels. I've never stopped
you."

"No, you haven't." No, she'd never stopped him making
love to her nor discouraged him at all. But did she really want
him or was she merely being accommodating? That question
plagued him.

Had she married him only for the children's sakes?

"These last few nights..." Touching her face, he let his fingers slide against her smooth cheek, testing the way her lashes
felt against his thumb pad. "You have such pretty skin. Soft.
Soft as a newborn chick."

He bent to kiss her, coaxing her mouth into a full, all-out
response in a matter of seconds, and he thought he'd been
starved long enough. He didn't want it to stop. "Let's find our
own bed, okay?"

Outside, the bluster increased, the wind whistled harder. A
roll of thunder sounded, long and rumbly. Kelsey lifted his head
and stilled to listen. Something hadn't sounded right. A noise
that shouldn't have been.

"What is it?"

He merely shook his head. After a moment he let his hands
fall from around her and took a step toward the open door. A
heavy gust of wind slammed it shut before he could reach it.

"Surely it's only the storm."

He pivoted and strode through the house to the back door,
hitting the outdoor floodlight switches, illuminating the house
and barnyard. "Heard something else. Think I should go check
on things."

"What are you worried about?" Meg, following, pulled the
kitchen window curtain aside and looked out. Dust and leaves
swept against the panes. Through the edges of light and beginning rain, the barn looked old and shimmery, like an Impres-
sionist painting. Over the wind she could hear a faint bawling
of cattle and a heavy thudding.

Kelsey tipped his head to listen a scant second, then grabbed his boots and sat on the bench to yank them on. "I put my cattle in that old corral behind the barn ready for the loading tomorrow. Normally they'd be okay there for a day or two, but with this weather brewing..."

"What is it, Daddy?" Lissa asked from her bedroom door. A streak of lightning darted overhead making the outside floodlighting look eerie and false with blue edges. Immediately after, a crack and roll of thunder shook the house.

"Is it just the storm?" Her voice held a tremor.

Meg turned from the window, but Kelsey was already gone.

"Lissa, watch out for the others," Meg ordered, making an instant decision. "I'm going with your dad."

She ran out to the laundry porch and searched in the box of various boots stacked in the corner. Finding an old pair of rubber knee-highs that looked like they would fit her, she kicked off her tennies and yanked the boots on, tucking her jeans inside. They had to be Kelsey's; no one else in the house had feet big enough for her.

"Where to?"

"To check on the animals," Meg replied. Glancing up, she noted Phillip, his reddish brown hair sticking up, crowding behind. Lissa chewed worriedly at her bottom lip.

"It's all right, honey. We'll be close to the barn. I'll come back to check on you kids in a little while, but just now your dad might need me."

The wind gusted against the house, and upstairs something crashed to the floor.

"Uh-oh, those shutters need closing or—" Meg took a step toward the doorway leading to the stairs "—I'll have a soggy mess for a bed. And my clothes! Last time it rained, there was a leak in the roof right over those hooks where I hang my night things."

"I'll shut 'em," Phillip offered, turning back into the tiny hall. "I'm not scared of a little wind."

"Me, either," Thad said, coming up behind his brother, snapping a pair of denims. "I'll come out to help you and Dad."

"No. Stay with your sisters, Thad. If Heather wakes..."

"Don't worry about Heather," Lissa said. "I can take care

of her. And I'll get your clothes away from where it might blow in around the shutter edges. And we know what to do if it gets worse."

"Where's Aimee?" Meg asked.

"Aw, she sleeps through everything," Thad said in disgust. "Never mind. I'll get some blankets and flashlights in case we need 'em. And I'll get out the camping gear, too."

"Flashlights. Glad you remembered, Thad." She swung a box down from a nearby shelf, choosing one, and passed the box over to the boy. "Okay, kids. Stay put in the house and don't worry, okay?"

Lightning jagged overhead as Meg slipped through the back door and headed toward the barn. Dangerously near. Something sizzled and snapped close to the road and all the floodlights went out. She halted abruptly in the sudden pitch-black night.

No lights shone from the house, either. She could see only a dark outline to tell her where the structure stood. Had the lightning hit anything more than a power line? She held her breath, glancing this way and that, praying against the danger such an occurrence might bring. Fire—anywhere—they could do without. Or a live electricity wire.

The children would be scared. She should go back. But Kelsey was out there somewhere. What if he needed her more?

A sudden dim light went on in the house and she sighed. They'd lit the lantern they used for camping, no doubt.

She turned once more toward the barn. Strands of hair whipped across her face and into her eyes; she brushed it aside and silently scolded herself for forgetting to tie it back.

A sharp whistle pierced the night gloom. She strode toward it around the outside of the barn, waving her flashlight against the rough path.

"Hiyah...git!" Kelsey's voice cut through the noisy blow and bawling cattle. She followed the call to where the ground dropped away in a gradual slope. The old slatted fencing that enclosed about half an acre of rocky ground had been there for ages, she thought. Since long before Kelsey had owned the farm. About thirty beeves circled restlessly or huddled near the barn.

A few wilder critters seemed bent on testing their limits against the fence.

She heard Kelsey whistle again and spotted him at the bottom of the slope, his hands stretched against the top board. He seemed to be holding it in place against a black, stiffly lowered head trying to butt through a section of splintering fence. She signaled her presence with her flashlight and, almost at a run, hurried to reach him.

"Hiyah, git back there!" The steer shied back and ran a few paces, but then turned and stared at them as though making up its mind whether to try its luck again.

"Kelsey!" she shouted to be heard. "What can I do? How can I help?"

"Meg. Shine that light onto me."

She angled the light as he directed, its radiance barely reaching past his shoulders. He'd come out without a hat or outer garment. His hair, dark and matted with rain was plastered flat to his head, while his wet T-shirt lay molded to his muscled chest. He looked almost like a stranger, but a very attractive one. She stared in mesmerized fascination and thought every female cell in her body must respond. When he jumped and howled to frighten the steer back to its mates, she jumped, too.

The steer darted away, circling back toward the herd. He stopped just short of joining them, turning to stare back at her and Kelsey.

She took a deep breath.

"We've lost power," she remarked, shaking off her fanciful response to her husband and edging closer to him.

"Yeah," Kelsey acknowledged without further concern. "This ol' boy has delusions he's still a bull." He jiggled the fence where the steer had butted. The two bottom slats fell, broken completely, to the ground. The upper section sagged. "I knew I should've replaced this whole thing last spring. Been waiting..." He let his words go to heave a huge rock into place, propping two of the broken boards on it.

"What can we do?" she asked as he dusted his hands against each other.

"Got some wire in the barn. Just stay here a minute with that flashlight till I get back. If any of those ornery candidates for the best steer-imitating-a-wild-bull contest tries to get out again, holler like I did. I'll come running.''

"Um, all right."

He disappeared into the dark. Another lightning flash showed him turning the corner out of sight. A few steers nervously bawled a protest, huddling as near the barn as they could...except for the ornery one, who seemed determined to stand out from his buddies. He didn't seem nearly as frightened of the storm as he was of her. But then, the heavenly light show was moving on.

"That's all right, there. You can stay on your side of the yard," she muttered, wondering if the steer would soon lose his fear and try the fence again. "I'll stay on mine."

The rain slashed heavier. She stood and waited a long time, checking to see where the one steer was each time the sky gave her a minor flash. What seemed like half the night later, Kelsey came striding toward her, an old-fashioned kerosene lantern swinging from one hand, a toolbox in the other and a roll of wire over one shoulder.

They started to work, Kelsey directing her every move. Tossing her a pair of leather gloves, he ordered her to put them on. When he said "higher" Meg held the lantern above his head; when he told her to stretch as much as she could, she pulled on the wire; when he even grunted a "hold it" she froze in place. He snipped the final cut and tossed the wire clippers into the box.

"That should do it." He straightened. "For now."

"You need to replace this old corral fence altogether, Kelsey."

"Don't I know it. Haven't had the time or money." He picked up the remainder of the wire and his toolbox, his body moving with tired response. "Well, come on, sweetheart. We've done everything we can tonight."

She held the lantern high and handed him her flashlight. "Kels, I could—"

"Uh-uh! Don't even offer, Meg." He headed around to the front of the barn.

"But if you need it—"

"Meg, I'm not going to borrow any money from you. Got that?"

The kerosene lantern took on a brighter glow, its light reaching farther in the barn's interior blackness. He hung it high on a nail, then went to put the wire in its proper storage place. Meg waited against the post, the soft lantern light making shadows around her and on the planes of her face. She looked a little pensive, almost woebegone.

Inside him, he sighed at his own clumsiness. *Lord, help me bridge this gap between us. Show me how to love her better.*

"But, I do appreciate the offer, sweetheart. I know you only want to help. And I've been thinking." He wiped his face on his sleeve and leaned an arm against the post beside her head, continuing in a conversational tone. "I still have money I put aside to buy Miss Maybelle's land, so now that it's not being used, I think I'll use it for just those kinds of things. New fencing—of good quality—and a few other odds and ends that need doing around here. Even spruce up the old house a bit. What do you think?"

"That's a great idea, Kelsey. And I've wondered what we could do with the little house once we move out. I thought..."

"Go on," he said, his tone rich with honest encouragement. "What have you been thinking?"

"Well," she said, more enthusiastically, "I had thought you might get someone in to help you part-time, and the little house, once we do some work on it, might be a good part of the package."

"Have to admit it, Meg. That had crossed my mind, too. Having help would give me the push to expand like I've wanted to. Bennie, now..."

"Oh, yes, just who I'd pick."

"Mmm..." He gazed at her thoughtfully, listening to the muffled rain, breathing in the smell of straw and old wood, of animals and the rain itself. "Meg, I haven't told you...shown you how grateful—"

"You don't need to be grateful, Kels. Anything I've done is because I've wanted to. Sometimes I'm selfish that way."

"Me too, I s'pose. Self-centered. And I'm going to be self-centered one more time and say what I want to say. I like having you with me, Meg. Like tonight when we worked side by side. Always did like it. But you're going to have to teach me how to stand by your side when you need me there in the things that are important to you. Even when it takes me time to understand."

"All right," she said, tentatively.

"Even when you have to sit me down with a scold to do it."

"All right," she said, less uncertain.

"Even when you have to ask the Lord to bring me up short until I do."

"All right," she conceded, laughing. "It's a promise."

The distant hum of a machine began to thrum and the house lights suddenly lit. A second later, the floodlights in front of the barn came on as well. They both glanced toward the house.

"One of the kids turned on the generator, I guess," he said, looking out.

"Mmm...I forgot about that." Her hands hurt. Even wearing gloves, the wire had dug into her palms. She'd barely noticed it until now. And she was wet and cold and starting to shiver. So was Kelsey. But she felt as though she'd crawl a mile for a chance to do it all over again—they'd worked in such complete harmony, the way they'd done when they were young. And he'd made some real strides in making up for their quarrel. She'd noticed a rapidly returning feeling of trust in him, too. Trust in the Lord to make things right.

"Will this put a crimp in your hauling them to market tomorrow?" she asked as they slogged toward the house.

"Don't know. I'll have to wait till morning to see."

Chapter Twenty-One

All the children were up. Or rather, they were awake, though they slumped to varying degrees over the board game in the center of the kitchen table. The overhead light was on, but the camp lantern remained lit.

Lissa broke out in a smile when she saw them, her face losing the pinched look around her eyes. She jumped up to get them some towels. "Everything okay out there?"

"Sure, honey," Kelsey answered, automatically accepting one. Then taking a closer look at her worried expression, he reached out to pat her cheek and run a hand against her hair. "It's only a little storm and it's already on the wane. Everything will be right by tomorrow."

"Daddy," Heather cried as she threw herself against Kelsey.

"Why aren't you in bed, sprite? You couldn't stand to be left out, huh?"

"Naw," Thad said, pushing the game pieces away and getting up from the table. "She squeals no matter what you do."

Meg struggled to kick out of her rubber boots. "I'm so cold I'm shivering in my boots," she tried to joke.

"Here, I'll help," Thad said. "Sit down."

Meg dutifully sat on the bench and stuck out her feet. Phillip and Thad each grabbed a boot and pulled. They came off with a sudden little plopping sound and the boys ended up squarely on their bottoms on the floor. The worried tension broke with the responsive laughter.

"I'll make you some hot chocolate," Aimee said and turned the stove on under the tea kettle. "We took care of things in here Dad."

"I see you did. Glad I can count on you," he gave an appreciative answer. He hugged Heather close for a moment, then set her down. "I'll get you all wet, sweetie. C'mon, Meg, let's get out of these things."

Meg and Kelsey shed their soaked clothing for dry robes. Meg wandered back to the kitchen, so tired she thought she could curl up on one of the benches to sleep. She sank down and brought her cold bare feet up under her robe, her chin on her knees. Aimee brought over two mugs of steaming hot chocolate.

"Mmm...this is just the thing, Aimee," Meg said, lifting one of the mugs to take a sip.

"Heather, get Meg some socks, would you?" Kelsey asked when he settled beside her. For once, Heather responded without a fuss and found two pairs of her daddy's clean heavy boot socks.

"Good girl," Kelsey said, handing one to Meg.

Pride in his children shone from Kelsey's gaze at he praised their efforts to work as a family team. Meg had always known that Kelsey was a good father. He loved his kids wholeheartedly. But she'd refrained from thinking too deeply about their own relationship since that night of Thad's breakthrough, and for the first time, she starkly wondered if Kelsey would ever be able to love another woman as he'd loved their mother. Would he ever have those deepest feelings for her? They'd functioned once again like comrades, like teammates, but not necessarily as lovers.

"You can have my bunk, Mom," Phillip offered, interrupting her thoughts. "We put the sleeping bags out in the living room. I don't mind sleeping there."

"Me, either," Thad jumped in. "And you'll like my bunk

better. It's the bottom one,'' he reminded as though she wouldn't remember.

"Why, that's a lovely thing to do, boys,'' she praised, turning to set her mug on the table behind her. "I'll take you up on that, thank you.'' And she would, too. Where else could she find a spot to sleep in this overcrowded house? Kelsey had his old bed.

"Who turned on the generator?'' Kelsey asked, curious.

"Me and Aimee,'' Thad said, offhand.

"You mean you actually got along together long enough to accomplish something? Well, let's write this one up for the town headlines.''

"Come on, Dad. We're not that bad,'' Aimee insisted.

Kelsey tugged at his ear and sipped his hot chocolate. And grinned. "Well, who remembered to do it?''

"That was Aimee,'' Thad admitted. "I, um, I was really trying to get the battery radio to hold a good station so we could hear about the storm. 'Sides, we were hauling a bunch of Meg's stuff down from upstairs so it wouldn't get wet. Rain was coming in between the shutters. Everywhere. Sorry, Meg.''

"Things are...''. She shrugged, then made a face. "Just things.'' She drew a deep breath. "Don't worry about it.''

"Well, I never said my girls were less bright than my boys,'' Kelsey remarked with a huge yawn. "Good thinking, Aimee.''

"Let's all get to bed now,'' Meg said, her voice raspy with exhaustion. "It's one-thirty. Nobody'll want to get up in the morning.''

No one argued the point. She turned to shut off the overhead light as they filed out of the kitchen. Kelsey waited in the kitchen door, his face reflected softly in the camp lantern. He wore that arrested expression, the one she'd noticed the night he'd understood Thad's deep unexpressed grief. She looked at him in question as she paused. What was it he wanted to say?

"I, um, appreciate all the help tonight, Meg,'' he said in a low and intimate voice. He reached out to run a thumb against her cheek. "Sorry about your bed.''

He touched his tongue to his teeth as though he had something on his mind, but said nothing more as he searched her

gaze. She'd sensed a change in him lately and tried now to put
a thought to what it might be. Tired lines stretched around his
mouth and circles were beginning to form under his eyes. Perhaps it was simply very late after a long, exhausting day, she
mused. He needed sleep as much as she. And maybe that was
why she felt a bit dispirited.

"Can't be helped," she murmured as she slipped past him to
enter the boys' room. "Don't let it plague you, Kels. I'll sort it
all out tomorrow. You'll have enough to do yourself without
worrying about my stuff."

"Yeah..." He followed her and paused, glancing at the bunk
beds in distaste as she curled onto the lower one. She didn't
bother to remove her robe. She wondered why he didn't seek
his own bed, the one in that tiny room next door. Maybe she
was missing something.

"Is there anything more—" she said, smothering a huge
yawn "we can do tonight, Kels?"

"No. There's nothing. We both need some sleep. It's only..."

"Mmm..." Somewhere in the back of her mind she knew he
was trying to tell her something. But her eyes simply wouldn't
stay open another minute.

"...that I'll, um, be doggone glad when the new house is
done."

She woke suddenly the next morning with that awful feeling
of being very late for an appointment and sat up. Aimee stood
in her door. Only a gloomy half light from the overcast sky told
her it was daylight.

"Sorry, Meg. We didn't want to wake you but—"

"You missed the bus."

"Yeah."

"So don't sweat it, hon. We'll make it, even late." She swung
out of bed, knowing the day ahead would be a mad scramble
without ever looking at her daily schedule. *Whatever today's
needs are, Lord, I can do it as long as I can draw on your
strength. But, oh boy! Am I going to need it today.*

"Where's your dad?"

"Out already."

Meg nodded, and hurried to dress. She peeked out, noting a number of light tree limbs and twigs were down and wondering what else there might be.

"There's a utility truck down on the road," Thad announced. "Making repairs."

"Well, let's not worry about it and do a drive-by breakfast this morning, what do you say?

"Forgive me, Lord, for taking the easy way out," she muttered under her breath. She just didn't feel like tackling breakfast in uncertain conditions and the kids being an additional thirty minutes or so late to school didn't seem to matter.

"Yeah, I could get into a biscuit and egg sandwich," Thad replied.

"I'll get my shoes on," Aimee said, her way of agreeing.

By the time Meg combed Heather's hair and all five of the children climbed into the van, they were already an hour behind. She didn't try to find Kelsey and his truck was gone from its usual spot.

They saw limbs down everywhere as they pulled onto the highway. She slowed the van as they approached the new home site; Kelsey's truck sat next to one she recognized as belonging to Carter's Construction. He must be checking to see how the place looked after the storm.

Her heart warmed. He *did* want to know about the new house, she hadn't dreamed it up. Did that mean he was eager to move into a shared room?

Kelsey was gone by the time she and Heather returned home soon after lunch. His note, stuck to the answering machine, told her he'd gone to see the man about the trucks. That night he came in late, too tired to say much, and everyone went to bed at an early hour. Beginning at dawn the next day Kelsey loaded his market cattle. He left again at noon.

The next day, Meg instructed Heather to take the bus home so she could work longer at the office. Then surprise caught her when she drove into the farm yard to discover Mary Claire's car still there. So was Kelsey's truck, telling her he was home from his trip. Wasn't Heather home yet? What if there'd been an accident? Or was Heather lost?

"What's wrong?" Meg rushed through the back door, her heart in her throat.

"Why, nothing," Mary Claire said, startled. She held a glass of iced tea halfway to her lips. Heather sat across from her, downing a chocolate chip cookie, dark smears on her cheek. "Why would you think it?"

"Oh," she gulped and let her breath out on a long sigh while her heart settled back to where it belonged.

Oh, Father, how foolish of me. How could I have ever worried about having enough time for business when these children are my business. And yours...anything else and everything else is in your keeping. Including my love for Kelsey, just as always.

She drew another steadying breath. "Well, usually you've gone by now. Where's...?" But she didn't have to ask. Her husband's voice murmured from the next room, the pause and cadence of his speech letting her know he spoke with someone on the telephone.

"He said," Mary Claire talked as she jerked her head toward the living room, "for me to stay if I could. Said you two was goin' out an' Lissa had studyin' to do. Fine with me, I told him. I ain't got no date with Brad or Kevin or Mel."

"Oh?" Meg glanced toward the living room. Kelsey had made plans?

"Fact is, he said not to expect you back 'til late and was that all right? Shoot, I told him it was 'bout time the two of you took some time off for yourselves. Ain't been married but a couple of months or so, seems like I remember. An' your mother says you didn't have no real honeymoon."

"Um, what about dinner for the kids?"

"Pizza!" mumbled Heather around another cookie.

"Well, but—"

"That's okay, Meg. We'll make it ourselves. Got everything I need 'cause Kelsey brought groceries when he came in."

Kelsey'd thought of everything.

He swung through the doorway then, freshly shaved and wearing the last new outfit she'd bought him when she'd made the round for school clothes with the kids, and his soft, half-teasing grin. The taupe shirt blended well with the darker pants, and the total outfit set off his auburn brown hair and glinting green eyes.

"A successful cattle trade, I see," she murmured, feeling her response to his smile run all the way to her toes.

"Yes, and I think I'll deal more with this packer in the future. Meg, sweetheart, you look great in what you have on," he stated, letting his gaze run down her navy slacks and cotton sweater "but you have time to shower and change into that nice rosy thingamabob you wear sometimes to church if you want to."

"Give me half an hour," she said. It was the first hint she'd had that he even liked the deep rose knit she had from two years back.

"Take your time. But we have reservations at that steak place..."

They stood ready to leave just after the school buses dropped off the older children. Kelsey verbally tossed out chores for the kids to complete, ordered them to go to bed on time and said not to wait up. He handed Meg into the van with all the pomp and style of a real date. But he didn't drive far. He turned off onto the dirt road that led to the river picnic spot.

"Why are we stopping here?" she asked.

"We have a couple of hours before we go to dinner, Meg. I just wanted to have time for a talk before we got there. Privately, without the kids."

"All right." What could be so serious that he had to make time in so spectacular a way? They hadn't come back here since they'd decided to marry.

He parked in the usual spot and rolled down his window. He pulled the latch to release his seat and pushed it back to give him a stretch for his long legs before turning in her direction. He didn't say anything for a long moment, but reached out to smooth back the print scarf she wore draped about her shoulders. It was the gesture of a man who was afraid of saying what he must.

"Kels, you're scaring me. What's wrong? Something is wrong, isn't it?"

"Yeah...yes. But not wrong so much as...out of balance."

"All right. So tell me."

"Meg, I know we, um, agreed on a partnership in this marriage, but..."

"But?"

"I want to renegotiate our agreement."

"Our agreement," she repeated, feeling momentarily blank. "What don't you like? Well, I know you're still upset over the house—"

"No. No, Meg, that's not it," he said, placing a finger against her mouth. "Once I got over my hurt pride, I realized just how proud I am of your business talents. I don't want you to give up your work and we'll just have to keep on working the schedules out. Building the new house is the best solution for all of us. I'm very glad about it, it's exactly what we need."

Her heart eased its tightness. "Then?"

"I don't want a partnership between you, me, and the kids any longer."

Meg felt the blood drain out of her face. "You don't?"

"No!" he cried out in passion. "I want a marriage between you and me. A true marriage between a man and a woman who love each other first, before anything or anyone else except God."

"Do we love each other, Kels?" she threw at him bluntly, the words an immediate self-defensive reaction.

"Don't we?" he threw back. "Yes...the answer is yes, we do. That's the thing I've been getting straight in my mind these last few weeks. I love you so much it's making me wacky because there's a part of you I don't know half, even a quarter as well as I want to in spite of our shared youth, and because I can't make love to you every time I want to with so little privacy and—Lord knows, I love my kids, Meg. But if I don't get some time with you alone I might be tempted to throw you over my shoulder and carry you off to the wilds. I mean, this is *seriously* serious stuff I'm feeling."

A burst of laughter erupted from her very soul. "I—you—I doubt you even could, Kels. I'm no lightweight, you know. Not like—" She'd been going to say not like Dee Dee. Her laughter died. Dee Dee had only been a lightweight in physical size.

Would Dee Dee always be between them? They'd both loved her, but she'd been Kelsey's wife first. Would she always be first in his heart for the rest of their lives?

"No..."

For a moment, Meg thought he'd read her thoughts, but then she realized he'd answered the surface banter. She was twice Dee Dee's size and not easily pitched over a shoulder.

He leaned his head back against the seat, staring straight ahead, and remained quiet a moment, thoughtful. "You know, Meg...I don't have to tell you how much I loved Dee Dee. I know you remember. But I've discovered something recently..." He rolled his head slightly, looking at her steadily. His mouth was pensive, as though hardly daring to put expression to his deepest thoughts.

"I've discovered something I'd forgotten. That God's timing is perfect. Because fifteen, sixteen years ago I didn't recognize I loved you, too."

"You did?" Stunned, she could only look at him. And listen.

"I mean, if it's possible to be in love with two women at once. Maybe what I felt was simply sexual attraction. Somewhere, deep inside me...I don't know, Meg. I'm having a hard time with it because it makes me feel horribly disloyal to Dee Dee and you at the same time. But there it is. You were still a kid and you had things to do and places to go with all those brains and talent. Maybe if you'd been older...I guess I just buried those feelings."

He'd been attracted to her? When she'd thought she was too big, too awkward, too *anything* that would explain why she couldn't gain his attention.

"We were all very young, Kels. Emotions at that age are hard to confine. They're all over the place." Hers weren't much different now.

"True. On the other hand, Meg, I never once felt tempted to ask you for more than friendship while Dee Dee was alive."

It was her turn to be thoughtful. She stared down at her hands, turning the simple gold wedding ring round and round on her finger.

"You did better than I did, Kels," she finally murmured, her voice husky with tears. "I loved you with everything I had in me to love. Many a time…no, *every day* after you and Dee Dee got married I had to ask the Lord to wipe the desire for you from my heart. That's why I—"

"Left?"

She nodded. He took her hand, splaying her fingers, pressing his mouth to her thumb, sending her into shivers of longing.

"Dee Dee hinted at how you felt once or twice. But we never talked about it openly. She kept a lot of things to herself, didn't she?"

"Yeah, sometimes she did. I'm glad, though, that she never told you." He kissed another finger, and another. "I might have felt, oh, betrayed, somehow, to know she'd shared my secret. It's hard to love someone when the person doesn't love you back." He pressed a kiss to the corner of her mouth. "I tried hard to move on to a new love, but I never could."

Keeping her hand in his, he drew back a little. "Perhaps it was more than just discretion on her part. Knowing could have stirred up all kinds of trouble and might have damaged what we all had. That deep a friendship is rare. But—" he drew a solid breath "—all that's in the past, now, sweetheart. And while I want to keep the friendship we've always had, I want to live with you—love you—in the now. Can we renegotiate this partnership into a real one? The way God intends marriage to be?"

"Yes." She smiled, her heart lifting as though taking on new life. "Yes, let's do that. Kelsey Jamison, I love you more than anything on earth. I'd love to be married to you. Honestly married, sharing a room, sharing a bed."

"You got it. We're now entering into an honest marriage. Two of us in a love match. And I love you, Meg Jamison, to the ends of time. And I'm counting on a real honeymoon with you when we attend that Serenity opening bash. In fact, I can hardly wait. As for right now, I have a reservation at the closest motel to that steak place."

"You do? What about the kids?"

"Forget about the kids. Mary Claire agreed to stay the night. And I've packed the only things you'll need for an overnight stay. Remember that black lacy thing someone gave you?"

"Oh...oh, my...you did?"

After his next kiss she wondered if they'd ever make dinner at all.

Well, maybe breakfast. Eventually.

Epilogue

Kelsey stood with his hand entwined with Meg's in front of the floor to ceiling brick fireplace in the huge gathering room of their new house and lifted his cup of mulled cider high in salute. Behind him, a softly lit Nativity scene took pride of place on the polished black walnut mantel, a gift from Miss Maybelle and Bennie. Fragrances of cooking turkey and ham, cinnamon and nutmeg, and new wood filled the house. He glanced from face to face; to each of his children, and his in-laws, Jack and Kathy, Sara and Andy, and Audrey, who'd become a friend. And the friends so close to their hearts: Paul Lumbar, Miss Maybelle and Bennie, Justine, her husband and son.

"Thanks for sharing our best Christmas ever," he said. Gratitude and soul-deep love for their presence and God's filled his heart to overflowing. "I praise God for each of you. Thanks for coming and being our family."

Everyone lifted their cups to sip. "Dinner is ready, folks," Meg said after licking a drop of the honeyed cider from her lip. "But before we sit, Kelsey and I'd like to share the best gift yet..."

Her mother, already turned toward the two cloth-covered, china-laded tables at the end of the room turned back, her eyebrows raised. Kelsey squeezed Meg's hand encouragingly.

"Kelsey and I think our five children are lovely, but...six will be even better." She smiled with pride. "We're going to have a baby."

Exclamations, hugs and excited congratulations followed. Lissa and Aimee immediately began to plan the nursery. Thad decided they needed another boy to even the balance and started to choose names. Phillip said he'd teach him to climb trees.

"A baby?" Heather frowned, then her face cleared and brightened. "A little baby...well that's okay. 'Cause *I* get to be the big sister this time."

"Oh-oh," Kelsey murmured. "I think we're in for big trouble."

"That's *major* trouble if you ask me," Meg replied with a chuckle. "But in God's own time..."

* * * * *

Dear Reader,

Times and technology change with each generation. My mother, born in 1907, saw life go from horse-and-buggy days to men walking on the moon, meals cooked on a wood-burning stove to those heated in a microwave. In my teen years I never dreamed that to write novels I'd eventually use a personal computer that could correct my spelling with a button touch.

Yet since the dawn of time, mankind's character traits remain unchanged. The ugly ones, like greed, hate, bitterness, anger, spitefulness, dishonesty, lying and selfishness are still present. And the lovely ones like kindness, compassion, patience, honesty, love and forgiveness, are there, as well. Even the best of us sometimes struggle with choosing the better ones over the undesirables. Maybe *especially* the best of us.

God's commandments haven't changed, either. They're still valid. If we honor them, they teach us how to get along with each other—they're the ground rules for good relationships. He also tells us we have His help in our struggles.

All writers are observers of life. They watch what people do, listen to what they say, study attitudes and motives for their actions, and assimilate that into their writing, be that fiction, nonfiction, or simply reporting.

I'm the same. I *love* writing love stories. I like writing stories about real problems and how people either solve them, learn to live with them, or change their life focus because of them. I love success stories and happy endings where love and goodness triumph.

Ruth Scofield

Take 3 inspirational love stories FREE!

PLUS get a FREE surprise gift!

Special Limited-time Offer

Mail to Steeple Hill Reader Service™
P.O. Box 609
Fort Erie, Ontario
L2A 5X3

YES! Please send me 3 free Love Inspired™ novels and my free surprise gift. Then send me 3 brand-new novels every month, which I will receive months before they appear in bookstores. Bill me at the low price of $3.46 each plus 25¢ delivery and GST*. That's the complete price and a saving of over 10% off the cover prices—quite a bargain! I understand that accepting the books and gift places me under no obligation ever to buy any books. I can always return a shipment and cancel at any time. Even if I never buy another book from Steeple Hill, the 3 free books and the surprise gift are mine to keep forever.

303 IEN CFAK

Name	(PLEASE PRINT)	
Address		Apt. No.
City	Province	Postal Code

Welcome to *Love Inspired*™

A brand-new series of contemporary inspirational love stories.

Join men and women as they learn valuable lessons about facing the challenges of today's world and about life, love and faith.

Look for the following July 1998 Love Inspired™ titles:

SHELTER OF HIS ARMS
by Sara Mitchell

SWEET CHARITY
by Lois Richer

EVER FAITHFUL
by Carolyne Aarsen

Available in retail outlets in June 1998.

LIFT YOUR SPIRITS AND GLADDEN YOUR HEART
with *Love Inspired!*™

Steeple Hill™

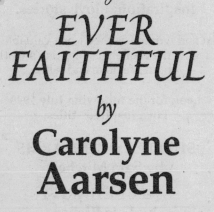